The New York Times

LOOKING FORWARD

DNA Testing

GENEALOGY AND FORENSICS

I0800908

EDUCATIONAL PUBLISHING BOOKS

THE NEW YORK TIMES EDITORIAL STAFF

Published in 2019 by New York Times Educational Publishing in association with The Rosen Publishing Group, Inc.
29 East 21st Street, New York, NY 10010

First Edition

The New York Times
Alex Ward: Editorial Director, Book Development
Phyllis Collazo: Photo Rights/Permissions Editor
Heidi Giovine: Administrative Manager

Rosen Publishing
Megan Kellerman: Managing Editor
Michael Hessel-Mial: Editor
Greg Tucker: Creative Director
Brian Garvey: Art Director

Cataloging-in-Publication Data
Names: New York Times Company.
Title: DNA testing: genealogy and forensics / edited by the New York Times editorial staff.
Description: New York : New York Times Educational Publishing, 2019. | Series: Looking forward | Includes glossary and index.
Identifiers: ISBN 9781642821284 (library bound) | ISBN 9781642821277 (pbk.) | ISBN 9781642821291 (ebook)
Subjects: LCSH: Genetic genealogy—Juvenile literature. | Forensic genetics—Juvenile literature. | Genetics—Juvenile literature.
Classification: LCC CS21.3 D63 2019 | DDC 929.1072—dc23

Manufactured in the United States of America

On the cover: The forensic biology laboratory of the chief medical examiner in New York, N.Y. The medical examiner uses DNA testing to identify the remains of 9/11 victims; Fred R. Conrad/The New York Times.

Contents

7 Introduction

CHAPTER 1

The Revolution of Personal Genetic Testing

10 My Genome, My Self BY STEVEN PINKER

33 23andMe Will Resume Giving Users Health Data BY ANDREW POLLACK

36 With a Simple DNA Test, Family Histories Are Rewritten BY GINA KOLATA

43 Are Genetic Testing Sites the New Social Networks? BY ALYSON KRUEGER

48 The Online Gene Test Finds a Dangerous Mutation. It May Well Be Wrong. BY GINA KOLATA

CHAPTER 2

Genetic Testing and Medicine

53 DNA Blueprint for Fetus Built Using Tests of Parents BY ANDREW POLLACK

58 The Path to Reading a Newborn's DNA Map BY ANNE EISENBERG

62 New York's Chief Medical Examiner Seeks to Lead in DNA Research BY J. DAVID GOODMAN

66 In Iceland's DNA, New Clues to Disease-Causing Genes
BY CARL ZIMMER

70 U.S. Introduces New DNA Standard for Ensuring Accuracy of Genetic Tests BY ROBERT PEAR

73 Pursuit of Cash Taints Promise of Gene Tests BY REED ABELSON AND JULIE CRESWELL

81 New Gene Tests Pose a Threat to Insurers BY GINA KOLATA

86 The Struggle to Build a Massive 'Biobank' of Patient Data
BY GINA KOLATA

CHAPTER 3

The Adoption of Genetics by Law Enforcement

92 Biologist Teaches the Nation's Judges About Genetics
BY CLAUDIA DREIFUS

97 DNA Evidence Can Be Fabricated, Scientists Show
BY ANDREW POLLACK

99 Falsely Convicted, Freed and No Longer Quiet BY MARTIN FACKLER

104 Genetic Basis for Crime: A New Look BY PATRICIA COHEN

108 Helping Decide Guilt or Innocence BY LIZ ROBBINS

114 Seeking Answers in Genome of Gunman BY GINA KOLATA

118 Using DNA to Sketch What Victims Look Like; Some Call It Science Fiction BY ASHLEY SOUTHALL

123 In Africa, Geneticists Are Hunting Poachers BY GINA KOLATA

128 The Golden State Killer Is Tracked Through a Thicket of DNA, and Experts Shudder BY GINA KOLATA AND HEATHER MURPHY

CHAPTER 4

Ethical Issues in Genetic Testing

132 Ethics Questions Arise as Genetic Testing of Embryos Increases
BY GINA KOLATA

138 The Fault in Our DNA BY DAVID DOBBS

142 White? Black? A Murky Distinction Grows Still Murkier
BY CARL ZIMMER

146 Disability and the Right to Choose BY JENNIFER BARTLETT

150 My 'Orphan Disease' Has Given Me a New Family
BY ROSEMARIE GARLAND-THOMSON

155 How Genetics Is Changing Our Understanding of 'Race'
BY DAVID REICH

164 The Racial Spectacle of DNA Test Result Videos BY AMANDA HESS

169 Scientists Can Design 'Better' Babies. Should They?
BY CLYDE HABERMAN

173 Why Many Native Americans Are Angry With Elizabeth Warren
BY MAGGIE ASTOR

CHAPTER 5

Scientific Frontiers Opened by Genetic Testing

176 DNA Double Take BY CARL ZIMMER

184 The Upside of Bad Genes BY MOISES VELASQUEZ-MANOFF

189 The Famine Ended 70 Years Ago, but Dutch Genes Still Bear Scars BY CARL ZIMMER

193 David Reich Unearths Human History Etched in Bone
BY CARL ZIMMER

203 As D.I.Y. Gene Editing Gains Popularity, 'Someone Is Going to Get Hurt' BY EMILY BAUMGAERTNER

211 Glossary
213 Media Literacy Terms
215 Media Literacy Questions
217 Citations
221 Index

Introduction

IN 1953, JAMES WATSON and Francis Crick published their landmark paper on the structure of DNA, inaugurating the field of modern genetics. Based on prior research by Maurice Wilkins and Rosalind Franklin, Watson and Crick's paper outlined for the first time the "double helix" structure of DNA, along with the relationship between genes and the chemical sequence that comprises them. Though Gregor Mendel and countless unnamed experimenters in selective breeding learned by trial and error how traits are inherited over the centuries, it was not until Watson and Crick's paper that heredity became known as the "genetic code," a long sequence of four molecules that was understood as the blueprint for a living organism.

Though genetics research is often used to understand evolution and its history, the applications occurred most in fields like health care and law enforcement. In the following decades, researchers devised tests for specific genetic disorders, including Tay-Sachs, sickle cell anemia and Down syndrome. These prenatal and neonatal tests helped identify possible health risks in our genes, becoming a standard part of medical care. Likewise, in the 1980s law enforcement began using DNA profiles as evidence in criminal investigations, which helped solve old cases and free the wrongly convicted. These applications were focused on particular genes, without a complete picture of human DNA.

Personal genetic testing was not too far behind. In 1990, a team of scientists launched the Human Genome Project, with the goal of mapping the entirety of a single human's genetic makeup. Thirteen years and $2.7 billion later, the project was complete, and the fundamental tools were in place for the revolution in personal genetic testing. At first, the service was prohibitively expensive, costing tens of thousands of dollars for a personal genome readout. However, services like 23andMe eventually found ways to market the service for mere hundreds of dollars, opening a lucrative market for direct-to-consumer genetic testing.

As a result, genetic testing became not only a medical tool, but a tool for exploring our own identity. While some consumers sought insights into genetic risks for cancer, Alzheimer's and other afflictions, many consumers sought answers about their racial ancestry. Genetic tests provided racial data in tidy percentages, and many people found surprise and delight in backing their racial heritage with hard numbers.

But how much do these tests tell us? While personal genetic testing gave people more complex understandings of their ancestry, the troubled concept of race remained a contentious issue. Some voices in this collection, especially with regard to Native American ancestry, argue that genetics alone do not connect one to an ethnic culture. Others argue that the historical concept of race is no longer a useful scientific

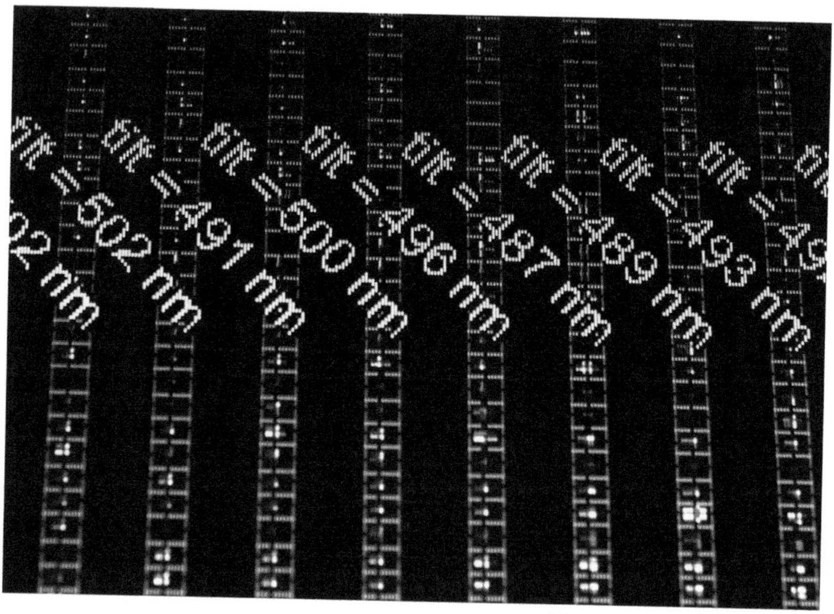

NOAH BERGER FOR THE NEW YORK TIMES

DNA sequencing elements displayed on a monitor.

term to describe human diversity and ancestral origin. Still others find a new self-understanding in knowing the story of their ethnic background.

Genetics is frequently assumed to give final answers to questions related to health, crime and identity, but the articles in this collection often complicate those answers. Along with the fraught discussions of racial identity, new research in gene editing and epigenetics offers new perspectives on how genes work. In the former, new technologies like Crispr are allowing independent researchers to genetically modify themselves, often without any regulatory oversight. In the latter, research is finding that experiences change gene expression in ways that are often passed onto one's offspring. Furthermore, genes once only associated with disease are revealing healthy purposes, and criminal genetic evidence is coming under scrutiny for what it can and cannot prove. These examples reveal that while genetics offers revolutionary insights, the discipline does not offer simple ones.

As our understanding of genetics grows and genetic modification of humans becomes a greater possibility, the question of genetics and identity will take on an increasingly ethical character. What will it mean to link genes with desirable or undesirable traits? What will it mean if people decide to edit them in their children, as technologies like Crispr promise? Will we think critically of the choices at stake, or will "designer babies" and the belief in inherent "crime genes" be strong enough to shape human behavior? As genetics research enters the cultural mainstream, informed readers may find themselves forced to make decisions of great ethical importance.

CHAPTER 1

The Revolution of Personal Genetic Testing

In 2009, personal genetic testing was still too expensive for the general public. In less than a decade, companies like 23andMe made genetic testing a popular consumer item. Users thrilled in the surprises their genetic backgrounds promised and reconnected with distant family. However, many who purchased the product found their senses of themselves changed, as they learned of their tangled racial ancestries. In addition, genetic testing provided information on genetic health risks, despite some doubts about these companies' medical credibility.

My Genome, My Self

BY STEVEN PINKER | JAN. 7, 2009

ONE OF THE PERKS of being a psychologist is access to tools that allow you to carry out the injunction to know thyself. I have been tested for vocational interest (closest match: psychologist), intelligence (above average), personality (open, conscientious, agreeable, average in extraversion, not too neurotic) and political orientation (neither leftist nor rightist, more libertarian than authoritarian). I have M.R.I. pictures of my brain (no obvious holes or bulges) and soon will undergo the ultimate test of marital love: my brain will be scanned while my wife's name is subliminally flashed before my eyes.

Last fall I submitted to the latest high-tech way to bare your soul. I had my genome sequenced and am allowing it to be posted on the Internet, along with my medical history. The opportunity arose when the biologist George Church sought 10 volunteers to kick off his audacious Personal Genome Project. The P.G.P. has created a public database that will contain the genomes and traits of 100,000 people. Tapping the magic of crowd sourcing that gave us Wikipedia and Google rankings, the project seeks to engage geneticists in a worldwide effort to sift through the genetic and environmental predictors of medical, physical and behavioral traits.

The Personal Genome Project is an initiative in basic research, not personal discovery. Yet the technological advance making it possible — the plunging cost of genome sequencing — will soon give people an unprecedented opportunity to contemplate their own biological and even psychological makeups. We have entered the era of consumer genetics. At one end of the price range you can get a complete sequence and analysis of your genome from Knome (often pronounced "know me") for $99,500. At the other you can get a sample of traits, disease risks and ancestry data from 23andMe for $399. The science journal Nature listed "Personal Genomics Goes Mainstream" as a top news story of 2008.

Like the early days of the Internet, the dawn of personal genomics promises benefits and pitfalls that no one can foresee. It could usher in an era of personalized medicine, in which drug regimens are customized for a patient's biochemistry rather than juggled through trial and error, and screening and prevention measures are aimed at those who are most at risk. It opens up a niche for bottom-feeding companies to terrify hypochondriacs by turning dubious probabilities into Genes of Doom. Depending on who has access to the information, personal genomics could bring about national health insurance, leapfrogging decades of debate, because piecemeal insurance is not viable in a world in which insurers can cherry-pick the most risk-free customers, or in which at-risk customers can load up on lavish insurance.

The pitfalls of personal genomics have already made it a subject of government attention. Last year President Bush signed the Genetic Information Nondiscrimination Act, outlawing discrimination in employment and health insurance based on genetic data. And the states of California and New York took action against the direct-to-consumer companies, arguing that what they provide are medical tests and thus can be ordered only by a doctor.

With the genome no less than with the Internet, information wants to be free, and I doubt that paternalistic measures can stifle the industry for long (but then, I have a libertarian temperament). For better or for worse, people will want to know about their genomes. The human mind is prone to essentialism — the intuition that living things house some hidden substance that gives them their form and determines their powers. Over the past century, this essence has become increasingly concrete. Growing out of the early, vague idea that traits are "in the blood," the essence became identified with the abstractions discovered by Gregor Mendel called genes, and then with the iconic double helix of DNA. But DNA has long been an invisible molecule accessible only to a white-coated priesthood. Today, for the price of a flat-screen TV, people can read their essence as a printout detailing their very own A's, C's, T's and G's.

A firsthand familiarity with the code of life is bound to confront us with the emotional, moral and political baggage associated with the idea of our essential nature. People have long been familiar with tests for heritable diseases, and the use of genetics to trace ancestry — the new "Roots" — is becoming familiar as well. But we are only beginning to recognize that our genome also contains information about our temperaments and abilities. Affordable genotyping may offer new kinds of answers to the question "Who am I?" — to ruminations about our ancestry, our vulnerabilities, our character and our choices in life.

OVER THE YEARS I HAVE COME to appreciate how elusive the answers to those questions can be. During my first book tour 15 years ago, an interviewer noted that the paleontologist Stephen Jay Gould had dedicated his first book to his father, who took him to see the dinosaurs when he was 5. What was the event that made me become a cognitive psychologist who studies language? I was dumbstruck. The only thing that came to mind was that the human mind is uniquely interesting and that as soon as I learned you could study it for a living, I knew that that was what I wanted to do. But that response would not just have been charmless; it would also have failed to answer the question. Millions of people are exposed to cognitive psychology in college but have no interest in making a career of it. What made it so attractive to me?

As I stared blankly, the interviewer suggested that perhaps it was because I grew up in Quebec in the 1970s when language, our preeminent cognitive capacity, figured so prominently in debates about the future of the province. I quickly agreed — and silently vowed to come up with something better for the next time. Now I say that my formative years were a time of raging debates about the political implications of human nature, or that my parents subscribed to a Time-Life series of science books, and my eye was caught by the one called "The Mind," or that one day a friend took me to hear a lecture by the great Canadian psychologist D. O. Hebb, and I was hooked. But it is all humbug. The very fact that I had to think so hard brought home what scholars of autobiography and memoir have long recognized. None of us know what made us what we are, and when we have to say something, we make up a good story.

An obvious candidate for the real answer is that we are shaped by our genes in ways that none of us can directly know. Of course genes can't pull the levers of our behavior directly. But they affect the wiring and workings of the brain, and the brain is the seat of our drives, temperaments and patterns of thought. Each of us is dealt a unique hand of tastes and aptitudes, like curiosity, ambition, empathy, a thirst for novelty or for security, a comfort level with the social or the mechanical or the abstract. Some opportunities we come across click with our constitutions and set us along a path in life.

This hardly seems radical — any parent of more than one child will tell you that babies come into the world with distinct personalities. But what can anyone say about how the baby got to be that way? Until recently, the only portents on offer were traits that ran in the family, and even they conflated genetic tendencies with family traditions. Now, at least in theory, personal genomics can offer a more precise explanation. We might be able to identify the actual genes that incline a person to being nasty or nice, an egghead or a doer, a sad sack or a blithe spirit.

LOOKING TO THE GENOME for the nature of the person is far from innocuous. In the 20th century, many intellectuals embraced the idea that babies are blank slates that are inscribed by parents and society. It allowed them to distance themselves from toxic doctrines like that of a superior race, the eugenic breeding of a better species or a genetic version of the Twinkie Defense in which individuals or society could evade responsibility by saying that it's all in the genes. When it came to human behavior, the attitude toward genetics was "Don't go there." Those who did go there found themselves picketed, tarred as Nazis and genetic determinists or, in the case of the biologist E. O. Wilson, doused with a pitcher of ice water at a scientific conference.

Today, as the lessons of history have become clearer, the taboo is fading. Though the 20th century saw horrific genocides inspired by Nazi pseudoscience about genetics and race, it also saw horrific genocides inspired by Marxist pseudoscience about the malleability of human nature. The real threat to humanity comes from totalizing ideologies and the denial of human rights, rather than a curiosity about nature and nurture. Today it is the humane democracies of Scandinavia that are hotbeds of research in behavioral genetics, and two of the groups who were historically most victimized by racial pseudoscience — Jews and African-Americans — are among the most avid consumers of information about their genes.

Nor should the scare word "determinism" get in the way of understanding our genetic roots. For some conditions, like Huntington's disease, genetic determinism is simply correct: everyone with the defective gene who lives long enough will develop the condition. But for most other traits, any influence of the genes will be probabilistic. Having a version of a gene may change the odds, making you more or less likely to have a trait, all things being equal, but as we shall see, the actual outcome depends on a tangle of other circumstances as well.

WITH PERSONAL GENOMICS in its infancy, we can't know whether it will deliver usable information about our psychological traits. But evidence from old-fashioned behavioral genetics — studies of twins, adoptees and other kinds of relatives — suggests that those genes are in there somewhere. Though once vilified as fraud-infested crypto-eugenics, behavioral genetics has accumulated sophisticated methodologies and replicable findings, which can tell us how much we can ever expect to learn about ourselves from personal genomics.

To study something scientifically, you first have to measure it, and psychologists have developed tests for many mental traits. And contrary to popular opinion, the tests work pretty well: they give a similar measurement of a person every time they are administered, and they statistically predict life outcomes like school and job performance, psychiatric diagnoses and marital stability. Tests for intelligence might ask people to recite a string of digits backward, define a word like "predicament," identify what an egg and a seed have in common or assemble four triangles into a square. Personality tests ask people to agree or disagree with statements like "Often I cross the street in order not to meet someone I know," "I often was in trouble in school," "Before I do something I try to consider how my friends will react to it" and "People say insulting and vulgar things about me." People's answers to a large set of these questions tend to vary in five major ways: openness to experience, conscientiousness, extraversion, agreeableness (as opposed to antagonism) and neuroticism. The scores can then be compared with those of relatives who vary in relatedness and family backgrounds.

The most prominent finding of behavioral genetics has been summarized by the psychologist Eric Turkheimer: "The nature-nurture debate is over … . All human behavioral traits are heritable." By this he meant that a substantial fraction of the variation among individuals within a culture can be linked to variation in their genes. Whether you measure intelligence or personality, religiosity or political orientation, television watching or cigarette smoking, the outcome is the same. Identical twins (who share all their genes) are more similar than fraternal twins (who share half their genes that vary among people). Biological siblings (who share half those genes too) are more similar than adopted siblings (who share no more genes than do strangers). And identical twins separated at birth and raised in different adoptive homes (who share their genes but not their environments) are uncannily similar.

Behavioral geneticists like Turkheimer are quick to add that many of the differences among people cannot be attributed to their genes. First among these are the effects of culture, which cannot be measured by these studies because all the participants come from the same culture, typically middle-class European or American. The importance of culture is obvious from the study of history and anthropology. The reason that most of us don't challenge each other to duels or worship our ancestors or chug down a nice warm glass of cow urine has nothing to do with genes and everything to do with the milieu in which we grew up. But this still leaves the question of why people in the same culture differ from one another.

At this point behavioral geneticists will point to data showing that even within a single culture, individuals are shaped by their environments. This is another way of saying that a large fraction of the differences among individuals in any trait you care to measure do not correlate with differences among their genes. But a look at these non-genetic causes of our psychological differences shows that it's far from clear what this "environment" is.

Behavioral genetics has repeatedly found that the "shared environment" — everything that siblings growing up in the same home have in common, including their parents, their neighborhood, their home, their peer group and their school — has less of an influence on the way they turn out than their genes. In many studies, the shared environment has no measurable influence on the adult at all. Siblings reared together end up no more similar than siblings reared apart, and adoptive siblings reared in the same family end up not similar at all. A large chunk of the variation among people in intelligence and personality is not predictable from any obvious feature of the world of their childhood.

Think of a pair of identical twins you know. They are probably highly similar, but they are certainly not indistinguishable. They clearly have their own personalities, and in some cases one twin can be gay and the other straight, or one schizophrenic and the other not. But where could these differences have come from? Not from their genes, which are identical. And not from their parents or siblings or neighborhood or school either, which were also, in most cases, identical. Behavioral geneticists attribute this mysterious variation to the "nonshared" or "unique" environment, but that is just a fudge factor introduced to make the numbers add up to 100 percent.

No one knows what the nongenetic causes of individuality are. Perhaps people are shaped by modifications of genes that take place after conception, or by haphazard fluctuations in the chemical soup in the womb or the wiring up of the brain or the expression of the genes themselves. Even in the simplest organisms, genes are not turned on and off like clockwork but are subject to a lot of random noise, which is why genetically identical fruit flies bred in controlled laboratory conditions can end up with unpredictable differences in their anatomy. This genetic roulette must be even more significant in an organism as complex as a human, and it tells us that the two traditional shapers of a person, nature and nurture, must be augmented by a third one, brute chance.

The discoveries of behavioral genetics call for another adjustment to our traditional conception of a nature-nurture cocktail. A common finding is that the effects of being brought up in a given family are sometimes detectable in childhood, but that they tend to peter out by the time the child has grown up. That is, the reach of the genes appears to get stronger as we age, not weaker. Perhaps our genes affect our environments, which in turn affect ourselves. Young children are at the mercy of parents and have to adapt to a world that is not of their choosing. As they get older, however, they can gravitate to the micro-environments that best suit their natures. Some children naturally lose themselves in the library or the local woods or the nearest computer; others ingratiate themselves with the jocks or the goths or the church youth group. Whatever genetic quirks incline a youth toward one niche or another will be magnified over time as they develop the parts of themselves that allow them to flourish in their chosen worlds. Also magnified are the accidents of life (catching or dropping a ball, acing or flubbing a test), which, according to the psychologist Judith Rich Harris, may help explain the seemingly random component of personality variation. The environment, then, is not a stamping machine that pounds us into a shape but a cafeteria of options from which our genes and our histories incline us to choose.

All this sets the stage for what we can expect from personal genomics. Our genes are a big part of what we are. But even knowing the totality of genetic predictors, there will be many things about ourselves that no genome scan — and for that matter, no demographic checklist — will ever reveal. With these bookends in mind, I rolled up my sleeve, drooled into a couple of vials and awaited the results of three analyses of my DNA.

THE OUTPUT OF A COMPLETE GENOME scan would be a list of six billion A's, C's, G's and T's — a multigigabyte file that is still prohibitively expensive to generate and that, by itself, will always be perfectly useless. That is why most personal genomics ventures are starting with smaller portions of the genome that promise to contain nuggets of interpretable information.

The Personal Genome Project is beginning with the exome: the 1 percent of our genome that is translated into strings of amino acids that assemble themselves into proteins. Proteins make up our physical structure, catalyze the chemical reactions that keep us alive and regulate the expression of other genes. The vast majority of heritable diseases that we currently understand involve tiny differences in one of the exons that collectively make up the exome, so it's a logical place to start.

Only a portion of my exome has been sequenced by the P.G.P. so far, none of it terribly interesting. But I did face a decision that will confront every genome consumer. Most genes linked to disease nudge the odds of developing the illness up or down a bit, and when the odds are increased, there is a recommended course of action, like more frequent testing or a preventive drug or a lifestyle change. But a few genes are perfect storms of bad news: high odds of developing a horrible condition that you can do nothing about. Huntington's disease is one example, and many people whose family histories put them at risk (like Arlo Guthrie, whose father, Woody, died of the disease) choose not to learn whether they carry the gene.

Another example is the apolipoprotein E gene (APOE). Nearly a quarter of the population carries one copy of the E4 variant, which triples their risk of developing Alzheimer's disease. Two percent of people carry two copies of the gene (one from each parent), which increases their risk fifteenfold. James Watson, who with Francis Crick discovered the structure of DNA and who was one of the first two humans to have his genome sequenced, asked not to see which variant he had.

As it turns out, we know what happens to people who do get the worst news. According to preliminary findings by the epidemiologist Robert C. Green, they don't sink into despair or throw themselves off bridges; they handle it perfectly well. This should not be terribly surprising. All of us already live with the knowledge that we have the fatal genetic condition called mortality, and most of us cope using some combination of denial, resignation and religion. Still, I figured that my current burden of existential dread is just about right, so I followed Watson's lead and asked for a line-item veto of my APOE gene information when the P.G.P. sequencer gets to it.

The genes analyzed by a new company called Counsyl are more actionable, as they say in the trade. Their "universal carrier screen" is meant to tell prospective parents whether they carry genes that put their potential children at risk for more than a hundred serious diseases like cystic fibrosis and alpha thalassemia. If both parents have a copy of a recessive disease gene, there is a one-in-four chance that any child they conceive will develop the disease. With this knowledge they can choose to adopt a child instead or to undergo in-vitro fertilization and screen the embryos for the dangerous genes. It's a scaled-up version of the Tay-Sachs test that Ashkenazi Jews have undergone for decades.

I have known since 1972 that I am clean for Tay-Sachs, but the Counsyl screen showed that I carry one copy of a gene for familial dysautonomia, an incurable disorder of the autonomic nervous system that causes a number of unpleasant symptoms and a high chance of premature death. A well-meaning colleague tried to console me, but I was pleased to gain the knowledge. Children are not in my cards, but my nieces and nephews, who have a 25 percent chance of being carriers, will know to get tested. And I can shut the door to whatever wistfulness I may have had about my childlessness. The gene was not discovered until 2001, well after the choice confronted me, so my road not taken could have led to tragedy. But perhaps that's the way you think if you are open to experience and not too neurotic.

Familial dysautonomia is found almost exclusively among Ashkenazi Jews, and 23andMe provided additional clues to that ancestry in my genome. My mitochondrial DNA (which is passed intact from mother to offspring) is specific to Ashkenazi populations and is similar to ones found in Sephardic and Oriental Jews and in Druze and Kurds. My Y chromosome (which is passed intact from father to son) is also Levantine, common among Ashkenazi, Sephardic and Oriental Jews and also sprinkled across the eastern Mediterranean. Both variants arose in the Middle East more than 2,000 years ago and were probably carried to regions in Italy by Jewish exiles after the Roman destruction of Jerusalem, then to the Rhine Valley in the Middle Ages and eastward to the Pale of Settlement in Poland and Moldova, ending up in my father's father and my mother's mother a century ago.

It's thrilling to find yourself so tangibly connected to two millenniums of history. And even this secular, ecumenical Jew experienced a primitive tribal stirring in learning of a deep genealogy that coincides with the handing down of traditions I grew up with. But my blue eyes remind me not to get carried away with delusions about a Semitic essence. Mitochondrial DNA, and the Y chromosome, do not literally tell you about "your ancestry" but only half of your ancestry a generation ago, a quarter two generations ago and so on, shrinking exponentially the further back you go. In fact, since the further back you go the more ancestors you theoretically have (eight great-grandparents, sixteen great-great-grandparents and so on), at some point there aren't enough ancestors to go around, everyone's ancestors overlap with everyone else's, and the very concept of personal ancestry becomes meaningless. I found it just as thrilling to zoom outward in the diagrams of my genetic lineage and see my place in a family tree that embraces all of humanity.

As fascinating as carrier screening and ancestry are, the really new feature offered by 23andMe is its genetic report card. The company directs you to a Web page that displays risk factors for 14 diseases and 10 traits, and links to pages for an additional 51 diseases and 21 traits for which the scientific evidence is more iffy. Curious users can browse a list of markers from the rest of their genomes with a third-party program that searches a wiki of gene-trait associations that have been reported in the scientific literature. I found the site user-friendly and scientifically responsible. This clarity, though, made it easy to see that personal genomics has a long way to go before it will be a significant tool of self-discovery.

The two biggest pieces of news I got about my disease risks were a 12.6 percent chance of getting prostate cancer before I turn 80 compared with the average risk for white men of 17.8 percent, and a 26.8

percent chance of getting Type 2 diabetes compared with the average risk of 21.9 percent. Most of the other outcomes involved even smaller departures from the norm. For a blessedly average person like me, it is completely unclear what to do with these odds. A one-in-four chance of developing diabetes should make any prudent person watch his weight and other risk factors. But then so should a one-in-five chance.

It became all the more confusing when I browsed for genes beyond those on the summary page. Both the P.G.P. and the genome browser turned up studies that linked various of my genes to an elevated risk of prostate cancer, deflating my initial relief at the lowered risk. Assessing risks from genomic data is not like using a pregnancy-test kit with its bright blue line. It's more like writing a term paper on a topic with a huge and chaotic research literature. You are whipsawed by contradictory studies with different sample sizes, ages, sexes, ethnicities, selection criteria and levels of statistical significance. Geneticists working for 23andMe sift through the journals and make their best judgments of which associations are solid. But these judgments are necessarily subjective, and they can quickly become obsolete now that cheap genotyping techniques have opened the floodgates to new studies.

Direct-to-consumer companies are sometimes accused of peddling "recreational genetics," and there's no denying the horoscopelike fascination of learning about genes that predict your traits. Who wouldn't be flattered to learn that he has two genes associated with higher I.Q. and one linked to a taste for novelty? It is also strangely validating to learn that I have genes for traits that I already know I have, like light skin and blue eyes. Then there are the genes for traits that seem plausible enough but make the wrong prediction about how I live my life, like my genes for tasting the bitterness in broccoli, beer and brussels sprouts (I consume them all), for lactose-intolerance (I seem to tolerate ice cream just fine) and for fast-twitch muscle fibers (I prefer hiking and cycling to basketball and squash). I also have genes that are nothing to brag about (like average memory performance and lower efficiency at learning from errors), ones whose meanings are a bit baffling (like a gene that gives me "typical odds" for having red hair, which I don't have), and ones whose predictions are flat-out wrong (like a high risk of baldness).

For all the narcissistic pleasure that comes from poring over clues to my inner makeup, I soon realized that I was using my knowledge of myself to make sense of the genetic readout, not the other way around. My novelty-seeking gene, for example, has been associated with a cluster of traits that includes impulsivity. But I don't think I'm particularly impulsive, so I interpret the gene as the cause of my openness to experience. But then it may be like that baldness gene, and say nothing about me at all.

Individual genes are just not very informative. Call it Geno's Paradox. We know from classic medical and behavioral genetics that many physical and psychological traits are substantially heritable. But when scientists use the latest methods to fish for the responsible genes, the catch is paltry.

Take height. Though health and nutrition can affect stature, height is highly heritable: no one thinks that Kareem Abdul-Jabbar just ate more Wheaties growing up than Danny DeVito. Height should therefore be a target-rich area in the search for genes, and in 2007 a genomewide scan of nearly 16,000 people turned up a dozen of them. But these genes collectively accounted for just 2 percent of the variation in height, and a person who had most of the genes was barely an inch taller, on average, than a person who had few of them. If that's the best we can do for height, which can be assessed with a tape measure, what can we expect for more elusive traits like intelligence or personality?

GENO'S PARADOX ENTAILS that apart from carrier screening, personal genomics will be more recreational than diagnostic for some time to come. Some reasons are technological. The affordable genotyping services don't actually sequence your entire genome but follow the time-honored scientific practice of looking for one's keys under the lamppost because that's where the light is best. They scan for half a million or so spots on the genome where a single nucleotide (half a rung on the DNA ladder) is likely to differ from one person to the next. These differences are called Single Nucleotide Polymorphisms, or SNPs (pronounced "snips"), and they can be cheaply identified en masse by putting a dollop of someone's DNA on a device called a microarray or SNP chip. A SNP can be a variant of a gene, or can serve as a signpost for variants of a gene that are nearby.

But not all genetic variation comes in the form of these one-letter typos. A much larger portion of our genomes varies in other ways. A chunk of DNA may be missing or inverted or duplicated, or a tiny substring may be repeated different numbers of times — say, five times in one person and seven times in another. These variations are known to cause diseases and differences in personality, but unless they accompany a particular SNP, they will not turn up on a SNP chip.

As sequencing technology improves, more of our genomic variations will come into view. But determining what those variants mean is another matter. A good day for geneticists is one in which they look for genes that have nice big effects and that are found in many people. But remember the minuscule influence of each of the genes that affects stature. There may be hundreds of other such genes, each affecting height by an even smaller smidgen, but it is hard to discern the genes in this long tail of the distribution amid the cacophony of the entire genome. And so it may be for the hundreds or thousands of genes that make you a teensy bit smarter or duller, calmer or more jittery.

Another kind of headache for geneticists comes from gene variants that do have large effects but that are unique to you or to some tiny fraction of humanity. These, too, are hard to spot in genomewide scans. Say you have a unique genetic variant that gives you big ears. The problem is that you have other unique genes as well. Since it would be literally impossible to assemble a large sample of people who do and don't have the crucial gene and who do and don't have big ears, there is no way to know which of your proprietary genes is the culprit. If we understood the molecular assembly line by which ears were put together in the embryo, we could identify the gene by what it does rather than by what it correlates with. But with most traits, that's not yet possible — not for ears, and certainly not for a sense of humor or a gift of gab or a sweet disposition. In fact, the road to discovery in biology often goes in the other direction. Biologists discover the genetic pathways that build an organ by spotting genes that correlate with different forms of it and then seeing what they do.

SO HOW LIKELY IS IT THAT future upgrades to consumer genomics kits will turn up markers for psychological traits? The answer depends on why we vary in the first place, an unsolved problem in behavioral genetics. And the answer may be different for different psychological traits.

In theory, we should hardly differ at all. Natural selection works like compound interest: a gene with even a 1 percent advantage in the number of surviving offspring it yields will expand geometrically over a few hundred generations and quickly crowd out its less fecund alternatives. Why didn't this winnowing leave each of us with the best version of every gene, making each of us as vigorous, smart and well adjusted as human physiology allows? The world would be a duller place, but evolution doesn't go out of its way to keep us entertained.

It's tempting to say that society as a whole prospers with a mixture of tinkers, tailors, soldiers, sailors and so on. But evolution selects among genes, not societies, and if the genes that make tinkers outreproduce the genes that make tailors, the tinker genes will become a monopoly. A better way of thinking about genetic diversity is that if everyone were a tinker, it would pay to have tailor genes, and the tailor genes would start to make an inroad, but then as society filled up with tailor genes, the advantage would shift back to the tinkers. A result would be an equilibrium with a certain proportion of tinkers and a certain proportion of tailors. Biologists call this process balancing selection: two designs for an organism are equally fit, but in different physical or social environments, including the environments that consist of other members of the species. Often the choice between versions of such a trait is governed by a single gene, or a few adjacent genes that are inherited together. If instead the trait were controlled by many genes, then during sexual reproduction those genes would get all mixed up with the genes from the other parent, who might have the alternative version of the trait. Over several generations the genes for the two designs would be thoroughly scrambled, and the species would be homogenized.

The psychologists Lars Penke, Jaap Denissen and Geoffrey Miller argue that personality differences arise from this process of balancing selection. Selfish people prosper in a world of nice guys, until they become so common that they start to swindle one another, whereupon nice guys who cooperate get the upper hand, until there are enough of them for the swindlers to exploit, and so on. The same balancing act can favor rebels in a world of conformists and vice-versa, or doves in a world of hawks.

The optimal personality may also depend on the opportunities and risks presented by different environments. The early bird gets the worm, but the second mouse gets the cheese. An environment that has worms in some parts but mousetraps in others could select for a mixture of go-getters and nervous nellies. More plausibly, it selects for organisms that sniff out what kind of environment they are in and tune their boldness accordingly, with different individuals setting their danger threshold at different points.

But not all variation in nature arises from balancing selection. The other reason that genetic variation can persist is that rust never sleeps: new mutations creep into the genome faster than natural selection can weed them out. At any given moment, the population is laden with a portfolio of recent mutations, each of whose days are numbered. This Sisyphean struggle between selection and mutation is common with traits that depend on many genes, because there are so many things that can go wrong.

Penke, Denissen and Miller argue that a mutation-selection standoff is the explanation for why we differ in intelligence. Unlike personality, where it takes all kinds to make a world, with intelligence, smarter is simply better, so balancing selection is unlikely. But intelligence depends on a large network of brain areas, and it thrives in a body that is properly nourished and free of diseases and defects. Many genes are engaged in keeping this system going, and so there are many genes that, when mutated, can make us a little bit stupider.

At the same time there aren't many mutations that can make us a whole lot smarter. Mutations in general are far more likely to be harmful than helpful, and the large, helpful ones were low-hanging fruit that were picked long ago in our evolutionary history and entrenched in the species. One reason for this can be explained with an analogy inspired by the mathematician Ronald Fisher. A large twist of a focusing knob has some chance of bringing a microscope into better focus when it is far from the best setting. But as the barrel gets closer to the target, smaller and smaller tweaks are needed to bring any further improvement.

THE PENKE/DENISSEN/MILLER THEORY, which attributes variation in personality and intelligence to different evolutionary processes, is consistent with what we have learned so far about the genes for those two kinds of traits. The search for I.Q. genes calls to mind the cartoon in which a scientist with a smoldering test tube asks a colleague, "What's the opposite of Eureka?" Though we know that genes for intelligence must exist, each is likely to be small in effect, found in only a few people, or both. In a recent study of 6,000 children, the gene with the biggest effect accounted for less than one-quarter of an I.Q. point. The quest for genes that underlie major disorders of cognition, like autism and schizophrenia, has been almost as frustrating. Both conditions are highly heritable, yet no one has identified genes that cause either condition across a wide range of people. Perhaps this is what we should expect for a high-maintenance trait like human cognition, which is vulnerable to many mutations.

The hunt for personality genes, though not yet Nobel-worthy, has had better fortunes. Several associations have been found between personality traits and genes that govern the breakdown, recycling or detection of neurotransmitters (the molecules that seep from neuron to neuron) in the brain systems underlying mood and motivation.

Dopamine is the molecular currency in several brain circuits associated with wanting, getting satisfaction and paying attention. The gene for one kind of dopamine receptor, DRD4, comes in several versions. Some of the variants (like the one I have) have been associated with "approach related" personality traits like novelty seeking, sensation seeking and extraversion. A gene for another kind of receptor, DRD2, comes in a version that makes its dopamine system function less effectively. It has been associated with impulsivity, obesity and substance abuse. Still another gene, COMT, produces an enzyme that breaks down dopamine in the prefrontal cortex, the home of higher cognitive functions like reasoning and planning. If your version of the gene produces less COMT, you may have better concentration but might also be more neurotic and jittery.

Behavioral geneticists have also trained their sights on serotonin, which is found in brain circuits that affect many moods and drives, including those affected by Prozac and similar drugs. SERT, the serotonin transporter, is a molecule that scoops up stray serotonin for recycling, reducing the amount available to act in the brain. The switch for the gene that makes SERT comes in long and short versions, and the short version has been linked to depression and anxiety. A 2003 study made headlines because it suggested that the gene may affect a person's resilience to life's stressors rather than giving them a tendency to be depressed or content across the board. People who had two short versions of the gene (one from each parent) were likely to have a major depressive episode only if they had undergone traumatic experiences; those who had a more placid history were fine. In contrast, people who had two long versions of the gene typically failed to report depression regardless of their life histories. In other words, the effects of the gene are sensitive to a person's environment. Psychologists have long known that some people are resilient to life's slings and arrows and others are more fragile, but they had never seen this interaction played out in the effects of individual genes.

Still other genes have been associated with trust and commitment, or with a tendency to antisocial outbursts. It's still a messy science, with plenty of false alarms, contradictory results and tiny effects. But consumers will probably learn of genes linked to personality before they see any that are reliably connected to intelligence.

PERSONAL GENOMICS IS HERE TO STAY. The science will improve as efforts like the Personal Genome Project amass huge samples, the price of sequencing sinks and biologists come to a better understanding of what genes do and why they vary. People who have grown up with the democratization of information will not tolerate paternalistic regulations that keep them from their own genomes, and early adopters will explore how this new information can best be used to manage our health. There are risks of misunderstandings, but there are also risks in much of the flimflam we tolerate in alternative medicine, and in the hunches and folklore that many doctors prefer to evidence-based medicine. And besides, personal genomics is just too much fun.

At the same time, there is nothing like perusing your genetic data to drive home its limitations as a source of insight into yourself. What should I make of the nonsensical news that I am "probably light-skinned" but have a "twofold risk of baldness"? These diagnoses, of course, are simply peeled off the data in a study: 40 percent of men with the C version of the rs2180439 SNP are bald, compared with 80 percent of men with the T version, and I have the T. But something strange happens when you take a number representing the proportion of people in a sample and apply it to a single individual. The first use of the number is perfectly respectable as an input into a policy that will optimize the costs and benefits of treating a large similar group in a particular way. But the second use of the number is just plain weird. Anyone who knows me can confirm that I'm not 80 percent bald, or even 80 percent likely to be bald; I'm 100 percent likely not to be bald. The most charitable interpretation of the number when applied to me is, "If you knew nothing else about me, your subjective confidence that I am bald, on a scale of 0 to 10, should be 8." But that is a statement about your mental state, not my physical one. If you learned more clues about me (like seeing photographs of my father and grandfathers), that number would change, while not a hair on my head would be different. Some mathematicians say that "the probability of a single event" is a meaningless concept. Even when the effect of some gene is indubitable, the sheer complexity of the self will mean that it will not serve as an oracle on what the person will do. The gene that lets me taste propylthiouracil, 23andMe suggests, might make me dislike tonic water, coffee and dark beer. Unlike the tenuous genes linked to personality or intelligence, this one codes for a single taste-bud receptor, and I don't doubt that it lets me taste the bitterness. So why hasn't it stopped me from enjoying those drinks? Presumably it's because adults get a sophisticated pleasure from administering controlled doses of aversive stimuli to themselves. I've acquired a taste for Beck's Dark; others enjoy saunas, rock-climbing, thrillers or dissonant music. Similarly, why don't I conform to type and exploit those fast-twitch muscle fibers (thanks, ACTN3 genes!) in squash or basketball, rather than wasting them on hiking? A lack of coordination, a love of the outdoors, an inclination to daydream, all of the above? The self is a byzantine bureaucracy, and no gene can push the buttons of behavior by itself. You can attribute the ability to defy our genotypes to free will, whatever that means, but you can also attribute it to the fact that in a hundred-trillion-synapse human brain, any single influence can be outweighed by the product of all of the others.

Even if personal genomics someday delivers a detailed printout of psychological traits, it will probably not change everything, or even most things. It will give us deeper insight about the biological causes of individuality, and it may narrow the guesswork in assessing individual cases. But the issues about self and society that it brings into focus have always been with us. We have always known that people are liable, to varying degrees, to antisocial temptations and weakness of the will. We have always known that people should be encouraged to develop the parts of themselves that they can ("a man's reach should exceed his grasp") but that it's foolish to expect that anyone can accomplish anything ("a man has got to know his limitations"). And we know that holding people responsible for their behavior will make it more likely that they behave responsibly. "My genes made me do it" is no better an excuse than "We're depraved on account of we're deprived."

MANY OF THE DYSTOPIAN FEARS raised by personal genomics are simply out of touch with the complex and probabilistic nature of genes. Forget about the hyperparents who want to implant math genes in their unborn children, the "Gattaca" corporations that scan people's DNA to assign them to castes, the employers or suitors who hack into your genome to find out what kind of worker or spouse you'd make. Let them try; they'd be wasting their time.

The real-life examples are almost as futile. When the connection between the ACTN3 gene and muscle type was discovered, parents and coaches started swabbing the cheeks of children so they could steer the ones with the fast-twitch variant into sprinting and football. Carl Foster, one of the scientists who uncovered the association, had a better idea: "Just line them up with their classmates for a race and see which ones are the fastest." Good advice. The test for a gene can identify one of the contributors to a trait. A measurement of the trait itself will identify all of them: the other genes (many or few, discovered or undiscovered, understood or not understood), the way they interact, the effects of the environment and the child's unique history of developmental quirks.

It's our essentialist mind-set that makes the cheek swab feel as if it is somehow a deeper, truer, more authentic test of the child's ability. It's not that the mind-set is utterly misguided. Our genomes truly are a fundamental part of us. They are what make us human, including the distinctively human ability to learn and create culture. They account for at least half of what makes us different from our neighbors. And though we can change both inherited and acquired traits, changing the inherited ones is usually harder. It is a question of the most perspicuous level of analysis at which to understand a complex phenomenon. You can't understand the stock market by studying a single trader, or a movie by putting a DVD under a microscope. The fallacy is not in thinking that the entire genome matters, but in thinking that an individual gene will matter, at least in a way that is large and intelligible enough for us to care about.

So if you are bitten by scientific or personal curiosity and can think in probabilities, by all means enjoy the fruits of personal genomics. But if you want to know whether you are at risk for high cholesterol, have your cholesterol measured; if you want to know whether you are good at math, take a math test. And if you really want to know yourself (and this will be the test of how much you do), consider the suggestion of François La Rochefoucauld: "Our enemies' opinion of us comes closer to the truth than our own."

STEVEN PINKER is Harvard College professor of psychology at Harvard University and the author of "The Stuff of Thought: Language as a Window Into Human Nature."

23andMe Will Resume Giving Users Health Data

BY ANDREW POLLACK | OCT. 21, 2015

THE GENETIC TESTING company 23andMe became a Silicon Valley sensation by providing consumers with health and ancestry information based on a sample of their saliva, but suffered a setback when the Food and Drug Administration told it to stop presenting health data in 2013.

Now, after nearly two years, 23andMe is announcing on Wednesday that it will begin providing customers with health information again, though much less than before and with F.D.A. approval.

The company hopes the information, which relates to the risk of passing certain inherited diseases to one's children, will reignite growth in its subscriptions — even as the company evolves from being just a consumer testing service into a drug developer. It has also revamped its website to make the genetic information easier to understand and is raising the price of its service to $199, from $99.

"Part of what we tried to do over the last two years is take advantage of being off the market to redesign the entire experience," said Anne Wojcicki, co-founder and chief executive of 23andMe.

The company, based in Mountain View, Calif., initially offered consumers information on their risks of developing various diseases based on an analysis of the DNA in their saliva sample. The company created a buzz with its celebrity-filled "spit parties" and its message that consumers have the right to their own genetic information, without a doctor or regulatory agency being involved. It did not hurt that Ms. Wojcicki, now divorced, was married at the time to Sergey Brin, a co-founder of Google, and that Google invested in her company.

But in November 2013, the F.D.A. demanded that 23andMe stop providing health information until it could obtain regulatory approval by demonstrating that its results were accurate.

The setback was somewhat similar to what is occurring now with Theranos, another hot Silicon Valley medical testing company run by an entrepreneurial young woman, Elizabeth Holmes. In articles last week, The Wall Street Journal raised questions about Theranos's accuracy (the company says the doubts are unfounded), and the F.D.A. has asked the company to stop using its method of drawing blood from a finger instead of the arm until it wins regulatory approval for the device used.

The new health-related information 23andMe will provide is called carrier status. That relates to whether people have genetic mutations that could lead to a disease in their offspring, presuming the other parent has a mutation in the same gene and the child inherits both mutated genes. There will be information on 36 diseases, including cystic fibrosis, sickle cell anemia and Tay-Sachs.

Whether that information, which is of most interest to people planning to have babies, will be compelling is unclear, and there are separate carrier tests available through doctors from other laboratories.

Ms. Wojcicki said 23andMe still hoped to gain F.D.A. approval to provide information on health risks, but she would not estimate how long it might take to win that approval.

From a rebel fighting the system, she said, 23andMe is now "working from within the system and saying the consumer will have a sense of ownership and a voice in that system."

Ms. Wojcicki said that when the company stopped providing health information, the rate of new customer sign-ups dropped by more than half. The company continued to offer information on ancestry.

But the business still grew. This year it surpassed one million users, compared with half a million at the time of the F.D.A. action. She declined to disclose the current figure.

Many of the customers allow their genetic information to be used for medical studies, and some also provide additional information, such as what diseases they have. Companies like Pfizer and Genentech are paying 23andMe to use the data to search for insights that could be useful in developing drugs.

In May, 23andMe decided to go into drug discovery and development itself. That effort is being led by Richard Scheller, who had headed research and early development at Genentech.

Many earlier genomics companies, including Celera Genomics and DeCode Genetics, also tried their hand at drug development. Companies can make much more money from a successful drug than from selling genetic data. But drugs are also riskier and costly to develop, and many of those early attempts failed.

Ms. Wojcicki said 23andMe hoped to learn from those previous failures. She said that pharmaceutical companies would prefer to license an experimental compound rather than just acquire raw data.

The company recently raised $115 million from investors, led by Fidelity Management & Research, bringing its total raised to $241 million. Ms. Wojcicki said that 23andMe was not yet profitable and that the investment in drug development might prevent it from turning a profit in the short term.

With a Simple DNA Test, Family Histories Are Rewritten

BY GINA KOLATA | AUG. 28, 2017

Widespread DNA testing has shed light on the ancestry of millions of Americans. But these services have limitations, and the results can be uncertain.

BOB HUTCHINSON'S MOTHER told him and his siblings almost nothing about her family, no matter how often they asked. "She was good at brushing people off," said Mr. Hutchinson, 60.

Growing up, there were no photos of his mother as a child in the home, or of her own parents. She said that she was an only child, that her parents were dead. Her heritage, she claimed, was Italian and Swedish.

Mr. Hutchinson suspected there was more to the story. Then his sister-in-law, digging into the family past, found his mother's childhood home listed in a 1930 census.

The family had lived in Montclair, N.J., and was described as "Negro." Mr. Hutchinson, who runs an advertising agency and lives in Pacifica, Calif., had never been told he had African-American heritage.

These days, family secrets like this one are becoming harder to keep.

A growing number of companies now offer DNA tests that promise to pinpoint a customer's heritage and, with permission, to identify genetic relatives. The firms include generalists like 23andMe and Ancestry.com and specialty companies like African Ancestry.

Millions of people have signed up for the tests, sending saliva samples to laboratories and paying $100 to $350 or more for an analysis.

The customers are eager to know where they came from, to find a familial context that may be lacking. The answers hidden in DNA can be revelatory, shedding light on hidden events occurring decades earlier and forever changing the family narrative.

But a new analysis of DNA test kits by The Wirecutter, a review site owned by The New York Times, finds that the services also have limitations that the providers do not always fully acknowledge.

BRIAN FLAHERTY FOR THE NEW YORK TIMES

Bob Hutchinson at his home in Pacifica, Calif. He learned of his mixed-race ancestry through a genetic test and discovered relatives.

Mr. Hutchinson decided to have his DNA analyzed by 23andMe. The report revealed he is one-eighth sub-Saharan African, which means that his mother was of mixed race. There was some Italian and Swedish heritage.

Mr. Hutchinson also learned that his mother was not an only child, but had a brother. A genealogist helped him track down some first cousins in Alabama, who said they had been told never to contact Mr. Hutchinson or his family.

The cousins were delighted to hear from him. He plans to visit next year at Mardi Gras.

Mr. Hutchinson's results were enlightening, but in other contexts ethnicity has posed a particularly knotty problem for DNA testing firms. The very definitions of "race" and "ethnicity" are fuzzy, said Joseph Pickrell, a computational geneticist at the New York Genome Center laboratory, affiliated with Columbia University.

"Different people mean different things when they say 'race,' " he said. In the United States, for example, a person with almost any African ancestry often is identified as black.

"That's not necessarily the case in other parts of the world," Dr. Pickrell said.

Researchers at 23andMe acknowledged the difficulty in a recent paper, writing, "It is important to note that ancestry, ethnicity, identity and race are complex labels that result both from visible traits, such as skin color, and from cultural, economic, geographical and social factors."

In a recent study, the researchers decided to use Census Bureau definitions — black, white, Hispanic — to ask how often people who identify as one race actually have genetic markers indicating a mixed heritage.

After examining data from 160,000 customers who agreed to participate, the geneticists learned that 3.5 percent of those who said they were white actually had DNA that was 1 percent or more African in origin.

BRIAN FLAHERTY FOR THE NEW YORK TIMES

Mr. Hutchinson's family photographs. Through the genetic testing service 23andMe, Mr. Hutchinson learned that his mother had a brother, and a genealogist helped him track down some first cousins in Alabama, who said they had been told never to contact Mr. Hutchinson or his family.

The chances of having African ancestry were highest in the South, and highest of all in South Carolina, where at least 13 percent of those who said they were white had African ancestors.

Among those who said they were black, genetic ancestry over all was 73.2 percent African, 0.8 percent Native American and 24 percent European. Experts say the large proportion of European DNA found in African-Americans can be traced to before the Civil War, and the rape of enslaved African women.

The ancestry of those who said they were Hispanic was something of a hodgepodge. Some had no Native American ancestry; others had 50 percent or more.

Hispanics living in the South tended to have more African ancestry. As a group, their DNA was 6.2 percent African, 18 percent Native American and 65.1 percent European.

Jewish ancestry, on the other hand, is far easier to discern. Historically, these populations were small and Jews tended not to marry outsiders. As a result, they share telltale sequences of DNA, easily identified by testing.

But is this sort of ethnic categorization really instructive? Human beings share more than 99.9 percent of their DNA; what makes us different is vanishingly insignificant in terms of genetics.

If testing "tells me I'm 95 percent Ashkenazi Jewish and 5 percent Korean, is that really different from 100 percent Ashkenazi Jewish and zero percent Korean?" Jonathan Marks, an anthropology professor at the University of North Carolina at Charlotte, wondered in The Wirecutter.

The question of ethnicity is enmeshed with another difficult challenge for DNA testers: geography.

Genetics researchers generally know which DNA sequences originated on which continents. But pinpointing a particular country of origin, as many testing services claim to do, is far trickier.

Scientists simply do not have good data on the genetic characteristics of particular countries in, say, East Africa or East Asia. Even in more developed regions, distinguishing between Polish and, for instance, Russian heritage is inexact at best.

The precise numbers offered by some testing services raise eyebrows among genetics researchers. "It's all privatized science, and the algorithms are not generally available for peer review," Dr. Marks said.

"That's why their ads always specify that this is for recreational purposes only: lawyer-speak for, 'These results have no scientific standing.' "

For many, though, the point of DNA testing has nothing to do with ethnicity. Theresa Musumeci, 49, of Hockessin, Del., wanted to solve a longstanding mystery in her family. Who was her biological grandmother?

Decades ago, Ms. Musumeci's mother had discovered she had been adopted after she overheard the nuns at her Catholic high school in Camden, N.J., talking about it.

For years, she searched for clues to her birth mother's identity, eventually learning her name: Mary Culliton. But Ms. Musumeci's mother died in 1995, at 55, without learning much more.

Ms. Musumeci decided to continue the quest by submitting a sample to Ancestry.com, which also will notify users of relatives in its database if they have given permission.

Among the matches were Ms. Musumeci's half brother and a few well-known cousins — but also a man she had never heard of. His great-aunt, it turned out, was Ms. Musumeci's great-grandmother — Mary Culliton's mother. He filled her in on the woman's life.

Eventually Ms. Musumeci discovered other long-lost aunts and uncles. "I found five great family members," she said. Yet there is one regret: Her mother did not survive long enough to learn the story.

"I feel bad that the technology was not available for her," Ms. Musumeci said.

If DNA testing has the potential to shed light on new family relationships, it also can muddy those that had seemed settled. While putting together The Wirecutter's own report, one researcher learned that a grandparent was in fact not biologically related.

Such news can be burdensome — or freeing.

Mark, a banker in Delaware, got his test results back from Ancestry.com along with a list of relatives in its database. Oddly, there was no one on the list from his father's side of the family.

There was one name he recognized, though: his father's best friend. Who, it turned out, actually was his biological father.

Mark, 43, whose last name was withheld to protect his family's privacy, is estranged from his mother, and the man he knew as his father died more than a decade ago. So he reached out to his father's best friend, who confirmed an affair with his mother decades ago.

The two live near each other and have gotten together several times recently. The secret that the older man thought he would take to his grave is well out of the bag.

On one recent outing, Mark said, "he even showed me the place where I probably was conceived."

Are Genetic Testing Sites the New Social Networks?

BY ALYSON KRUEGER | JUNE 16, 2018

Like Facebook, but for fifth cousins, adoptive mothers and sperm-donor dads.

THREE YEARS AGO Dyan deNapoli, a 57-year-old author and TED speaker who specializes in penguins, was given a 23andMe genetic testing kit for her birthday. Intrigued, she spit in the tube and sent the results to a lab in Burlington, N.C.

About two months later she received a pie chart breaking down where her ancestors lived (99.4 percent of them were from Europe). What she was most giddy about, however, was a 41-page list of all the people who had done the test and were genetically related to her: 1,200 in all. (Customers can choose whether their information is shared with others.)

"I had the names of everyone from my immediate family members to my first cousins, second cousins, third. Once I got past fourth cousins, it went to my fifth cousins, and beyond," said Ms. deNapoli, who lives in Georgetown, Mass. "It started me down this genealogical rabbit hole."

Using the website's internal messaging system supplemented with Facebook, she connected with three second cousins, who were in neighboring towns. She met each one for breakfast in a local diner, where they spent hours drinking coffee and poring over family trees and photos, marveling at various resemblances.

"Jorge is an older cousin, a very young 90," Ms. deNapoli said. "Everybody agreed he looks just like my dad."

Last June she visited a third cousin and other relatives in a mountainous village in the Campania region of Italy, her paternal grandmother's place of origin, walking the narrow streets, eating four-course meals and learning stories of her ancestors, including a long-ago Hatfield-McCoy-level feud. "That's why I really didn't know this side of my family," Ms. deNapoli said in wonderment.

'ARE YOU SURE YOU ARE MY SISTER?'

At-home genetic testing services have gained significant traction in the past few years. 23andMe, which costs $99, has over five million customers, according to the company; AncestryDNA (currently $69), over 10 million.

The companies use their large databases to match willing participants with others who share their DNA. In many cases, long-lost relatives are reuniting, becoming best friends, travel partners, genealogical resources or confidantes.

The result is a more layered version of what happened when Facebook first emerged and out-of-touch friends and family members found one another. Children of long-ago casual sperm donors are finding their fathers. Adoptees are bonding to biological family members they've been searching for their entire lives.

Sherri Tredway, 55, is a marketing and development director for a social service agency based in Washington, Ind. She was adopted as a baby, and in January she drove two and a half hours to Bowling Green, Ky., to meet her biological half sister, Patty Roberts-Freeman, 60, with whom she connected through AncestryDNA.

Ms. Roberts-Freeman needed an outfit for a wedding, so they arranged to meet at a shopping mall to find one together. They started in the food court, where they bought sodas and talked for over an hour about their mother, their current lives, their upbringings.

They then went to a Belk department store, where they tried on outfits. "I was looking at some dressy dresses and showed her a few, and she said, 'No, no dresses for me!' " Ms. Tredway recalled. "I remember saying, 'O.K., are you sure you are my sister?' which we both laughed about. She found a silky floral shell and a beautiful sweater in rose, pink and cream to wear with some slacks. It was very classy.' "

The half sisters have since seen each other several times, meeting in restaurants between their homes. They also see other relatives including two more half siblings, Sissy Bonham, 51, and Michael Clavette, 54, as well as their biological mother's sister, Nancy Kalman Bell.

"Not a day goes by when I don't talk to Aunt Nan," Ms. Tredway said. "I call her to talk, when I'm upset, anything. She's my family now."

Josh Broadwater, 44, a deputy sheriff in California, was abandoned when he was 1 day old in a gas station bathroom in California. When he was in his 30s, he implored the agency that placed him with adoptive parents to give him whatever information they had about his biological ones but ran into constant dead ends.

In July 2015 he sent a kit to AncestryDNA and found a cousin who shared DNA with him. That led to him discovering his biological father: a man who had had a one-night stand in the front seat of a '69 pickup truck and never knew he existed. They connected over the phone, and soon Mr. Broadwater was driving 500 miles to go elk hunting on his father's farm in Kingston, Utah.

"He kind of sat there quiet for 10 to 15 seconds," said Mr. Broadwater about their first conversation. "And then in his cute little country voice he said, 'Well, if Gloria is your mom, and this thing says I'm your dad, there is a damn good chance I am your dad.' He is just the coolest person."

The two got along so well that they now talk on the phone once a week about the weather, what is going on with the children, about the hunting season. "I never thought finding my biological dad, he would be the one calling me," Mr. Broadwater said.

He also talks to a half brother who is eight months older than him. "I just got a text message from him that I'm going to be an uncle in October," Mr. Broadwater said. "I don't know how much I will be involved. This whole new family is new to me."

THE GENETIC GLOBAL VILLAGE

Others who have their DNA tested are forming relationships not with specific people, but with their family's places of origin.

One example is Leah Madison, 32, an education outreach coordinator for the Desert Research Institute in Reno, Nev. She was planning trips to Peru and Korea when she learned a year and a half ago from 23andMe that her family came from Greece, Italy and the Iberian Peninsula.

Over the winter she and her father went to the Iberian Peninsula for two weeks. She felt an ineluctable connection to the people as she ate their bread masterpieces, toured buildings by Antoni Gaudí and danced to flamenco music.

"I had a piece of paper that tells me I'm from Spain," Ms. Madison said. "But then I went there and I noticed all these people have curly hair, and maybe that is where mine comes from?" Now she feels compelled to visit the other places as well.

But other testers have found their results more alienating.

In February 2016 Christine Carter, a marketing strategist, was on a business trip to London when she decided to open her 23andMe dossier. She was in her hotel room, rushing to dinner. "I thought it would be a quick reveal," she said. "I was going to learn that I was Native American and black, and maybe learn a little bit more about the stories I heard as a child."

Ms. Carter was shocked when the results showed she was 31.5 percent white or European. She struggled through dinner, keeping this revelation mostly to herself, until she got back to her home in Baltimore and contended with her feelings.

She wrote a Huffington Post blog post, "I Celebrated Black History Month ... By Finding Out I Was White" that went viral. It attracted thousands of comments, from white supremacists who berated her, to people who had a similar experience and shared her sentiments.

"It took me less than 30 minutes to write the post, it was like journaling, something to get it off my chest," said Ms. Carter, 32. "So to have that reaction was insane."

Perhaps the most frustrating reality is when users don't have any known connections at all. This can happen to people in certain ethnic groups, including Latinos and Asians, that thus far have fewer people using the services and a smaller database.

"Diversity in genetic research is a global problem," said Joanna Mountain, the senior director of Research at 23andMe, adding that the company is offering free testing in some countries to begin to rectify that. "The results for Hispanics and Asians aren't there yet, but they are coming," said Jenn Utley, a family historian at Ancestry (the parent company of AncestryDNA). "The database keeps growing."

FINDING YOUR TRIBE

Even for those privy to rich data, using a genetic-testing service as social network poses challenges. Ms. deNapoli has written to 25 people related to her and has heard back from only nine. "I guess a lot of people aren't doing the tests to connect with family," she said.

Ms. Tredway said she had a difficult experience after reaching out to her biological mother, getting an out-of-the-blue phone call from North Carolina while she was getting a haircut: "She said, 'There is no way you could be my daughter,' even though I knew I was."

And then there is David Hughes, 38, the owner of an executive search firm, Sandbox Partners, who was ecstatic when he got his results back from 23andMe. "My breakdown is basically 60 percent Balkan, which is Mediterranean or Greek, 25 percent Native American Indian, 11 percent Middle Eastern and 4 percent Eastern African," he said. "I'm like the heritage of warriors or something."

But as much as Mr. Hughes wants to explore the different regions he comes from and meet the family members whom he got that DNA from, he hasn't matched with anyone through the genetic testing service.

"My biological dad is 50 percent Native American Indian, so I eventually hope to find which tribe I am from," he said. "But I have nothing yet."

The Online Gene Test Finds a Dangerous Mutation. It May Well Be Wrong.

BY GINA KOLATA | JULY 2, 2018

Third-party analysis of raw DNA is not as rigorous as that done in a certified laboratory. But many consumers don't understand that their results are not conclusive.

DR. JOSHUA CLAYTON, a 29-year-old radiology resident at Baylor University Medical Center in Dallas, wanted to learn about his ancestry. So he sent a sample of his saliva to 23andMe, the genetic testing company.

His report was pretty mundane — no new revelations. But then he sent the profile created by 23andMe to a separate company called Promethease, which promises to do a more in-depth analysis for genetic mutations that cause disease.

The news was not good. Dr. Clayton got back a report with a sinister red box at the top saying he had a mutation linked to Lynch syndrome, a frightening genetic disorder that leads to potentially deadly cancers at an early age.

In an interview, Dr. Clayton said he "knew, at least cursorily, that false positives were common with these tests." But "that didn't change the frightened feelings or concern, because I certainly couldn't blow it off."

After two weeks of panic and yet another genetic test at a company with expertise in medical diagnostics, he learned the red box result was wrong. He simply didn't have the mutation.

More Americans are embracing consumer genetic testing, but the Food and Drug Administration limits what major firms like 23andMe or Ancestry.com can say about a consumer's health.

So many people are taking an additional step: uploading all the raw data created by these companies to second companies for additional

ALLISON V. SMITH FOR THE NEW YORK TIMES

Joshua Clayton was erroneously told he had a mutation associated with Lynch syndrome, a genetic disorder that can lead to fatal cancers at an early age.

analysis. But these are not firms certified to provide medical diagnoses, nor are they sophisticated academic centers.

Companies like Promethease warn customers not to regard their results as medical diagnoses. Mostly, they are comparing a consumer's raw data to gene variants reported to be linked to disease.

But it's not at all clear that consumers understand how uncertain their results may be.

There are no systematic studies of how often the direct-to-consumer results and third-party analyses are wrong. In one small study, Ambry Genetics — a lab certified to do medical testing — looked at 49 samples sent in by physicians whose patients had been told that they had disease-causing mutations by third-party interpreters.

Ambry found that 40 percent were wrong. In addition, some genetic variations classified by second companies as threatening actually were benign.

This tiny sample doesn't prove that the false-positive rate is 40 percent. But patients like Dr. Clayton are not uncommon, genetic counselors say. And they are increasingly worried about the flip side: false negatives that reassure consumers who actually should be worried.

Dr. Judy Garber, director of the Center for Cancer Genetics and Prevention at the Dana-Farber Cancer Institute in Boston, said one of her patients was told by a consumer testing company she had Li-Fraumeni syndrome, which greatly raises the risk of a number of rare cancers.

Further testing showed that diagnosis was wrong. "It makes you worry about the people who don't come in," said Dr. Garber.

"People think they are getting the same kind of genetic testing as they would get from a certified clinical laboratory," said Stephany Tandy-Connor, a genetic counselor at Ambry. "Nothing could be further from the truth."

Even some doctors are misled by the reports, she said.

Of course, companies like Ambry have an interest in making sure their business is not usurped by consumer testing firms. But it's also true that the method used by consumer companies is very different from those used by certified clinical laboratories.

Consumer companies look for changes in tiny segments of genes, rather than examining the entire gene and looking for alterations. That is cheap but not comprehensive.

And because they are not making medical diagnoses, these companies are not subject to the sort of quality controls as certified labs, which require extensive confirmation that results are free of errors.

Compounding the problem, the second companies rely on databases that may contain errors — so even if the genetic alteration found by the first company is correct, the analysis can be wrong. Ambry found such patients in its recent analysis.

Greg Lennon, a co-founder of Promethease, said that the company's reports include a disclaimer saying the data are "not intended for medical or health purposes." Customers are warned to seek out "an independent, clinically validated test" if they are told of a mutation and to seek out a genetic counselor.

When errors occur, they usually derive from mistakes in the raw DNA data, said Mike Cariaso, also a co-founder of Promethease.

23andMe offers limited medical testing — for example, looking for three of the most common mutations in breast cancer genes that occur mostly in Ashkenazi Jews. But there are thousands of other alterations in those genes that the company does not track.

The F.D.A. has given 23andMe approval to do similar testing for 10 disorders linked to genetic mutations, but not for the huge number of others, including Lynch syndrome, that companies like Promethease look for.

The variations in DNA in 23andMe's raw data "are not for medical or diagnostic use," said Shirley Wu, the company's director of product science. "The data hasn't undergone the same kind of quality control and validation as our variations in our health reports."

The company warns customers of this before providing their raw data, Dr. Wu said.

For the consumer who expects validated diagnoses, it's all a bit confusing.

Testing companies like 23andMe say they are not at fault, because they make it clear that their data are not meant to be used for medical diagnoses.

The companies that provide deeper analyses, like Promethease, say they take only raw genetic profiles created elsewhere and use publicly available data to scan for mutations that can increase disease risk. Promethease didn't author any of it.

"So much of what I have seen in these D.T.C. tests are false positives and cannot be trusted," said Dr. Robert Nussbaum, chief medical officer at Invitae, a medical testing lab.

Still, he added, false negatives are even more worrisome.

Dr. Clayton learned only after weeks of agonizing that his Lynch syndrome diagnosis wasn't really a diagnosis at all. "My wife and I were talking about having children," he recalled. "What do you do? Do you make that decision to pass this on to them?"

And what about disability insurance? If he got cancer, he might not be able to work. But could he even get insurance?

Dr. Clayton searched online for Lynch syndrome experts and found Dr. Theodora Ross, director of the cancer genetics program at the University of Texas Southwestern Medical Center in Dallas.

She had Dr. Clayton's DNA tested at a lab certified to make the diagnosis. That was how he found out the report was wrong.

He was lucky, he said, that he had medical training and knew where to find help.

"I don't think that applies to a lot of people," he said.

GINA KOLATA writes about science and medicine. She has twice been a Pulitzer Prize finalist and is the author of six books, including "Mercies in Disguise: A Story of Hope, a Family's Genetic Destiny, and the Science That Saved Them."

CHAPTER 2

Genetic Testing and Medicine

Though genes associated with risk for disease have been tested for decades, the increased availability of genetic testing has allowed for more advanced genetic health screenings. In addition, gene-editing technologies like Crispr are beginning to promise more widespread use of gene therapy. To support this work on a larger scale, many institutions are exploring genetic databases to identify the range of genetic diversity in the general public, as well as common genetic diseases.

DNA Blueprint for Fetus Built Using Tests of Parents

BY ANDREW POLLACK | JUNE 6, 2012

FOR THE FIRST TIME, researchers have determined virtually the entire genome of a fetus using only a blood sample from the pregnant woman and a saliva specimen from the father.

The accomplishment heralds an era in which parents might find it easier to know the complete DNA blueprint of a child months before it is born.

That would allow thousands of genetic diseases to be detected prenatally. But the ability to know so much about an unborn child is likely to raise serious ethical considerations as well. It could increase abortions for reasons that have little to do with medical issues and more to do with parental preferences for traits in children.

"It's an extraordinary piece of technology, really quite remarkable," said Peter Benn, professor of genetics and developmental biology at the University of Connecticut, who was not involved in the work. "What I see in this paper is a glance into the future."

The paper, published Wednesday in the journal Science Translational Medicine, was written by genome scientists at the University of Washington. They took advantage of new high-speed DNA sequencing and some statistical and computational acrobatics to deduce the DNA sequence of the fetus with about 98 percent accuracy.

The process is not practical, affordable or accurate enough for use now, experts said. The University of Washington researchers estimated that it would cost $20,000 to $50,000 to do one fetal genome today.

But the cost of DNA sequencing is falling at a blistering pace, and accuracy is improving as well. The researchers estimated that the procedure could be widely available in three to five years. Others said it would take somewhat longer.

It is already possible to determine the DNA sequence of a fetus by acquiring fetal cells through amniocentesis or chorionic villus sampling, which involves testing the placental tissue. But these procedures are invasive and carry a slight risk of inducing a miscarriage.

For couples worried about passing on a genetic disease, it is also possible to use in vitro fertilization and have an embryo genetically tested before implantation into the womb.

But the technique described in the paper would not require complete cells from the fetus and would make such DNA testing easier and less risky.

"If this sort of thing is ever to be used on a widespread basis, I think it necessarily has to be noninvasive," said Jay Shendure, associate professor of genome sciences at the University of Washington, who supervised the research team.

The genome was determined from blood samples taken 18.5 weeks into the pregnancy, although the researchers said the technique could probably be applied in the first trimester, as early as or even earlier than some invasive techniques.

The technique takes advantage of the discovery in the 1990s that fragments of DNA from the fetus can be found in a pregnant woman's blood plasma, probably the result of fetal cells dying and breaking apart.

These fragments can be genetically analyzed, providing that the fetal DNA fragments can be distinguished from the far more numerous fragments that come from the mother herself.

The analysis of fetal DNA fragments found in a pregnant woman's blood is already used in new commercially available tests of the fetus's gender, its paternity and whether it has Down syndrome. But reconstructing an entire genome from DNA fragments is much more difficult.

Such information would allow detection of so-called Mendelian disorders, like cystic fibrosis, Tay-Sachs disease and Marfan syndrome, which are caused by mutations in a single gene.

More than 3,000 such diseases collectively occur in about 1 percent of births. The mutations can be inherited from the parents or they can arise spontaneously in the fetus.

Researchers led by Dennis Lo at the Chinese University of Hong Kong first showed in 2010 that reconstructing a fetal genome would be possible. Other work toward this goal has been done by Stephen Quake and colleagues at Stanford University.

But Dr. Lo's team used a maternal sample obtained invasively. And it could determine only the inherited mutations, not the spontaneous ones.

The University of Washington researchers, using an approach partly developed by a graduate student, Jacob O. Kitzman, did not need an invasive test. And they were able to detect 39 of 44 such spontaneous mutations, though with a huge number of false positives.

"This will be a step toward having a better and better prenatal diagnosis that detects more and more at a reliable cost," said Dr. Arthur L. Beaudet, chairman of molecular and human genetics at Baylor College of Medicine in Houston.

Dr. Beaudet, who was not involved in the work, said that spontaneous mutations account for about 10 percent of cases of mental retardation and other learning disabilities.

The ability to sequence an entire fetal genome is likely to raise numerous issues. "There are some scenarios that are extremely troubling," said Marcy Darnovsky, associate executive director of the Center for Genetics and Society, a public interest group in Berkeley, Calif. The tests will spur questions on "who deserves to be born," she said.

Use of the approach could lead to an increase in abortions because some parents might terminate the pregnancy if the fetus was found to have a genetic disease. But it is also possible that parents may be tempted to terminate if the fetus lacked a favorable trait like athletic prowess.

"You could start doing things more toward the direction of positive selection," said Dr. Stephen A. Brown, associate professor of obstetrics and gynecology at the University of Vermont.

Moreover, a full fetal genome sequence would turn up numerous mutations for which information is lacking as to whether they cause disease, posing a dilemma for expectant parents and their doctors.

"Our capacity to generate data is outstripping our ability to interpret it in ways that are useful to physicians and patients," the University of Washington researchers wrote their paper. "That is, although the noninvasive prediction of a fetal genome may be technically feasible, its interpretation — even for known Mendelian disorders — will remain a major challenge."

The researchers sequenced the genomes of the mother and father. They then sequenced nearly three billion DNA fragments from the mother's blood. The samples, obtained from a tissue bank, were from unknown donors.

Since people have two copies of each chromosome, they have two versions of each gene. Only one version is passed to the baby.

Determining which version at any given spot in the father's genome was passed to the fetus was fairly straightforward, since any fragments of DNA in the mother's blood containing a sequence unique to the father had to have come from the fetus.

Determining which of two variants at a given location — call them A and B — the fetus inherited from the mother was more difficult. If the fetus inherited version A, then fragments containing A (which could come from either the fetus or the mother) would outnumber fragments containing B (which could come only from the mother). But since there are relatively few fetal fragments, the difference would be small and hard to detect.

The researchers used an approach they developed to figure out which variations in the mother's genome were likely to be passed to the baby together. That made the problem more tractable than trying to make a call individually at three million locations in the genome.

After it was determined what the fetus inherited from the mother and father, what was left in the fetus's DNA was considered a possible spontaneous mutation. There were initially 25 million such candidates, though statistical approaches narrowed that to 3,800. That still vastly exceeded the 44 such spontaneous mutations found after the baby was born and its cord blood sequenced. Having so many false positive findings of spontaneous mutations could worry parents and doctors.

"There's definitely plenty of room for improvement," Professor Shendure said. But, he added, "This is not science fiction anymore."

The Path to Reading a Newborn's DNA Map

BY ANNE EISENBERG | FEB. 8, 2014

WHAT IF LABORATORIES could run comprehensive DNA tests on infants at birth, spotting important variations in their genomes that might indicate future medical problems? Should parents be told of each variation, even if any risk is still unclear? Would they even want to know?

New parents needn't confront these difficult questions just yet. The more than four million babies born in 2014 in the United States will likely be screened in traditional ways — by public health programs that check for sickle cell anemia and several dozen other serious, treatable conditions. So far, DNA-based tests of infants play only a small part in screening.

But that may change in the next few years, as technology that can sequence and analyze the entire genome of a child becomes available, potentially detecting a range of inherited genetic conditions at birth. It's the same type of analysis that now can tell adults — if they choose to ask for it — whether they are at high risk for a certain type of cancer, for example. As the technology becomes more sophisticated, it will inevitably expand into the world of newborns.

To begin dealing with the complexities of that new world, the National Institutes of Health have awarded $5 million in four pilot grants under a research program.

Genomic sequencing may reveal many problems that could be treated early in a child's life, avoiding the diagnostic odyssey that parents can endure when medical problems emerge later, said Dr. Cynthia Powell, winner of one of the research grants and chief of the division of pediatric genetics and metabolism at the University of North Carolina School of Medicine.

The research projects are unusual in that they tightly link technical and clinical problems with ethical ones, said Dr. Edward McCabe, chief medical officer at the March of Dimes in White Plains. "So often in biomedical research, there is a siloed way of thinking," in which technical problems are considered independent of their social implications, he said. "Here we have transdisciplinary thinking at the core."

Jaime King, a professor at the University of California Hastings College of the Law, is, among other things, trying to create screening guidelines to suggest which genetic conditions might be mandatory for testing and follow-up, and which might be optional and left up to parents.

"This will take the wisdom of Solomon," she said. "We will be debating it for years to come."

One of the drawbacks of DNA tests for children — as well as for adults — is that they reveal many mutations that don't pose problems for the people who carry them. "Many changes in the DNA sequence aren't disease-causing," said Dr. Robert Nussbaum, chief of the genomic medicine division at the School of Medicine of the University of California, San Francisco, and leader of one of the pilot grants. "We aren't very good yet at distinguishing which are and which aren't."

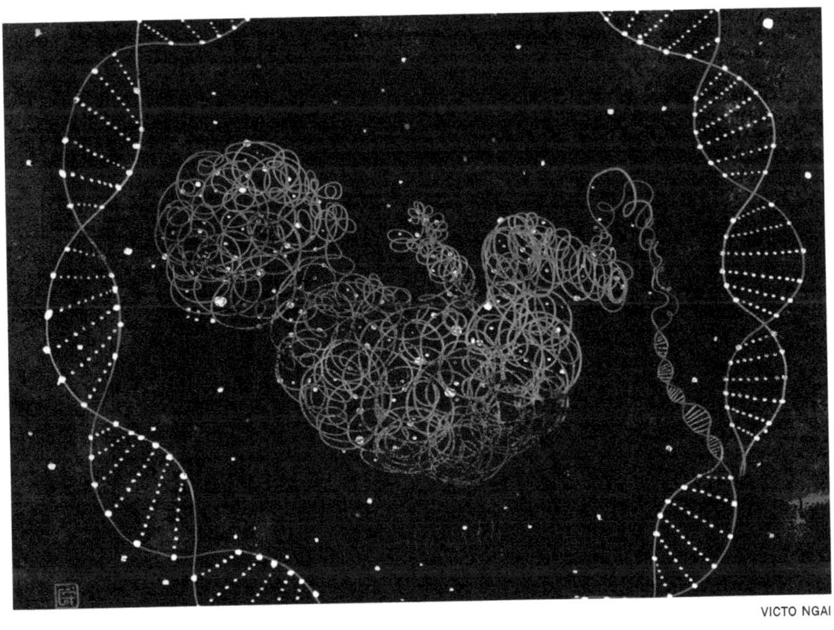

VICTO NGAI

For this reason, Dr. Jeffrey Botkin, a professor of pediatrics and chief of medical ethics at the University of Utah, said it was far too soon to consider comprehensive genome sequencing as a primary screening tool for newborns.

"You will get dozens of findings per child that you won't be able to adequately interpret," he said. "Imagine trying to explain dozens of these unknown variants to parents. And it's an enormous psychological burden on the parents, who can't know whether the child has an actual problem or not." The ethical issues of sequencing are sharply different when children, rather than adults, undergo comprehensive DNA tests, he said.

Adults can decide which test information, if any, they want to receive about themselves. But children won't usually have that option — their parents will decide. "We can't presume that children would want or benefit from the information," he said.

The first human genome was decoded only a decade ago, but genomics has already become a multibillion-dollar industry. If screening of newborns gains traction, established genomics companies that make DNA testing and analysis tools — companies like Illumina and Pacific Biosciences — may be beneficiaries.

Dr. Powell of the University of North Carolina wants the pilot projects to establish research data before consumer-directed programs offering comprehensive genome sequencing and analysis become widespread.

"It won't be long before people are offered this kind of genomic screening commercially," she said. "We want to look at it in a much more controlled setting before consumer companies get hold of it."

Dr. Eric Green, director of the National Human Genome Research Institute, which is part of the N.I.H. and is a funding organization for the pilot grants, agreed that skepticism was warranted. "We are not ready now to deploy whole genome sequencing on a large scale," he said, "but it would be irresponsible not to study the problem," using the time before the technology matures to hash out difficult issues.

“We are doing these pilot studies so that when the cost of genomic sequencing comes down, we can answer the question, ‘Should we do it?’ ” he said.

“There will be an industry setting up around this,” he said. “We need to be ahead of that. We should get data to see if there is any value in sequencing all newborns.”

New York's Chief Medical Examiner Seeks to Lead in DNA Research

BY J. DAVID GOODMAN | FEB. 9, 2015

SHE IS THE closest thing to a hometown medical examiner that a city of eight million people could really expect to see. Born in the Village. Raised to be a doctor. Working at the local morgue.

Of course, that local morgue happens to be among the largest in the country, New York's Office of Chief Medical Examiner, which handles roughly 12,000 bodies and performs 5,500 autopsies each year. Since late last year, Dr. Barbara Sampson has occupied its title role, the first woman to head the agency since it began investigating deaths in 1918.

Dr. Sampson, who had been acting chief since 2013, officially took the helm in December with the goal of pushing state-of-the-art research in DNA evidence collection and genetic investigations of mysterious deaths. But she does so at a time when the office is seeking to right itself after high-profile mistakes — a technician's mishandling of rape evidence; a body that went missing — sparked city investigations and risked tarnishing its reputation.

More recently, the medical examiner's office also found itself thrust into the debate over the police killing of Eric Garner on Staten Island after the agency officially linked his death to an officer's chokehold.

In an interview in her office, shortly after her appointment, Dr. Sampson said she hoped that a focus on quality assurance, along with a new lab supervisor and a 24-hour operations center for tracking bodies as they move from street to morgue, would curb human errors. She said that those isolated mistakes had not undermined the advanced science that was performed at the lab and was often presented at trial.

"The science was never in question," she said.

Science is important to Dr. Sampson, 48, who besides being a physician, as all city medical examiners are, also holds a doctorate in molecular biology. She counts microbiology and cardiac pathology as "research loves."

At the dinner table, growing up, conversation turned around medicine, and the question from her physician parents was not if she would become a doctor but what type she would be.

"My father always had a great respect for the autopsy," she said. "Were we right? Could we have done better?" By 13, she settled on what would be her life's work: forensic pathology. In 1998, after a hospital residency in Boston, she found her first and only job as a medical examiner — in New York City.

On her desk sit a model of a human heart, because of her fascination with cardiac issues, and a pipe, "my nod to Dr. Hirsch," her predecessor and mentor.

Her devotion to Dr. Charles S. Hirsch, the city's longtime chief medical examiner who retired in early 2013, can also be seen on the walls: His portrait and photographs of the many teams of medical examiners he trained hang to the right of her desk; across the room is a picture of the official truck that he took to the World Trade Center on Sept. 11, 2001, and that was crushed in the collapse.

"It's a reminder of how precious life is," said Dr. Sampson, who was three months pregnant with her only child when the twin towers came down and the office began a day-and-night operation to identify the remains of thousands of victims. "I would want no medical examiner to work here who was not upset by the kinds of things that we have to see."

And the city's 30 medical examiners see a lot, each performing hundreds of autopsies each year in the agency's aging blue-brick headquarters in Manhattan, on First Avenue and 30th Street, or in exam rooms in each of the boroughs.

Add to that the expanding number of tasks performed by the office and its staff of 620, including analyzing DNA evidence for the

Police Department, around 52,000 items a year; its role as the city morgue, processing 6,000 deaths that do not require investigation; and so-called molecular autopsies, genetic tests that provide an exact cause of death in cases where it previously would have been unknown.

There is also a forensic anthropology lab in the First Avenue building, where, on a recent morning, skeletons in varying degrees of completeness lay on tables. One, the likely victim of a crime, was found by the police after a tip last fall. Con Edison workers discovered another, probably buried long ago, under a sidewalk in Queens.

Four blocks farther south, in a sleek tower built in 2007, DNA technicians in white protective gear and purple gloves cut test swabs from bloodstained jeans, half-smoked cigarettes and other criminal evidence. "We get a lot of hats from robberies and burglaries," said Ashley Rhodes, a forensic scientist. Bank robbers' notes are also brought in.

Though the medical examiner's office acts as the city's only DNA crime lab and medical examiners often testify in criminal cases for the prosecution, the agency is independent of the police, a fact occasionally highlighted in autopsies after officer-involved killings.

Among the most contentious came recently after the killing of Mr. Garner, a Staten Island man who died after police officers wrestled him to the ground to arrest him in July. In its official ruling, reached through autopsy and testing as well as a review of a widely circulated video of the encounter, the medical examiner's office used the word "chokehold" to describe the neck restraint, prompting criticism from police unions. Dr. Sampson, while declining to discuss the case specifically, stressed the independence of the office.

Mr. Garner's relatives enlisted Michael Baden, a former chief medical examiner in the city, to review the findings, but he advised that a second autopsy was not needed.

Elsewhere in the same building is a molecular genetics laboratory where the bodies of otherwise healthy people who died suddenly, including infants, are tested for a group of potentially fatal heart diseases known as cardiac channelopathies that are otherwise invisible to medical examiners. By doing so, Dr. Sampson said, the office has been able to give clarity to mysterious deaths and to help treat living relatives who may be similarly afflicted.

"That is the next step for medical examiners' offices," said Dr. James R. Gill, who worked with Dr. Sampson before leaving to run the medical examiner's office in Connecticut. "New York City is on the cutting edge of molecular genetics."

Although city money for the agency had been cut in recent years, the last two budget cycles have included increases. The office's total budget is set to rise to about $76 million in the next fiscal year.

Despite the sheen of forensic testing in television crime dramas, it remains a profession troubled by an image problem. "It's not a glamorous field," Dr. Sampson conceded.

At the same time, it is one that increasingly attracts women. A majority of the medical examiners in New York City are women, Dr. Sampson said.

While most of her own mentors were men, including Dr. Hirsch, she said she did have one important female role model: her mother, who graduated from medical school in 1960 when there were few women doing so.

"She always told me if you want to do it, you can do it," Dr. Sampson said. "That's how I was raised; that's how I hope I'm raising my daughter."

In Iceland's DNA, New Clues to Disease-Causing Genes

BY CARL ZIMMER | MARCH 25, 2015

SCIENTISTS IN ICELAND have produced an unprecedented snapshot of a nation's genetic makeup, discovering a host of previously unknown gene mutations that may play roles in ailments as diverse as Alzheimer's disease, heart disease and gallstones.

"This is amazing work, there's no question about it," said Daniel G. MacArthur, a geneticist at Massachusetts General Hospital who was not involved in the research. "They've now managed to get more genetic data on a much larger chunk of the population than in any other country in the world."

In a series of papers published on Wednesday in the journal Nature Genetics, researchers at Decode, an Icelandic genetics firm owned by Amgen, described sequencing the genomes — the complete DNA — of 2,636 Icelanders, the largest collection ever analyzed in a single human population.

With this trove of genetic information, the scientists were able to accurately infer the genomes of more than 100,000 other Icelanders, or almost a third of the entire country.

"From the technical point of view, these papers are a tour-de-force," said David Reich, a geneticist at Harvard Medical School who was not involved in the research.

While some diseases, like cystic fibrosis, are caused by a single genetic mutation, the most common ones are not. Instead, mutations to a number of different genes can each raise the risk of getting, say, heart disease or breast cancer. Discovering these mutations can shed light on these diseases and point to potential treatments. But many of them are rare, making it necessary to search large groups of people to find them.

The wealth of data created in Iceland may enable scientists to begin doing that.

In their new study, the researchers at Decode present several such revealing mutations. For example, they found eight people in Iceland who shared a mutation on a gene called MYL4. Medical records showed that they also have early onset atrial fibrillation, a type of irregular heartbeat.

Gilian McVean, a geneticist at the University of Oxford who was not involved in the study, said that discovering a rare association this way "is a bit of a holy grail" for geneticists.

Luke Jostins, also at Oxford, was intrigued by another rare mutation discovered by Decode, one that influences the level of a hormone that stimulates the thyroid gland.

When Icelanders get the mutation from their mother, they make more of the hormone, the researcher found. But when they get it from their father, they make less.

Dr. Jostins called the discovery "super-weird" and wants to see the result replicated elsewhere. "If it is real, it is quite the find, the sort of thing that could really inform some new biology," he said.

The scientists also found a rare mutation to a gene called ABDB4 that raises the risk of gallstones. And they identified a gene called ABCA7 as a risk factor for Alzheimer's disease.

Previous studies had suggested a gene in the genetic neighborhood of ABCA7 was associated with the disease.

But the Icelandic study pinpointed the gene itself — and even the specific mutation involved.

In recent years, geneticists have been searching for causes of disease not just by seeking out people who carry mutations, but also those who lack a working copy of a particular gene. Scientists call them human knockouts.

The Decode researchers looked for human knockouts in Iceland — and found a lot of them. Nearly 8 percent of Icelanders lack a working version of a gene. All told, the Decode team identified 1,171 genes shut down in Icelandic knockouts.

In a 2012 study, Dr. MacArthur and his colleagues were able to identify just 253 genes knocked out in humans.

In an interview, Dr. Kari Stefansson, the founder of Decode, said that he and his colleagues are now getting in touch with the Icelandic knockouts to see if they will consent to more studies designed to figure out the physiological consequences of the missing genes.

Since Dr. Stefansson and his colleagues submitted their initial results for publication, they have continued gathering DNA from Icelanders.

The scientists now have full genomes from about 10,000 Icelanders and partial genetic information on 150,000 more.

With a technique called imputation, the researchers say they are able to ascertain the full genomes of people they have not even examined. Dr. Stefansson said that means that his firm could generate a report for genetic disease on every person in Iceland.

With the push of a button, for instance, the firm can identify every person with the well-known BRCA2 mutation, which dramatically raises the risk of breast and ovarian cancer — even if they have not submitted to genetic testing themselves.

Currently, that information is withheld from Icelanders, but Dr. Stefansson hopes that the government will change its policy. "It's a crime not to approach these people," he said.

Iceland is a particularly fertile country for doing genetics research. It was founded by a small number of settlers from Europe arriving about 1,100 years ago. Between 8,000 and 20,000 people came mainly from Scandinavia, Ireland and Scotland. The country remained isolated for the next thousand years, and so living Icelanders have a relatively low level of genetic diversity. This makes it easier for scientists to detect genetic variants that raise the risk of disease, because there are fewer of them to examine.

Iceland also has impressive genealogical records. Through epic poems and historical documents, many Icelanders can trace their ancestry back to the nation's earliest arrivals. Geneticists use national genealogy databases to look for diseases that are unusually common in relatives — a sign that they share a mutation.

Dr. Stefansson founded Decode in 1996 to explore the genetic landscape of his country. Over the next few years, the government set up regulations enabling Icelanders to consent to have their DNA analyzed and compared with their medical records.

Initially, Decode researchers looked for a set of genetic markers known to vary from person to person. But promising links did not lead to new treatments, and in 2009 Decode filed for bankruptcy.

In 2012, the biotechnology giant Amgen bought Decode for $415 million. The company is looking at the newly published results for clues to effective new drugs.

Sean E. Harper, the head of research and development at Amgen, said that the company is now investigating a gene, found by Decode, with a strong link to cardiovascular disease in Iceland. (He declined to name the gene.)

While many researchers are trying to treat heart disease by targeting cholesterol levels, this new mutation seems to affect heart disease through a different route.

Dr. Harper said that he expected many more insights from the DNA of Icelanders.

"They can be guiding lights for us," he said.

U.S. Introduces New DNA Standard for Ensuring Accuracy of Genetic Tests

BY ROBERT PEAR | MAY 14, 2015

WASHINGTON — The federal government opened the door to a new era of genetic medicine on Thursday by introducing a standard way to ensure the accuracy of DNA tests used to tailor treatments for individual patients.

Scientists have identified hundreds of genetic mutations that appear to increase the risk of diseases, including cancer, Alzheimer's and cystic fibrosis. But laboratories often report different results when they analyze genes obtained from samples of the same blood or tissue, because of variations in their testing equipment and methods.

The National Institute of Standards and Technology said Thursday that it had developed "reference materials" that could be used by laboratories to determine whether their machines and software were properly analyzing a person's genetic blueprint, or genome.

The institute disseminates such reference materials for thousands of products including steel, concrete and peanut butter. These materials are used for myriad purposes — to calibrate instruments, to make sure buildings are safe, to ensure that nutritional labels are accurate.

Laboratories can use the new DNA standard to make sure their genetic testing is accurate. If labs get the right answers for the reference material — by finding the same mutations in the same places, for example — they can be confident that their testing of patient samples is similarly accurate.

The devices used by the laboratories, known as DNA sequencers, have greatly accelerated biomedical research and discovery, allowing scientists to pinpoint mutations and devise treatments tailored to the genetic characteristics of individual patients. Such tests and treatments, developed in research laboratories, are quickly moving into the practice of medicine.

In his State of the Union address this year, President Obama announced a "precision medicine initiative" to foster the development and adoption of such customized treatments.

For $450, scientists and laboratories can now buy a vial of the reference material from the national standards institute, a unit of the Commerce Department. The material, for sale on the agency's website, includes 10 micrograms of DNA from a Utah woman of European ancestry. That is enough for numerous tests.

"If you send a sample of blood or a tumor biopsy to different genetic testing laboratories, you can get different results," said Marc L. Salit, the leader of a genome measurement group at the institute. "While largely in agreement, they may have significant differences. Now, for the first time, we have a standard to check the reliability and quality of gene sequencing."

A laboratory can use the samples to demonstrate the quality of its work, and health insurance companies can have confidence in the results, increasing the likelihood that they will pay for genome-sequencing tests, Dr. Salit said. Costs have come down in recent years, he added, but it still costs about $5,000 to analyze and interpret a whole genome.

Elizabeth A. Mansfield, a geneticist at the Food and Drug Administration who supervises its work on personalized medicine, said the reference material could lead to "better instruments and better tests." As a result, she said, "health plans may be more willing to pay for such tests."

The F.D.A. worked with the standards institute to develop the DNA reference material, which gives regulators a new tool to assess the accuracy of tests.

"An inaccurate genome-sequencing test can lead to patients receiving the wrong diagnosis, the wrong treatment or no treatment at all, even when effective therapy is available," said Dr. Jeffrey E. Shuren, director of the F.D.A. Center for Devices and Radiological Health. Accurate tests have become more important, he said, as treatments are increasingly based on the type of mutations detected in genetic testing.

Dr. Francis S. Collins, director of the National Institutes of Health, said that information from the tests could benefit patients in many ways. "For example," he said, "an oncologist might use the results of a sequencing scan to choose the chemotherapy drug that is most likely to work."

The regulation of DNA tests and technology is complicated and in flux.

One agency, the Centers for Medicare and Medicaid Services, regulates and certifies clinical laboratories under a 1988 law. The F.D.A., a sister agency in the same department, regulates manufacturers and has authority over the actual tests. The food and drug agency has historically refrained from enforcing some of its requirements for "laboratory-developed tests," including many genetic tests, but it proposed to overhaul and tighten regulation of these products last year.

The new reference material is for tests that use advanced technology — "next-generation sequencing" — to analyze a person's DNA. Such tests are generally interpreted by doctors or genetic counselors and not sold directly to consumers.

In 2013, the food and drug agency told a Silicon Valley company, 23andMe, to stop selling health information reports that interpreted a person's DNA. In February, it allowed the company to offer a direct-to-consumer test to help identify carriers of a gene linked to a specific rare disorder, Bloom syndrome.

The food and drug agency, expecting a wave of new technology to analyze the human genome, helped finance the work of scientists and engineers at the standards institute in Gaithersburg, Md.

Pursuit of Cash Taints Promise of Gene Tests

BY REED ABELSON AND JULIE CRESWELL | JUNE 24, 2015

DR. SCOTT WILSON often participated in medical studies, so the one being proposed by the New Orleans laboratory Renaissance RX seemed reasonable.

An assistant would swab inside the cheeks of qualified patients and send the samples off to the company, which was doing research in the fast-growing arena of personalized genetic medicine.

Dr. Wilson signed on to what was supposed to be one of the largest and most definitive studies of its kind. In exchange, he and other doctors would be paid $75 for every patient they enrolled and tracked.

But Dr. Wilson left the study last year, saying the company pressured doctors to enroll patients regardless of whether they were eligible. In a lawsuit, he also accused the company of improper billing. Renaissance denies the accusations.

The story of Renaissance offers a view inside the intoxicating brew of hype and hope in the field of genetic testing. All over the country, labs and research firms are popping up, eager to study strands of DNA to better identify who is at risk for developing a disease, to guide existing treatments and to develop new ones. But the troubles at Renaissance speak volumes about how difficult it is for Medicare and private insurers to keep up with the proliferation of tests being offered.

After receiving $130 million in Medicare funds and $55 million from a unit of the private investment giant TPG, Renaissance halted its study late last year after Medicare suspended payments and began reviewing the company's billing practices.

The Justice Department is also looking at whether the company's billing and payment practices violated federal laws. Renaissance officials say the federal government is unfairly targeting the company.

"It is unfortunate that the Medicare review process has effectively crippled a burgeoning start-up," the company said in a statement. "While the principals of Renaissance RX have confidence about the eventual outcome of the review, this extended delay continues to create great challenges."

Nearly all of the company's 800 employees have been laid off and questions are swirling around its principals and top executives, three of whom came from a similar company in Washington State that wound up under criminal investigation by the Justice Department over similar problems.

The entire lab industry is undergoing heightened federal scrutiny over its relationship with doctors.

Across the industry, investors are pumping tens of millions of dollars into clinical laboratories that are developing and selling the genetic tests. President Obama recently called on Congress to spend $215 million next year on personalized medicine, calling it "one of the greatest opportunities for new medical breakthroughs that we have ever seen." A major use of the federal funds would be to create a research group of a million volunteers that would provide scientists with an enormous collection of data.

Doctors and their patients, finding it hard to resist the promise, are being swept up in the excitement. The number of tests has almost doubled in the last few years, creating a $6 billion industry.

"It sounds so legitimate — who doesn't want safe medicine?" asked Dr. Howard L. McLeod, who is medical director of the personalized medicine institute for Moffitt Cancer Center in Tampa, Fla.

Few doubt that some genetic testing companies are doing valuable, cutting-edge research — in cancer treatment, for example — that has the potential to change the course of medicine. But many of the genetic tests, which can cost $1,000 each, have not proved valuable in improving patient care.

Until the tests are proved useful, Medicare generally should not pay for them, said Dr. Elaine Jeter, a medical director at a Medicare contractor responsible for paying for care in Virginia and elsewhere.

She is trying to develop national guidelines on individual tests. The evidence, she said, "has to be compelling."

But aside from the question of the value of any particular tests, federal regulators have become increasingly worried that the area is a hotbed of fraud. In the summer of 2014, the Office of Inspector General for the Department of Health and Human Services, which oversees Medicare, said labs could be using improper tactics to get doctors to order tests. In April, federal officials reached a $47 million settlement with Health Diagnostic Laboratory in Richmond, Va., over improper payments as part of an industrywide crackdown.

Companies have run afoul of the law when they seem to offer the payments, not as compensation, but as a way to entice doctors to participate or to enroll more patients than they might otherwise.

Renaissance, for example, said that the $75 per patient payment it made to doctors reflected the amount of work the physician needed to do to select the patients and track their progress under the study. The company said two outside firms had vetted the appropriateness of the payments.

But an internal chart reviewed by The New York Times suggests the company was not shy about pointing out that doctors could amass a substantial income by participating. If a doctor enrolled five patients per day and took 110 swabs per month, that physician could earn as much as $125,400 in compensation from the study over a year, according to the document.

The company's general counsel, Brandy Sheely, who said she was unaware of any inappropriate attempts to persuade doctors to sign up patients, said the company forbade its sales force from engaging in such behavior. Through Ms. Sheely, the three principals of Renaissance RX declined to comment.

A COMPANY WITH TROUBLED ROOTS

Renaissance had relatively humble beginnings, opening in 2012 as UTC Laboratories. Originally a toxicology lab that did urine and saliva analysis, UTC soon added genetic testing and began operating as Renaissance RX, a nod to the rebirth of New Orleans after Hurricane Katrina. The company had applied for — although apparently never received — state grants to encourage business development.

At its helm was Dr. Tarun Jolly, a well-connected pain specialist in New Orleans. Dr. Jolly invested in real estate and took stakes in a variety of business ventures, including pharmacies and surgical centers. He has family ties to the wife of Gov. Bobby Jindal of Louisiana.

Two of Renaissance's three principals, Barry Griffith and Patrick Ridgeway, and the company's chief medical officer, Dr. Karthikeshwar Kasirajan, were all fresh from a Washington State company called Natural Molecular Testing Corporation.

Natural Molecular was also a laboratory that had offered pharmacogenomic testing, the kind of genetic testing used to determine response to medication.

Under the guidance of Dr. Kasirajan, a well-regarded vascular surgeon who trained at the Cleveland Clinic, Natural Molecular had established a national registry in 2012 that focused on whether doctors should change a patient's prescription for heart medicine based on that patient's genetically determined metabolism.

But by August of that year, after Medicare had paid Natural Molecular tens of millions of dollars for various genetic tests, the agency's fraud contractor began reviewing the company's billing. A separate private lawsuit filed in 2013 raised questions about the payments that Natural Molecular was making to physicians to be part of its registry.

In April 2013, Medicare suspended all reimbursements, citing "credible allegations of fraud," according to records in the company's bankruptcy filings in Seattle.

Medicare, according to bankruptcy records, had unearthed signs of potential fraud, including billing patients for tests to determine a genetic sensitivity to warfarin, a blood thinner, when the patients were not on the drug. The Justice Department began a criminal investigation. Natural Molecular filed for bankruptcy in October 2013.

By then, however, Mr. Ridgeway, Mr. Griffith and Dr. Kasirajan of Natural Molecular were already in place at Renaissance, where they had even bigger ambitions.

While other studies typically enroll a few hundred to a few thousand patients, Renaissance's study was unusually sweeping, aiming to enroll 250,000 patients. Rather than focusing on a particular drug or set of drugs, it included a wide variety, as diverse as painkillers and the anti-clotting drug Plavix.

Renaissance's executives needed Medicare's approval so the agency would pay for the tests. Company officials said they worked closely with Dr. Mitchell Burken, a medical director at Novitas Solutions, the local Medicare contractor for clinical laboratories in Louisiana, who eventually agreed, despite the study's scope and the investigation of Natural Molecular. He had also authorized payment for tests from two other labs that had similar registries.

FAST-PACED GROWTH

To enroll a quarter-million people in its study, Renaissance needed to grow quickly. It went from a company with a handful of employees in 2012 to one with hundreds by 2014.

With Medicare seeming to have blessed the study, Renaissance had little difficulty signing up doctors. Dr. John Fullerton, a San Francisco geriatrician, said company representatives "certainly indicated that they were endorsed by Medicare." The research was in the early stages, but the idea of helping his patients take less medication and experience fewer adverse reactions appealed to him. He ended his involvement in the study as he grew concerned about the company's tactics. "They seemed to push volume," he said.

The company appeared to prosper. It made a series of hires, including a new head of its lab operations and a chief financial officer. In September, Dr. Jolly announced plans to create 425 high-paying jobs by moving to a larger headquarters. To secure the project, the State of Louisiana offered a grant of nearly $1 million. Governor Jindal was expected to appear at a news conference announcing the state support for Renaissance RX but the event was abruptly canceled as the governor's staff raised questions over his relationship to Dr. Jolly and Dr. Jolly's financial interest in the company, according to internal emails obtained from state economic officials.

But signs that Renaissance RX was having difficulty began to emerge. A Duke University researcher, Dr. Deepak Voora, who was supposed to take the lead on the analysis necessary to publish the results in an academic journal, parted ways with the company in early 2014 because of differences over the research.

In October, Medicare stopped payments, according to Ms. Sheely.

Renaissance's chief medical officer, Dr. Kasirajan, said he immediately sent an email to Dr. Burken at Novitas, trying to determine what had happened.

"I said to him, 'Our data was looking so good,' " recalled Dr. Kasirajan. " 'Can we talk? What have we done? What was the mistake?' "

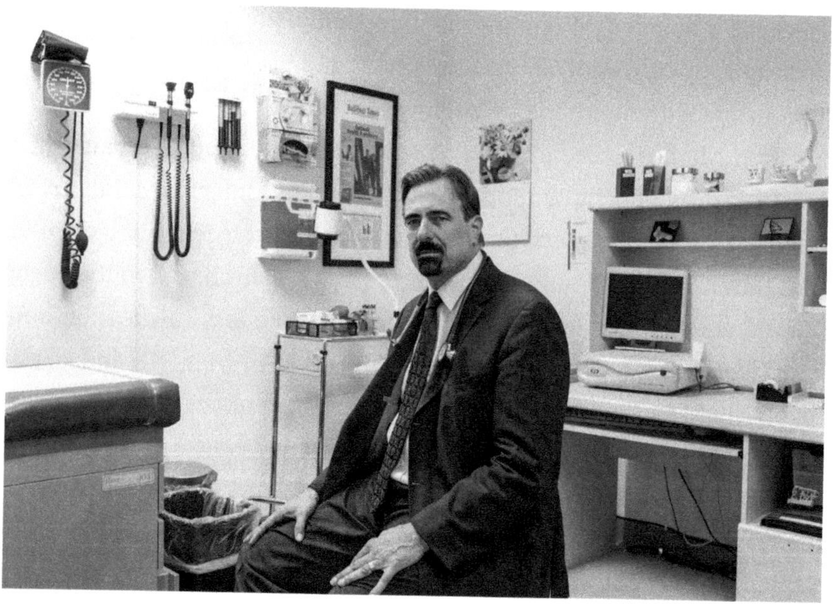

JASON HENRY FOR THE NEW YORK TIMES

Dr. John Fullerton, a geriatrician in San Francisco who administered gene tests on his patients as part of a study conducted by Renaissance RX, at his practice on Wednesday.

Dr. Kasirajan said he was told by Renaissance officials that all communications with Novitas needed to go through the legal department. Dr. Kasirajan said he knew the study was over and he left the company in late 2014.

The contractor and the agency declined to comment.

Dr. Burken, who is no longer reachable at Novitas, did not respond to multiple telephone calls seeking comment.

Despite the payment suspension, in mid-November 2014, TPG Growth, the venture capital arm of the private equity giant that invests in riskier start-up companies, invested $55 million for a 20 percent stake in the company.

Renaissance officials did not notify Louisiana officials of the Medicare review until after doctors and others raised concerns, emails from state officials show. The state says no payments from its development fund were ever made to Renaissance. A spokesman for TPG declined to comment on the record.

ENTHUSIASM OUTPACES EVIDENCE

Critics of the rapid rise in testing say Renaissance represents some of the perils of the industry.

"It's fairly easy to put a product out in the market," said Dr. Robert McDonough, senior director of clinical policy research and development at Aetna, the large insurer. Where the labs often fail, he said, is being able to show that the results can lead to better care. "We want to make sure the enthusiasm doesn't outpace the evidence," he said.

In some ways, that appears to have been the case at Renaissance. Its rapid rise and fall point to concerns about whether private investors and Medicare, which is heavily reliant on local contractors to make payment decisions, did enough due diligence. Did the study at Renaissance really qualify for Medicare funding — which generally pays for proved treatments, not experimentation?

Some experts said the study was disorganized and too big and unfocused to be of real value. And others in the industry say the payments, which are supposed to reimburse doctors for their time, may have been used to entice them to get their patients to participate.

Competition is fierce among labs, and success often depends on a lab's ability to persuade doctors to order a test from it rather than a competitor. The industry, which has a long history of companies paying doctors illegally to refer patients, is seeing a resurgence of these activities. "They seem to be coming back with a vengeance," said Marc Raspanti, a lawyer representing whistle-blowers in the Health Diagnostic Laboratory settlement.

The decision also points to a weakness in Medicare oversight in which contractors have different rules about what they will pay for and may not communicate effectively about areas of potential fraud or abuse. Kristine Ashcraft, an executive with Genelex, a personalized medicine competitor, says the government should be better at weeding out fraud because this kind of behavior makes the overall industry "tainted."

The proliferation of these tests is also making it challenging for local contractors to keep up with the science. Local contractors are known for making inconsistent decisions in this area, said Lakshman Ramamurthy, a consultant for Avalere Health, who describes it as "a symptom of a technology and science growing so fast." The agency is deciding whether to address the problem by selecting a handful of contractors, like the one run by Dr. Jeter, to make those determinations.

Whatever becomes of the review of Renaissance, its former leaders, including Dr. Jolly, are moving on. And the email domain of the company's chief counsel has been changed from Renaissance to UTC Labs.

At the same time, others are resurfacing in other laboratories.

Dr. Kasirajan, who left Renaissance, is now at Ally Clinical Diagnostics, a Texas lab whose chief executive came from a battery company. At Ally, Dr. Kasirajan published a paper last month on how the genomic tests can reduce bad drug reactions.

New Gene Tests Pose a Threat to Insurers

BY GINA KOLATA | MAY 12, 2017

PAT REILLY HAD good reason to worry about Alzheimer's disease: Her mother had it, and she saw firsthand the havoc it could wreak on a family, much of it financial.

So Ms. Reilly, 77, a retired social worker in Ann Arbor, Mich., applied for a long-term care insurance policy. Wary of enrolling people at risk for dementia, the insurance company tested her memory three times before issuing the policy.

But Ms. Reilly knew something the insurer did not: She has inherited the ApoE4 gene, which increases the lifetime risk of developing Alzheimer's. "I decided I'd best get long-term care insurance," she said.

An estimated 5.5 million people in the United States have Alzheimer's disease, and these patients constitute half of all nursing home residents. Yet very few people in the United States have been tested for the ApoE4 gene.

But last month, with the approval of the Food and Drug Administration, the gene testing company 23andMe began offering tests that reveal whether people have the variant, as well as assessing their risks for developing such conditions as Parkinson's and celiac disease.

Other genetics companies are planning to offer similar tests, and soon millions of people will have a better idea what their medical futures might be. Recent research has found that many, like Ms. Reilly, are likely to begin preparing for the worst.

But for companies selling long-term care insurance, these tests could be a disaster, sending risky patients in search of policies even as those with fewer risks shy away, damaging an already fragile business. "There is a question about whether the industry is in a

LAURA MCDERMOTT FOR THE NEW YORK TIMES

Pat Reilly, 77, at home in Ann Arbor, Mich., last week. Ms. Reilly found that she had inherited an ApoE4 gene that increases the risk of developing Alzheimer's disease and bought a long-term care policy in response.

death spiral anyway," said Robert Hunter, director of insurance at the Consumer Federation of America. "This could make it worse."

The tests are simple: All people have to do is send away a saliva sample and pay $199. Their disease risks, if they say they want to know them, will be delivered with a report on ancestry and on how their genes influence such traits as flushing when they drink alcohol or having straight hair.

The company will not reveal how many people have received disease-risk data, but it says that in Britain and Canada, where it has offered such testing for several years, about three-quarters of their customers have asked for it. 23andMe has sold its genetic services to more than two million people worldwide since 2007.

The issue for now is with long-term care insurance, not employment and not — at least so far — health insurance.

Under the Genetic Information Nondiscrimination Act, companies cannot ask employees to take gene tests and cannot use any such results in employment decisions; insurers are not permitted to require gene tests or to use the results in coverage decisions.

But legislation proposed in the House would exempt corporate "wellness" programs from some of these requirements. And the American Health Care Act, passed by the House, would permit states to waive some insurance safeguards regarding pre-existing conditions.

At the moment, companies selling long-term care insurance — unlike medical insurers — are permitted to ask about health status and take future health into consideration when deciding whom to insure and how much to charge.

The 23andMe test results will not appear in people's medical records, and the company promises not to disclose identifiable findings to third parties. It is up to the customers to reveal them — and the fear for insurers is that many will not.

Two-thirds of nursing home residents are on Medicaid, and the remaining private insurers are already struggling. In the early 2000s, more than 100 firms offered long-term care insurance, according to the Treasury Department. By the end of 2015, only 12 firms offered it, and new enrollees fell from 171,000 to 104,000.

The insurers charged too little for these policies, experts say; policyholders have turned out to be much sicker than anticipated. To pay for an unanticipated increase in policyholders who develop Alzheimer's, insurers would have to raise prices, said Don Taylor, a professor of public policy at Duke University who has studied the issue.

Increasing numbers of people at low risk might decide the insurance was not worth the rising price. Even many at high risk would eventually find the policies unaffordable. It is the definition of an insurance death spiral.

If that happens, said Mark Rothstein, the director of the bioethics institute at the University of Louisville's medical school, even more people with Alzheimer's will end up on Medicaid, with the federal government paying for their nursing home care.

Someone must pay, he said. The only question is whether it will be taxpayers or policyholders. "How do you want to spread the risk?" Mr. Rothstein asked.

For 23andMe, the new tests are simply a way to help people learn about their makeup. "People clearly want information about themselves," said Anne Wojcicki, the chief executive at 23andMe. "There is a demand."

Yet even if just a minority of 23andMe customers decided to game the current insurance system, "it's enough to perturb the market," said Dr. Robert Cook-Deegan, a professor at the school for the future of innovation in society at Arizona State University, who has studied the issue.

Research by Dr. Robert C. Green, a geneticist at Harvard University, indicates that this is exactly what is likely to happen. Drawing on data from his clinical trials involving more than 1,000 people, Dr. Green has found that people who learn they have the ApoE4 gene fare just as well if they get the results without counseling.

But he also found that those who learned they had the gene variant — Ms. Reilly was one of them — were nearly six times more likely to buy long-term care insurance than those who did not. The ApoE4 gene variant is present in about a quarter of the population.

Many thought there was no need to tell the insurer why they suddenly wanted a policy. "All the insurance companies are concerned about this," said Dr. Green, who has been discussing the problem with industry executives.

Major insurers declined to comment. A trade group, American Council of Life Insurers, issued an email statement by Mariana Gomez-Vock, the group's senior counsel.

"Though it is difficult to speculate on the potential impact of the latest 23andMe offering, any situation that has the ability to significantly increase adverse selection could impact the availability and affordability of products over time," she wrote. "We need to be on the same page with the applicant, where both sides share the same information," she added.

But will that happen? "I don't see a good outcome here," Mr. Taylor said.

The Struggle to Build a Massive 'Biobank' of Patient Data

BY GINA KOLATA | MARCH 19, 2018

THIS SPRING, the National Institutes of Health will start recruiting participants for one of the most ambitious medical projects ever envisioned.

The goal is to find one million people in the United States, from all walks of life and all racial and ethnic groups, who are willing to have their genomes sequenced, and to provide their medical records and regular blood samples.

They may choose to wear devices that continuously monitor physical activity, perhaps even devices not yet developed that will track heart rate and blood pressure. They will fill out surveys about what they eat and how much.

If all goes well, experts say, the result will be a trove of health information like nothing the world has seen. The project, called the All of Us Research Program, should provide new insights into who gets sick and why, and how to prevent and treat chronic diseases.

The All of Us program joins a wave of similar efforts to construct gigantic "biobanks" by, among others, the Department of Veterans Affairs, a British collaboration and private companies like Geisinger Health Systems and Kaiser Permanente.

But All of Us is the only one that attempts to capture a huge sample that is representative of the United States population. "It will be transformative," said Dr. Francis Collins, director of the National Institutes of Health.

It will also be expensive.

In 2017 alone, the budget for All of Us was $230 million, of which $40 million came from the 21st Century Cures Act. Congress has authorized an astounding $1.455 billion over 10 years for the project.

While supporters say the results will be well worth the money and effort, others have begun to question whether All of Us is just too ambitious, too loaded with cumbersome bureaucracy — and too duplicative of smaller programs that are moving much more quickly.

In the three years since the All of Us program was announced, not a single person's DNA has been sequenced. Instead, project leaders have signed up more than 17,000 volunteers as "beta testers" in a pilot phase of the program. They supplied blood and urine samples, had measurements taken, and filled out surveys.

Dr. George D. Yancopoulos, the president and chief scientific officer of the biotech company Regeneron, said the N.I.H. did not have much to show for three years of planning. Regeneron has been deeply involved in similar public and private efforts, sequencing the DNA of more than 300,000 participants.

The beta testers constitute just 1.7 percent of the program's target, Dr. Yancopoulos noted, and the investigators have collected only the simplest data, not genetic sequences.

"At this rate, when will they complete their one-million-person target?" he wondered. "And at what taxpayer cost?"

"I think someone needs to ask tough questions about whether this is the best use of precious N.I.H. resources," he added. "Should the funding instead go to individual researchers who are doing truly basic and innovative science?"

Two large health providers — Geisinger and Kaiser Permanente — both backed away from grants to participate in All of Us.

David Ledbetter, executive vice president and chief scientific officer of Geisinger, said that the program's complexity made it too time-consuming: conference calls upon conference calls, meetings upon meetings, without much progress.

"We decided it was not the right expenditure of our time," he said. Geisinger gave back its award that was potentially worth $50 million over five years.

Geisinger has enrolled more than 180,000 participants in a biobank of its own, and the health system already has years of their medical records. Regeneron is sequencing the participants' DNA and has completed more than 100,000.

Dr. Ledbetter said the N.I.H. program would be "very valuable someday." But Geisinger, he said, did not want to wait.

"Someday is today," he said.

Kaiser Permanente, too, is now far ahead in developing its own biobank. Originally, the company expected that the federal project would profit from Kaiser's experience with recruiting and data analysis, said Elizabeth McGlynn, vice president of Kaiser Permanente Research.

"We were not able to engage as a scientific partner," Dr. McGlynn said. "We felt increasingly that we were just being asked to give access to our members."

DeCode Genetics, a subsidiary of Amgen, a biotech company, is working with a biobank of 160,000 people from Iceland. Dr. Sean E. Harper, Amgen's executive vice president for research and development, says it is hard to imagine the complexity of analyzing the data.

"It took about 20 years and over a billion dollars of investment to get to the point where we are able to routinely extract from the data the necessary information to validate or invalidate drug targets," he said. Sequencing the DNA is the easy part, he said. "The hard part is to get all these medical records and lab tests curated in a computer system where they are query-able and to perfect the analytics."

Despite these concerns, All of Us has contracted with scientists at just about every leading university, as well as with companies like Verily, a subsidiary of Alphabet, parent company of Google.

"We will have an unprecedented amount of data at a scale never done before," said Eric Dishman, director of the program.

Investigators have grand plans for all that data once it becomes available.

Dr. Atul Butte, director of the Institute for Computational Health Sciences at the University of California, San Francisco, hopes to find the earliest signs of disease, especially of Type 2 diabetes.

"Do you go back and forth from diabetes for a while?" he asks. "Is it preventable?"

The Veterans Affairs Department began building a similar biobank, called the Million Veteran Program, in 2011 with a very lean budget: just $250 million over the past seven years.

The agency has recruited 650,000 vets so far and has years of their medical records, including prescription data. Investigators expect to sequence the DNA of 100,000 participants in the next two years, at a cost of $1,000 for each person's entire genome. The data will be available to approved researchers.

The British program, called the U.K. Biobank, has half a million participants with complete medical records and additional data for some, including body and brain scans.

Regeneron has committed to sequencing the DNA of all of the participants by the end of 2019. After a six to 12 month period of exclusivity, the company will make that data public.

But what All of Us is attempting to do is much more complex, said Dr. Dishman. The U.K. project and the program at Geisinger lack a representative range of racial and ethnic groups; the V.A.'s biobank has relatively few women.

All of Us will be built to reflect the United States population. The San Francisco General Hospital Foundation, for instance, was given a grant to recruit lesbian, bisexual, gay and transgender participants.

"I think what the U.S. project adds is that it reflects the diversity of the U.S.," said Dr. Sekar Kathiresan, a geneticist at the Broad Institute and an investigator with the N.I.H. program.

That's partly why planning for the project has dragged on. And the diversity of participants makes the daunting task of retrieving medical records even more difficult.

Americans tend to have medical records stored slapdash all over the place, and they change insurers and medical plans frequently. There is little uniformity in the country's electronic health systems.

Even the most straightforward part of the project — DNA sequencing — is formidable.

"There are not enough sequencing machines in the U.S. to just focus on our project," Dr. Dishman acknowledged. All of Us will depend on prices falling for sequencing — and more sequencers being built.

For participants, there will be a reward, Dr. Collins noted. The program will give them genetic information and health data, and tell them how they compare to others in the population.

To do that, All of Us plans to enlist genetic counselors. Yet right now, there are not nearly enough counselors to handle the task.

The counseling issue also bothered Kaiser, Dr. McGlynn said, and it was a factor in the decision to return the grant money.

"Genetic counselors are in terribly short supply," she said. "We wanted to be sure we were well organized to deliver results in a way that was ethical and not scary to members."

The accumulation of tremendous caches of medical data is raising troubling questions about what participants should be told. The U.K. Biobank, for instance, considered returning results to participants, but decided against it after an experiment.

It involved participants getting whole body scans for the program. For some subjects, a radiologist systematically assessed the scans to see if anything seemed abnormal. If it did, the patient and the patient's doctor were informed.

As it turned out, 20 percent of the participants had abnormalities. They often went on to have other tests, some of which were invasive and involved major surgery, like removal of a lobe of the lung.

Yet in the end, only one in eight with abnormal scans actually had a medical problem, and even then there was nothing they could do about it most of the time, said Dr. Rory Collins, chief executive of the U.K. project.

"What we are trying to do is not provide care to individuals, but to generate a resource that can provide health information," Dr. Collins said. "Feedback can cause more harm than good."

Other experts disagree with the British approach. At Geisinger, participants are told if they have a genetic variant that might affect their disease risk.

They are offered genetic counseling if they want it — and so far, about two-thirds do. The medical system has sufficient counselors to handle the demand, said Adam H. Buchanan, co-director of the counseling program.

Given the substantial obstacles, will the N.I.H. project, which has not even really begun, be worth the immense expense and effort?

Dr. Collins, an adviser to All of Us, thinks it will. Huge amounts of data will be needed to really understand interactions between genetics, environment and lifestyle.

"Half a million people isn't enough. Even a million isn't enough," he said.

Dr. Ledbetter was more circumspect. "I think the idea is great," he said. "It is ambitious. It is expensive. It will take a while."

"I wish the N.I.H. well."

CHAPTER 3

The Adoption of Genetics by Law Enforcement

Genetic testing has been widely implemented in the criminal justice system. Along with using genetic profiles to prove criminals' guilt or innocence, judges have used DNA evidence to take a second look at once settled cases. As genetic testing becomes increasingly accurate, standards for its use are coming into greater focus. A highlight of this work is the use of genetic ancestry websites to identify serial killers. More speculative research includes the reconstruction of faces from DNA evidence and the ongoing search for the "crime gene."

Biologist Teaches the Nation's Judges About Genetics

BY CLAUDIA DREIFUS | JULY 1, 2008

JAMES P. EVANS, a physician and molecular biologist, teaches genetics at the University of North Carolina School of Medicine. He also directs the school's Clinical Cancer Genetics Services, counseling patients about genetic testing. On weekends Dr. Evans, under the auspices of the Advanced Science and Technology Adjudication Resource Center — a Congressionally mandated program — teaches the nation's judges about genetics. Dr. Evans, 49, was interviewed recently in New York; he had come to speak at the World Science Festival.

Q: *Why do judges need to know their genetics?*

A: Because they are frequently trying cases that hinge on genetics. And many don't know what DNA is. They may have a rough idea. But they don't understand the fine points.

If they sit in a criminal court, they are increasingly seeing homicide and sexual assault cases where DNA evidence is used to identify defendants. In the civil court, they are seeing cases on who owns genetic information and on whether environment or a genetic disposition caused cancer in a plaintiff. Cancer is the largest single cause of medical negligence suits — and it is, at its most fundamental level, a genetic disease. These jurists are seeing cases where the question is, "Was this person's cancer triggered by environmental factors, or was it caused by a genetic predisposition?"

Many of the judges say that they fear their lack of scientific knowledge could cause them to make mistakes. They say they don't know how to weigh DNA evidence. They are afraid of being snookered by expert witnesses.

Q: *Are judges the sort of people who might be afraid of science?*

A: This is a huge issue. Yes! A lot of judges report that they did prelaw in college because it did not involve science. One of my favorite judges, a brilliant man, is fond of telling people he "flunked science in kindergarten." So in these workshops, I think of myself as a newfangled type of science teacher, instructing extremely smart and distinguished adults in science fundamentals.

Q: *How do you do that?*

A: I try to demystify all of science and, specifically, genetics. I begin by telling them exactly what DNA is, and how we find it. We do a mini-lab where they isolate their own DNA and look at it. When they can hold it in their hands, the mystique melts. Then, I describe how we use DNA to identify a unique individual. We talk about the pitfalls of doing DNA typing. Once we have the basics down, we do a practice court, where we make up fact patterns in hypothetic cases that might involve DNA. We ask the judges to speculate on how they might use DNA evidence and why. We might go: "You've got a murder case where some DNA from a suspect is found in the trunk of a victim's car. Under what conditions could this be evidence of guilt?"

Q: *And the answer is?*

A: If the defendant was a friend of the victim, they might have been lifting something into the car trunk and shed some DNA there. But if the defendant didn't know the victim at all, score one for the prosecution. Humans shed DNA easily. Our testing is highly sensitive. If it's in a place it shouldn't be — let's say in the vagina of a rape victim or at a crime scene — it can be incriminating.

I think the judges appreciate the hands-on nature of our course. After a recent workshop, a judge asked me, "Exactly how much DNA is a nanogram's worth?" When I informed him that the DNA in our test tube was 10,000 times more than a nanogram, he was relieved. He'd just decided a case that hinged on the quantity of DNA found at a crime scene. By working with his own DNA, he could see he'd rendered the right decision.

Q: *Behavioral genetics is the new hot area of study. Are criminal court judges beginning to see "my genes made me do it" defenses?*

A: Yup. We know some antisocial behaviors — drug addiction, alcoholism, a propensity toward violence — have genetic components. Therefore, one can easily imagine things reaching a certain level of predisposition and a lawyer going, "My client is not responsible for his actions any more than someone mentally ill is responsible."

In reality, those claims have not made it very far — yet. One judge, after learning about behavioral genetics, said to me, "If this proves out, our entire conception of culpability in crime and punishment will have to be reconsidered."

Q: *Do scientists and judges have much in common?*

A: Well, a scientist almost never says anything absolutely. Everything is a theory, to be disproved or adjusted later on. Judges worry a lot about the certainty of conclusions, too. Judges are used to thinking of truth as an elusive concept. A lot of judges, when you bring up "the truth," they roll their eyes. They say, "I don't know what to say about truth. I do know about probabilities."

Q: *And isn't that what you do — work with probabilities?*

A: Yup. That's what a geneticist does. We're all about probability. In my medical genetics clinic, when I counsel someone who's had a gene test, I might say: "The BRCA2 mutation you were found to carry confers about a 50 to 85 percent risk of breast cancer and a 25 percent risk of ovarian cancer."

Q: *That's a huge likelihood. What else do you tell her?*

A: I say: "You have two main choices. You can engage in heightened surveillance, but of course that isn't actually prevention. The most effective strategy is prophylactic mastectomy and removal of your ovaries, which reduce your risk of those cancers by over 90 percent."

Q: *That's a horrible choice.*

A: But it's all we've got right now. I can understand why many women wouldn't opt for it. Those who opt for it tend to be women who've seen a lot of family members die of breast cancer.

Listen, when it comes to genetic medicine, the only point to testing is to obtain information you can act on. Right now, there are only a handful of genetic diseases which we can do something to prevent. BRCA2 breast and ovarian cancers are among them. For other diseases, like Alzheimer's and Huntington's, the only value to knowing is for life-planning. There's no prevention.

Q: *Do you like your work?*

A: I sure do. With my patients, I can take a full hour with each one and show them how their genes might predict their future. An hour with an individual patient is a huge luxury these days, but it can save lives. With the judges, I feel gratified when a few of them tell me, "Gosh, now I understand what DNA is." What makes me feel even better is when one of them says, "I hated science in school, but genetics sounds real beautiful."

DNA Evidence Can Be Fabricated, Scientists Show

BY ANDREW POLLACK | AUG. 17, 2009

SCIENTISTS IN ISRAEL have demonstrated that it is possible to fabricate DNA evidence, undermining the credibility of what has been considered the gold standard of proof in criminal cases.

The scientists fabricated blood and saliva samples containing DNA from a person other than the donor of the blood and saliva. They also showed that if they had access to a DNA profile in a database, they could construct a sample of DNA to match that profile without obtaining any tissue from that person.

"You can just engineer a crime scene," said Dan Frumkin, lead author of the paper, which has been published online by the journal Forensic Science International: Genetics. "Any biology undergraduate could perform this."

Dr. Frumkin is a founder of Nucleix, a company based in Tel Aviv that has developed a test to distinguish real DNA samples from fake ones that it hopes to sell to forensics laboratories.

The planting of fabricated DNA evidence at a crime scene is only one implication of the findings. A potential invasion of personal privacy is another.

Using some of the same techniques, it may be possible to scavenge anyone's DNA from a discarded drinking cup or cigarette butt and turn it into a saliva sample that could be submitted to a genetic testing company that measures ancestry or the risk of getting various diseases. Celebrities might have to fear "genetic paparazzi," said Gail H. Javitt of the Genetics and Public Policy Center at Johns Hopkins University.

Tania Simoncelli, science adviser to the American Civil Liberties Union, said the findings were worrisome.

"DNA is a lot easier to plant at a crime scene than fingerprints," she said. "We're creating a criminal justice system that is increasingly relying on this technology."

John M. Butler, leader of the human identity testing project at the National Institute of Standards and Technology, said he was "impressed at how well they were able to fabricate the fake DNA profiles." However, he added, "I think your average criminal wouldn't be able to do something like that."

The scientists fabricated DNA samples two ways. One required a real, if tiny, DNA sample, perhaps from a strand of hair or drinking cup. They amplified the tiny sample into a large quantity of DNA using a standard technique called whole genome amplification.

Of course, a drinking cup or piece of hair might itself be left at a crime scene to frame someone, but blood or saliva may be more believable.

The authors of the paper took blood from a woman and centrifuged it to remove the white cells, which contain DNA. To the remaining red cells they added DNA that had been amplified from a man's hair.

Since red cells do not contain DNA, all of the genetic material in the blood sample was from the man. The authors sent it to a leading American forensics laboratory, which analyzed it as if it were a normal sample of a man's blood.

The other technique relied on DNA profiles, stored in law enforcement databases as a series of numbers and letters corresponding to variations at 13 spots in a person's genome.

From a pooled sample of many people's DNA, the scientists cloned tiny DNA snippets representing the common variants at each spot, creating a library of such snippets. To prepare a DNA sample matching any profile, they just mixed the proper snippets together. They said that a library of 425 different DNA snippets would be enough to cover every conceivable profile.

Nucleix's test to tell if a sample has been fabricated relies on the fact that amplified DNA — which would be used in either deception — is not methylated, meaning it lacks certain molecules that are attached to the DNA at specific points, usually to inactivate genes.

Falsely Convicted, Freed and No Longer Quiet

BY MARTIN FACKLER | AUG. 13, 2010

ASHIKAGA, JAPAN — On a December morning in 1991, Toshikazu Sugaya's quiet, anonymous existence in this sleepy city north of Tokyo ended abruptly with a knock on his door.

It was the police. They wanted to question Mr. Sugaya, then a 45-year-old divorced school bus driver with no friends, in connection with the grisly murder in 1990 of a 4-year-old girl. After 13 hours of interrogation, during which Mr. Sugaya says the police kicked his shins and shouted at him, he tearfully admitted to that murder and to killing two other girls. He was convicted of one murder and sentenced to life in prison.

But last year, after prosecutors admitted that his confession was a fabrication made under duress and that a DNA test used as evidence had been wrong, Mr. Sugaya was released. A court later acquitted him.

The disclosure that Mr. Sugaya had been wrongfully imprisoned for more than 17 years shocked Japan even more than his conviction as a serial killer had. His release drew a barrage of news media coverage, shaking the public's faith in the police and the courts at a time when Japan's prolonged economic decline has created growing doubts about Japan's national institutions in general.

Mr. Sugaya, now 63, has become a national figure, and perhaps the country's most vocal critic of forced confessions — a recurring problem here. He has written or co-written three books, including one titled "Falsely Convicted," and tours the country giving talks about his experience.

"I tell people not to believe the police," said Mr. Sugaya, a small, slightly built man whose face seems almost hidden behind a large pair of wire-rim glasses. "Look what they did to me."

Indeed, with slumped shoulders and an almost cowering demeanor that brings to mind a frightened animal caught in car headlights, Mr. Sugaya seems as unlikely a crusader against the abuse of power as he did a serial killer. But he can be disarmingly open, and his voice exudes a quiet confidence that he says he acquired in prison, where he learned to fend for himself.

During those years, he said, he met other convicts who told him they had been convicted because of false confessions. He said a desire to help them and others is one reason he has embraced his newfound celebrity, though he remains visibly uncomfortable with all the attention.

"I want to go back to my quiet life of before," Mr. Sugaya said. "But when I think that others have suffered the same treatment as me, I want to work to help them."

Before his ordeal, Mr. Sugaya described himself as a shy man who avoided conversations and rarely said more than a few words. After a marriage that lasted just three months, he divided his time between living with his parents and spending weekends alone at a small house he rented.

Unbeknown to him, the police had been following Mr. Sugaya for a year before his arrest. A witness had told them that Mr. Sugaya had been at a pachinko game parlor about the same time that the 4-year-old victim, Mami Matsuda, was last seen there.

In 1991, after his initial confession and subsequent arrest, Mr. Sugaya said he spent weeks concocting increasingly complex stories about how he murdered Mami and two other girls who had been killed in the 1980s. Mr. Sugaya, who said he had never really met any of the girls, said that at the time he was actually afraid that the police would discover he was lying and would start shouting at him again, a prospect he said paralyzed him with fear.

The police now admit that they missed glaring discrepancies between Mr. Sugaya's fabricated accounts of the killings and actual forensic evidence. Mr. Sugaya said he took the girl away on his bicycle; a witness reported seeing a man lead her away on foot. Mr. Sugaya also failed to identify the sites where the bodies had been buried.

SHIHO FUKADA FOR THE NEW YORK TIMES

Toshikazu Sugaya spent 17 years in prison. He now speaks out against the abuse of power.

Still, even when Mr. Sugaya started to proclaim his innocence midway through his trial, judges, prosecutors and Mr. Sugaya's own defense attorney ignored him, apparently in the belief that his initial confession was correct. Legal experts say this reflects the extreme importance that Japanese prosecutors and courts still place on confessions.

Mr. Sugaya said the question he is now asked the most is why he confessed so quickly to crimes he did not commit. Describing himself as insecure and "excessively spineless," he said his willpower just seemed to collapse after what he said were hours of police officers screaming at him so loudly that his ears still ring 19 years later. He said he finally confessed to all three killings just so the ordeal would end.

Hiroshi Sato, a defense lawyer who later took up Mr. Sugaya's case, said another problem was misplaced faith in a rudimentary DNA test that matched Mr. Sugaya with sperm found on one of the murdered girls. After years of fruitlessly petitioning courts for a retrial, Mr. Sato finally won Mr. Sugaya's freedom after a more advanced genetic test disproved the earlier result.

"We've had cases of false confessions before, but never one where the evidence was this clear-cut," said Akira Kitani, a former judge who now teaches law at Hosei University in Tokyo.

The police said mistakes were made because they were under pressure to solve the murders of the three girls, which shook this quiet community. The actual killer has never been found and could not be prosecuted now because Japan has a statute of limitations in murder cases.

Mr. Kitani said Mr. Sugaya's release has prompted broader moves to hold retrials in several similar cases, including one involving a 1967 robbery-murder in which two men were imprisoned based solely on confessions that they later recanted.

SHIHO FUKADA FOR THE NEW YORK TIMES

Mr. Sugaya, 63, with a supporter, Itoko Nishimaki.

As part of his efforts to draw attention to false confessions, Mr. Sugaya said he had visited that trial, which is now under way. He said his presence in the courtroom was intended to spur the news media to report that the two men might be innocent.

Still, he says, he finds his new prominence oppressively hard to escape. On a recent afternoon, just walking across a parking lot, Mr. Sugaya was stopped by uniformed attendants.

"You're Sugaya-san, aren't you?" asked one of the men.

"Before, I was famous for being a criminal," Mr. Sugaya said a few moments later. "Now I'm famous for being innocent."

He said the toughest part of his experience has been coming to terms with what he lost while in prison. In particular, he said, he was never able to meet his parents again. His father, a medicine salesman, died two weeks after the arrest, apparently of shock, Mr. Sugaya said.

His mother refused to visit him in prison, and once told the police that she wished they would execute him so he could be "sent home in a box." She died three years ago, before her son was exonerated.

"I wish I could explain to her what really happened," Mr. Sugaya said, his voice breaking the only time during a two-hour interview that touched on many painful topics.

Mr. Sugaya said that he felt a growing anger, and that he had started having trouble sleeping because of flashbacks to his interrogation. He also said that he had wanted to find some sort of closure by filing a lawsuit against the two detectives who forced him to confess, but that his lawyers and supporters advised against that because it could prove too emotionally traumatic.

"In the end, I still end up blaming myself," Mr. Sugaya said. "If I just had been a bit stronger in front of the police, none of this would have happened."

Genetic Basis for Crime: A New Look

BY PATRICIA COHEN | JUNE 19, 2011

IT WAS LESS than 20 years ago that the National Institutes of Health abruptly withdrew funds for a conference on genetics and crime after outraged complaints that the idea smacked of eugenics. The president of the Association of Black Psychologists at the time declared that such research was in itself "a blatant form of stereotyping and racism."

The tainted history of using biology to explain criminal behavior has pushed criminologists to reject or ignore genetics and concentrate on social causes: miserable poverty, corrosive addictions, guns. Now that the human genome has been sequenced, and scientists are studying the genetics of areas as varied as alcoholism and party affiliation, criminologists are cautiously returning to the subject. A small cadre of experts is exploring how genes might heighten the risk of committing a crime and whether such a trait can be inherited.

The turnabout will be evident on Monday at the annual National Institute of Justice conference in Arlington, Va. On the opening day criminologists from around the country can attend a panel on creating databases for information about DNA and "new genetic markers" that forensic scientists are discovering.

"Throughout the past 30 or 40 years most criminologists couldn't say the word 'genetics' without spitting," Terrie E. Moffitt, a behavioral scientist at Duke University, said. "Today the most compelling modern theories of crime and violence weave social and biological themes together."

Researchers estimate that at least 100 studies have shown that genes play a role in crimes. "Very good methodological advances have meant that a wide range of genetic work is being done," said John H. Laub, the director of the justice institute, who won the Stockholm Prize in Criminology last week. He and others take pains to emphasize, however, that genes are ruled by the environment, which can either mute or aggravate violent impulses. Many people with the same genetic tendency for aggressiveness will never throw a punch, while others without it could be career criminals.

The subject still raises thorny ethical and policy questions. Should a genetic predisposition influence sentencing? Could genetic tests be used to tailor rehabilitation programs to individual criminals? Should adults or children with a biological marker for violence be identified?

Everyone in the field agrees there is no "crime gene." What most researchers are looking for are inherited traits that are linked to aggression and antisocial behaviors, which may in turn lead to violent crime. Don't expect anyone to discover how someone's DNA might identify the next Bernard L. Madoff.

And that is precisely the problem, said Troy Duster, a professor of sociology and bioethics at New York University, who argues that studies examine not the remorseless and rapacious behavior of the rich and powerful, but the behavior of disadvantaged minorities. "Every era believes that the technology and the methodology have improved," he said, "but the science itself is problematic."

One gene that has been linked to violence regulates the production of the monoamine oxidase A enzyme, which controls the amount of serotonin in the brain. People with a version of the gene that produces less of the enzyme tend to be significantly more impulsive and aggressive, but, as Ms. Moffitt and her colleague (and husband) Avshalom Caspi discovered, the effect of the gene is triggered by stressful experiences.

Steven Pinker, a professor of psychology at Harvard whose forthcoming book, "The Better Angels of Our Nature," argues that humans have become less violent over the millenniums, suggests that the way to think about genetics and crime is to start with human nature and then look at what causes the switch for a particular trait to be flipped on or off.

"It is not a claim about how John and Bill differ, but about how every male is the same," he said. Understanding the genetics of violence can "tell you what aspect of the environment you should look at."

He mentioned one of the biggest risk factors leading to crime: remaining single instead of getting married, a link uncovered by

Mr. Laub and Robert J. Sampson, a Harvard sociologist who was a co-winner of the Stockholm Prize. Marriage may serve as a switch that directs male energies toward investing in a family rather than competing with other males, Mr. Pinker said.

Kevin Beaver, an associate professor at Florida State University's College of Criminology and Criminal Justice, said genetics may account for, say, half of a person's aggressive behavior, but that 50 percent comprises hundreds or thousands of genes that express themselves differently depending on the environment.

He has tried to measure which circumstances — having delinquent friends, living in a disadvantaged neighborhood — influence whether a predisposition to violence surfaces. After studying twins and siblings, he came up with an astonishing result: In boys not exposed to the risk factors, genetics played no role in any of their violent behavior. The positive environment had prevented the genetic switches — to use Mr. Pinker's word — that affect aggression from being turned on. In boys with eight or more risk factors, however, genes explained 80 percent of their violence. Their switches had been flipped.

A rash of new research has focused on self-control as well as callousness and a lack of empathy, traits regularly implicated in the decision to commit a crime. Like other personality traits, these are believed to have environmental and genetic components, although the degree of heritability is debated.

In findings from a long-term study of 1,000 babies born in 1972 in a New Zealand town, Ms. Moffitt and her colleagues recently reported that the less self-control a child displayed at 3 years of age, the more likely he or she was to commit a crime more than 30 years later. Forty-three percent of the children who scored in the lowest fifth on self-control were later convicted of a crime, she said, versus 13 percent of those who scored in the highest fifth.

But a predisposition is not destiny. "Knowing something is inherited does not IN ANY WAY tell us anything about whether changing the environment will improve it," Ms. Moffitt wrote in an e-mail. "For example, self-control is a lot like height, it varies widely in the human population, and it is highly heritable, but if an effective intervention such as better nutrition is applied to the whole population, then everyone gets taller than the last generation."

Criminologists and sociologists have been much more skittish about genetic causes of crime than psychologists. In 2008 a survey conducted by John Paul Wright, who heads graduate programs at the University of Cincinnati's School of Criminal Justice, discovered that "not a single study on the biology-crime link has been published in dissertation form in the last 20 years" from a criminal justice Ph.D. program, aside from two dissertations he had personally overseen (one of which was Mr. Beaver's). He also noted that the top four journals in the field had scarcely published any biological research in the past two decades.

Mr. Wright said he now thinks "in criminology the tide is turning, especially among younger scholars."

But recent work has tended to air outside the main criminology forums. Mr. Beaver, for example, published a paper in Biological Psychiatry in February that concluded that adoptees whose biological parents had broken the law "were significantly more likely to be arrested, sentenced to probation, incarcerated, and arrested multiple times when compared with adoptees whose biological parents had not been arrested."

At the American Association for the Advancement of Science's meeting in February, Adrian Raine, chairman of the criminology department at the University of Pennsylvania and a pioneer in the field, presented a paper showing how variations in the parts of a toddler's brain that regulate emotions — believed to be a product of genes and environment — turned out to be a good predictor of criminal behavior later in life.

Mr. Sampson, who planned to attend the opening day of the justice institute conference, said that "sociology has nothing to fear from genetic research," but he maintained that the most interesting questions about crime, like why some communities have a higher crime rate than others, are not traceable at all to genetics. "The more sophisticated the genetic research, the more it will show the importance of social context," he said.

Helping Decide Guilt or Innocence

BY LIZ ROBBINS | DEC. 15, 2012

A MAN WILL go on trial for attempted murder in Brooklyn. His fate may hang on the handlebars of a bicycle.

Prosecutors contend he shot a man from the bike, and may have left a DNA calling card on its surface. He may not have been the only one to touch the bicycle, though.

As DNA evidence is increasingly used in courtrooms, forensic scientists are struggling to find more-precise ways to analyze smaller and smaller samples that contain multiple contributors — scraped from, say, the trigger of a gun, the handle of a knife or the trim of a scarf.

Two scientists at the forensic biology laboratory of the New York City medical examiner's office have created a way. The scientists, Theresa A. Caragine and Adele A. Mitchell, produced the Forensic Statistical Tool, an algorithm for a software program that can analyze a mixture of DNA from a crime scene and determine the probability that it could include the defendant's profile.

"We said, 'Here's a problem. Let's do something about this,' " Dr. Caragine, the deputy director of the Office of the Chief Medical Examiner's forensic biology department, said in her office last week. "I like to think of it as the New York way. Just do it."

The tool has been used in New York City courts since July 2011, when it was approved by the New York State Commission on Forensic Science, which also accredits public laboratories, and the DNA Subcommittee, made up of statisticians and geneticists who review protocols.

What makes it innovative, but also controversial, is that in cases like the bicyclist's, where previously no conclusion could be made, the Forensic Statistical Tool, or FST, can now use the data to produce a ratio of the likelihood that the defendant's DNA is in the mixture compared to the DNA of random people. A lower value may help establish that a suspect is not the source of the DNA, while a higher value could point to a suspect.

In the bicyclist's case, the FST found that there was a relatively low likelihood that the suspect's DNA was part of the mixture on the left handlebar, but that the probability of it being part of the mixture on the right handlebar was quite high — 972,000 times more likely than the DNA of three random people.

The two scientists said that in general, differences might arise because of the amount and quality of DNA collected.

The Legal Aid Society filed a motion for a Frye hearing, which challenges the general scientific acceptance of new technology, to stop the introduction of the FST's conclusions as admissible evidence.

There are Frye hearings on FST scheduled in Manhattan, Brooklyn and the Bronx.

The first hearing, on both FST and DNA collection, began on Wednesday in Brooklyn. Dr. Caragine presented four hours of scientific

NICOLE BENGIVENO/THE NEW YORK TIMES

A new DNA tool was created at the New York City medical examiner's office.

testimony while the defendant peered numbly at the PowerPoint slides.

"It's very important, because DNA has such a powerful reputation in the legal community and the public, where it enjoys a gold standard. But it's not that simple," said Jessica Goldthwaite, one of the lead Brooklyn Legal Aid lawyers. "The FST must be subjected to scrutiny outside their inventors'."

The scientists say they are confident. "If I was nervous that it wasn't going to prevail, then we wouldn't be using it today," Dr. Caragine said.

Both 43 years old and mothers of boys under 2, Dr. Caragine and Dr. Mitchell work on the 13th floor in the $290 million laboratory that opened in Kips Bay, in Manhattan, in 2007. As the largest government forensics laboratory in the country, it examined 43,000 items for DNA last year. The department seems striking for another reason; it is 70 percent women, but that is actually common in forensic biology.

Dr. Caragine said the environment was supportive, rather than competitive. Her office has a plaque about teamwork, and there's also a signed book from the crime writer Patricia Cornwell and, one day last week, there was a cold cappuccino. Dr. Mitchell's office contains her foldup bike for her commute to Park Slope, Brooklyn.

Dr. Caragine and Dr. Mitchell are a well-balanced duo, finishing each other's sentences the way they finish formulas. Neither has ever watched "C.S.I." Dr. Caragine, who invented a DNA swab out of yarn in 2003 because she found the cotton ones insufficient to gather evidence, boldly proposes new ideas. Dr. Mitchell, a trained mediator, mathematician and private investigator (with her family's business in Seattle), tells her quietly when ideas do not work.

After earning her doctorate in molecular oncology and immunology from New York University, Dr. Caragine, from Mount Vernon, N.Y., started working for the medical examiner's office in 2001. She identified victims from the 9/11 attacks through DNA. "It was a place where you felt useful," she said.

In 2008, she hired Dr. Mitchell, who holds a doctorate in human

NICOLE BENGIVENO/THE NEW YORK TIMES

The medical examiner's practice lab.

genetics and molecular biology from Johns Hopkins University, to design the FST.

With the assistance of other deputies, researchers and programmers, Dr. Caragine and Dr. Mitchell spent two years validating the tool, conducting 557,000 test runs.

"We'd be partway through something and then find a better way to do it," Dr. Mitchell said. Dr. Caragine added, "There was never a moment that we didn't think it was going to work."

Mechthild Prinz, the director of the lab, praised their partnership. "Theresa really has the vision and the creative force, and Adele has the mathematical skills and the understanding of the problem," Dr. Prinz said, crediting Dr. Caragine's "chutzpah."

For their city service, Dr. Caragine and Dr. Mitchell won the Fred Hayes Award in 2012, named for Mayor John V. Lindsay's budget director whose hallmark was recruiting undaunted young talent. They split the $15,000 for traveling to international conferences.

In a tour of the lab last week, the researchers demonstrated the FST. From evidence collected by the New York Police Department, the lab uses high-sensitivity DNA testing to gather small amounts drawn from skin cells off objects possibly touched by the suspect. (Blood and semen usually produce larger DNA samples, often from one source.)

The lab interprets that DNA and puts the results into the FST, which compares it to the DNA profile drawn from the suspect. The tool factors in if a piece of DNA is missing or an extra one is present, which can happen with very small or degraded samples.

It then estimates the probability that the suspect is a contributor to the mixture of DNA versus a random member of the population, and how frequently one would expect to see the pieces of DNA from the evidence in the population. The FST estimates this based on four general New York City ethnic groups and reports the lowest likelihood ratio, underestimating the weight of the results, the scientists say, in favor of the defendant.

For now, the tool can only interpret a mix of up to three DNA samples and because of the similarities of DNA within families, it cannot be used to analyze samples from people who are related.

One former member of the DNA Subcommittee said he was concerned the formula was based on assumptions, not practice.

"As a pioneer, I am an advocate of DNA work," said Ranajit Chakraborty, the director of the Center for Computational Genomics at the University of North Texas. "At the same time, we should not push the envelope beyond what it is."

He eventually voted for it, in part because he said the technical discussions became "tedious."

Dr. Caragine said that from July 2011 to May 2012, they did 511 calculations with the FST, and 34 percent of the time, she noted, the evidence tended to exonerate the defendant.

"It is what it is, the evidence," Dr. Caragine said. "Sometimes it may free an innocent person or it may solve the crime. You don't always think about how it has a personal effect on people. It's easier not to think about it — we just have case files here and it's very clinical."

Seeking Answers in Genome of Gunman

BY GINA KOLATA | DEC. 24, 2012

IN A MOVE likely to renew a longstanding ethical controversy, geneticists are quietly making plans to study the DNA of Adam Lanza, 20, who killed 20 children and seven adults in Newtown, Conn. Their work will be an effort to discover biological clues to extreme violence.

The researchers, at the University of Connecticut, confirmed their plans through a spokeswoman but declined to provide details. But other experts speculated that the geneticists might look for mutations that might be associated with mental illnesses and ones that might also increase the risk for violence.

They could look at all of Mr. Lanza's genes, searching for something unusual like gene duplications or deletions or unexpected mutations, or they might determine the sequence of his entire genome, the genes and the vast regions of DNA that are not genes, in an extended search for aberrations that could determine which genes are active and how active they are.

But whatever they do, this apparently is the first time researchers will attempt a detailed study of the DNA of a mass killer.

Some researchers, like Dr. Arthur Beaudet, a professor at the Baylor College of Medicine and the chairman of its department of molecular and human genetics, applaud the effort. He believes that the acts committed by men like Mr. Lanza and the gunmen in other rampages in recent years — at Columbine High School and in Aurora, Colo., in Norway, in Tucson and at Virginia Tech — are so far off the charts of normal behavior that there must be genetic changes driving them.

"We can't afford not to do this research," Dr. Beaudet said.

Other scientists are not so sure. They worry that this research could eventually stigmatize people who have never committed a crime but who turn out to have a genetic aberration also found in a mass murder.

Everything known about mental illness, these skeptics say, argues that there are likely to be hundreds of genes involved in extreme violent behavior, not to mention a variety of environmental influences, and that all of these factors can interact in complex and unpredictable ways.

"It is almost inconceivable that there is a common genetic factor" to be found in mass murders, said Dr. Robert C. Green, a geneticist and neurologist at Harvard Medical School. "I think it says more about us that we wish there was something like this. We wish there was an explanation."

Scientists are well aware of the fraught history behind the questions of biology and violence.

In the early 20th century, claims that criminal behavior was inherited arose during the eugenics movement and led to sterilizations of mental patients and felons.

On Christmas Day in 1965, two researchers published a paper saying men with an extra Y chromosome, the chromosome that confers maleness, were "super males" and born criminals. The hypothesis was helped along by the fact that these men "fit the classic Hollywood criminal — big, awkward, thuglike and with low I.Q.'s," said Dr. Philip Reilly, a lawyer and clinical geneticist who has studied this history.

The idea persisted for about 15 years, Dr. Reilly said, but eventually the epidemiological evidence convinced scientists that these men were no more violent than men without an extra Y chromosome.

In 1993, in a paper published in the journal Science, researchers reported that a mutation leading to a lack of the enzyme monoamine oxidase caused violence in a Dutch family. Every family member who inherited the mutation was a violent criminal; those without it had no criminal behaviors.

"It was a stunning piece of work," said James Blair, the chief of the unit on affective cognitive neuroscience at the National Institute of Mental Health. But, he added, it turned out not to be generalizable. For the most part, "it was just this family," he said.

The National Institutes of Health was embroiled in controversy about 20 years ago simply for proposing to study the biological underpinnings of violence. Critics accused researchers of racism and singling out minorities, especially black men.

Shortly after, the N.I.H. took back financing for a conference at the University of Maryland to examine genetics and criminal behavior. The conference was canceled.

But genetics has come of age in recent years with new and powerful methods to determine DNA sequences and analyze the results. Studies of people at the far end of a bell curve can be especially informative, because the genetic roots of their conditions can be stark and easy to spot, noted J. H. Pate Skene, a Duke University neurobiologist.

"I think doing research on outliers, people at an end of a spectrum on something of concern like violent behavior, is certainly a good idea," he said, but he advised tempering expectations.

"I would call it a caution, not about whether to do this research but about what to expect," he added.

Perhaps it will be fruitless to search for one or a few major gene mutations that always lead to extreme violence, Dr. Beaudet said. But what if a significant fraction of the shootings were linked to gene variants? What if scientists were to discover genes that were risk factors, increasing a person's chance of violent behavior but not foreordaining it?

"If we know someone has a 2 percent chance or a 10 percent chance or a 20 percent chance of violent behavior, what would you do with that person?" Dr. Skene said. "They have not been convicted of anything — have not done anything wrong."

But a genetic profile might play a role if someone were convicted of violent offenses, Dr. Beaudet countered. Criminals are routinely denied parole based solely on psychiatric evaluations. Perhaps a genetic test could add to the certainty of the decision, he said.

Ultimately, understanding the genetics of violence might enable researchers to find ways to intervene before a person commits a horrific crime. But that goal would be difficult to achieve, and the pursuit of it risks jeopardizing personal liberties. Some scientists shudder at the thought of labeling people potential violent criminals.

"The idea of screening with a view of preventing those kinds of incidents is basically unthinkable," said Dr. Steven E. Hyman, director of the Stanley Center for Psychiatric Research at the Broad Institute of Harvard and M.I.T. "You would fail. You would stigmatize."

Some day, he added, it might be important to know the phenotypes — the characteristics — of violent killers and have their DNA, but not for the reasons many think.

"I am always happy to store DNA and phenotype information and freeze cells, thinking that one day we would have usable clues," Dr. Hyman added. "But that would be biology, not prevention."

Using DNA to Sketch What Victims Look Like; Some Call It Science Fiction

BY ASHLEY SOUTHALL | OCT. 19, 2017

FREEZING WINDS WHIPPED the snow-covered coastline of Brooklyn's Calvert Vaux Park on the day two years ago that a severed hand washed up on the rocks.

A bird-watcher found it on Jan. 4, 2015, according to the New York Police Department, which later recovered a foot and rib cage from the same body. The medical examiner determined the body parts had come from a woman between the ages of 20 and 45. A tattoo of a red heart and a rose on a patch of skin clinging to her calf offered what the police believed was her name: Monique. But what Monique looked like remained a mystery.

When a public appeal for help failed to generate leads, the Police Department turned to a forensic technique called phenotyping, which uses DNA from the biological matter people leave behind, like skin and blood, to predict their appearance.

"Once we identify the deceased, it'd go a long way to solving the crime itself," said Chief Patrick Conry, who was chief of Brooklyn detectives and is now a senior official at Police Headquarters.

In phenotyping, scientists scan a person's genes for variations known to influence traits like skin color, eye color, geographical ancestry and freckling. They then plug those markers into a set of algorithms to generate a profile. In recent years, pharmaceutical companies like Parabon NanoLabs of Virginia have begun recreating faces.

Parabon's tests revealed that Monique was primarily of sub-Saharan African descent, and not white as investigators had believed based on the color of the skin found on her remains.

Analysts used her sex and ancestry to create a generic sketch of a face from a database of demographic information, which they overlaid with traits gleaned from her genes: a deep brown complexion and brown eyes above a round nose.

As murder rates hover at historic lows, the Police Department is looking to emerging technologies like phenotyping to help solve old cases. The hope is that seeing a victim's likeness will jog people's memories. Deputy Chief Emanuel J. Katranakis, the commander of the Forensic Investigation Division, said the police have received several tips since releasing the likenesses of Monique and a male victim in another case in September.

But critics have raised concerns about the lack of peer-reviewed science behind the technology and the creeping expansion of how DNA is collected and used in criminal investigations, where it is susceptible to human bias, error and abuse.

Police officials have said they are focused on using phenotyping to help identify victims, though they have not ruled out using it to search for suspects. But relying on so few traits requires the police to cast a wide net, said Robert Perry, the legislative director of the New York Civil Liberties Union.

"The problem is, its use will place actual people, innocent of wrongdoing, under criminal suspicion without any basis in fact or science," he said.

Chief Katranakis said that criticism overlooks phenotyping's ability to help the police avoid targeting the wrong people in their investigations. "The power of exclusion from phenotyping is greater than that of inclusion," he said.

For example, he said, the Police Department used the technique to determine that the suspect in the 2016 murder of a Queens jogger, Karina Vetrano, was of African descent and eventually arrested a suspect, Chanel Lewis, who is black.

Dozens of law enforcement agencies in places like Louisiana and North Carolina have similarly used phenotyping to search for suspects in cases where investigators had exhausted traditional leads.

But New York regulators say any private lab seeking to perform testing on DNA samples from New York must have authorization from state health officials.

Chief Katranakis said state approval was not necessary because the Police Department was not using the technique to identify specific individuals. But the state Department of Health said Parabon is required to obtain a license to perform phenotyping on DNA samples from New York.

The agency sent Parabon a warning last month, and Ben Rosen, a Health Department spokesman, said the company is currently seeking a permit. In an interview, Dr. Steven L. Armentrout, Parabon's chief executive, declined to comment on the issue.

DNA testing has been around for decades, popularized on television and in the criminal justice system for its usefulness in determining paternity and ancestry. DNA collected from crime scenes is routinely used to identify suspects and to convict or exonerate the accused, usually by comparing it to a suspect's DNA or samples in a criminal database.

Increasingly, geneticists have been discovering ways to use variations to predict specific physical traits. The potential applications might someday include allowing doctors to detect genetic diseases by scanning a patient's face.

Parabon boasts that its Snapshot service, which police officials said cost $4,000 to $5,000 for each case, "accurately predicts the physical appearance and ancestry of an unknown person from DNA."

Although interest in its testing has grown, Parabon has yet to publish its detailed methodology for peer review.

Much of the science around how genetics determines facial appearance has focused on the role of individual genes. But Dr. Armentrout said Parabon's facial predictions are based on its research on how genes work together to shape the face.

"For a complex trait, this is unequivocally the way genetics works," he said.

But critics say the company is promising more than science has determined it can deliver. Dr. Yaniv Erlich, a computer science professor at Columbia University who studies genetics, said the idea that phenotyping could meaningfully predict something as complex as individual looks is "on the verge of science fiction."

"Ancestry?" he said. "Sure, that's fairly simple. Kinship, too. Phenotyping with faces? Forget about it."

The Police Department's announcement that it was using phenotyping came amid fresh controversy over forensic DNA techniques. The state inspector general is reviewing a request from criminal defense attorneys to investigate methods used for several years by the city medical examiner's office, an inquiry that could have implications for thousands of prosecutions.

Among scientists, the idea that phenotyping can predict faces has provoked debate. A geneticist was criticized for a recently published paper in which he claimed to be able to identify anonymous people's faces by sequencing their genes. Reviewers and a co-author said the paper, which was intended to raise privacy concerns, overstated what was achieved.

Dr. Erlich wrote that most of the trait predictions, such as height and face shape, were made using simple demographic data rather than trait-specific markers. "It is like the authors needed to get to the supermarket and decided to build a spacecraft to make the trip," he said.

Even amid such debates, the role of DNA in criminal investigations continues to expand in New York. The state Commission on Forensic Science, which approves methods used in state crime labs, adopted guidelines for familial testing — DNA searches for relatives of potential suspects — that took effect Wednesday, despite protests from criminal defense and civil liberties lawyers.

The Legal Aid Society, in a brief filed with the commission, said that the panel, which was lobbied by the police, prosecutors and Ms. Vetrano's family, does not have the authority to implement familial DNA testing.

Allison Lewis, a staff attorney in Legal Aid's DNA unit, and David Loftis, the attorney in charge of post-conviction and forensic litigation, said the expanded roles of DNA in the criminal justice system in recent years go far beyond what the Legislature had in mind when it adopted laws compelling people convicted of certain crimes to submit swabs.

They warned that without clear rules from lawmakers, the technology will be used to justify something akin to stop-and-frisk, where people in black and Latino communities are targeted for genetic surveillance, regardless of whether they are suspected of a crime.

Chief Katranakis said the Police Department was "fully aware" of the uncertainty surrounding phenotyping. Officials conducted a thorough evaluation of the science behind it and consulted with industry experts before deeming it appropriate for use in a limited number of cases where investigators have nothing to work with, he said.

Nothing is what the police had when a man's skull was found in July 2005 in a community garden in Bedford-Stuyvesant, Brooklyn. The teeth had been removed, preventing investigators from identifying the victim with dental records. Phenotyping analysts created an image from his DNA and adjusted it to his skull shape, getting closer to what he looked like, Chief Katranakis said.

Investigators found the victim's torso in a trash bin in East Williamsburg and traced it to 128 Gates Avenue in Bushwick, near where an accused serial killer lived when two of his teenage neighbors disappeared. Their bodies were found dismembered in 2004 and 2005.

The police are trying to determine whether the same suspect, Kwauhuru Govan, might be his killer.

DORIS BURKE contributed research.

In Africa, Geneticists Are Hunting Poachers

BY GINA KOLATA | JAN. 8, 2018

SOUTH AFRICAN AUTHORITIES long had eyes on Rogers Mukwena. They knew the former schoolteacher was wanted in Zimbabwe for poaching rhinoceroses and selling their horns, which can command hundreds of thousands of dollars.

He'd jumped bail and fled to northern Pretoria, but it was vexingly difficult to catch and prosecute him — until a scientist helped make the case against him with rhino DNA.

His subsequent conviction resulted from a new tactic in wildlife preservation: The genetic fingerprinting methods that have been so successful in the criminal justice system are now being used to solve poaching crimes.

First, researchers in South Africa had to build a large database of genetic samples drawn from African rhinoceroses. The DNA would be used to match a carcass to a particular horn discovered on a suspected poacher or trafficker, or to rhinoceros blood on his clothes, knives or axes.

To make that possible, Dr. Cindy Harper, a veterinarian at the University of Pretoria, and her colleagues collected DNA from every rhinoceros they could find — more than 20,000 so far. They have taught park rangers how to retrieve blood, tissue or hair samples from every rhinoceros that is killed, dehorned or moved.

The rangers have learned forensic crime-scene principles and the importance of the so-called chain of custody to ensure that the samples are not corrupted. Dr. Harper's lab performs the analysis and stores DNA fingerprints.

The scientists' database, which they call Rhodis, is modeled after Codis, the F.B.I. system used to link the DNA of suspects to evidence at a crime scene.

The approach is promising, said Crawford Allan, senior director of Traffic, which monitors illegal wildlife trade at the World Wildlife Fund.

A poaching scene is a crime scene, he said: "If you want to get through detection and investigation and prosecution, treat it as a crime scene and use forensics."

Poaching has escalated exponentially in the past decade, he noted. More than 7,000 rhinos have been killed in the past ten years. The World Wildlife Fund estimates that 20,00 to 30,000 African elephants are killed each year for their tusks.

Their tusks and horns are trafficked through experienced criminal networks. "You really need sophisticated tools to help solve these crimes," Mr. Allan said.

The rhino project provides "a 'cold hit' database," said Stephen J. O'Brien, referring to the identification of a perpetrator by DNA when there are no other apparent clues.

Dr. O'Brien, an expert on DNA fingerprinting and chief scientific officer of the Theodosius Dobzhansky Center for Genome Bioinformatics at St. Petersburg State University in Russia, is co-author of a new paper, published on Monday in Current Biology, describing the anti-poaching effort.

A similar attempt to use DNA to convict poachers is led by Sam Wasser, director of the Center for Conservation Biology at the University of Washington. His group's focus is African elephants.

Over a period of 15 years, he and his colleagues have collected and analyzed DNA from dung to create a map of the ranges of various elephant groups based on their genetic differences. It helps show where ivory seized from poachers originated.

The project has not linked specific carcasses to specific tusks recovered from traffickers. But the analysis has provided valuable clues about the regions in which poachers are operating.

"To our surprise, the ivory was consistently coming from two areas," Dr. Wasser said. Tusks from savanna elephants were initially coming

TYLER HICKS/THE NEW YORK TIMES

A pile of poached ivory is prepared for burning in Libreville, Gabon.

from southeastern Tanzania and northern Mozambique, the data showed, but the illegal trade then shifted northward to southern Kenya.

Tusks from forest elephants originated in a small triangular area in northeast Gabon, northwest Republic of the Congo, and southeastern Cameroon.

"Instead of focusing everywhere, if we really want the big criminals we should focus on those two spots," Dr. Wasser said.

The sale of ivory and rhino horns is hugely lucrative. Rhino horns may bring $60,000 or more per kilogram. A horn generally weighs a few kilograms, but a few have been as heavy as 10 kilograms, or about 22 pounds.

"Pound for pound, a rhino horn is worth more than heroin or gold or platinum," Mr. Allan said. And prosecutions are so rare that the risks for the traffickers are "very low."

The poacher sells horns to a trafficker, who disguises them and ships them to destination countries, mainly Vietnam and China. Some horns are carved into jewelry while still in South Africa, which can make it extremely difficult to trace them.

Most horns are ground and used as medicine in Asia, believed to cure cancer, impotence — or, Mr. Allan said, "you name it." More recently, people in Asia have begun wearing beads or bangles made from rhino horns thought to have curative powers and to be status symbols. Some horns are made into ceremonial cups.

Elephant tusks currently sell for $1,000 a kilogram, Dr. Wasser said. Unlike rhino horns, which are shipped in relatively small volumes, traffickers typically collect and ship at least half a ton of ivory, or 500 kilograms, in a container.

Some seizures have uncovered as much as seven tons of ivory in a single shipment, Dr. Wasser said. Ivory is primarily bought by collectors or as an investment.

Dr. Wasser's primary target is traffickers, not poachers. Even when poachers are caught and convicted, he said, "there are 10 more waiting in line to replace them."

But traffickers form the basis of the business that makes poaching profitable. "The analogy is, are you after a serial killer or a one-time murderer?" he asked.

To catch a serial killer, Dr. Wasser added, authorities require "intelligence-based forensics to prevent future crimes."

Dr. Harper also hopes to disrupt the criminal networks shipping contraband — in this case, rhino horns — to destination countries. So far, the rhino database has been used to convict hunters and traffickers in South Africa, Namibia, Kenya and Swaziland.

But the group has not disrupted the criminal conglomerates at the top of the chain, she said.

The rhinoceros project began in 2010, when poaching was skyrocketing. Thirteen were poached in South Africa in 2007; more than 1,000 are now killed each year.

In 120 criminal cases completed or still pending, Rhodis has linked DNA on horns, equipment or clothing to particular carcasses,

Dr. Harper said. But it can take years for a case to move through the courts and end in a conviction.

The first successful such conviction involved a Vietnamese smuggler who was caught with seven horns at O.R. Tambo International Airport in Johannesburg in 2010. Two were matched to carcasses, and he was sentenced to 10 years in prison.

But the case involving Mr. Mukwena was one of the first to involve a well-known smuggler. He was arrested on Jan. 16, 2012, after a police officer spotted him walking across a field carrying a black bag.

When the officer confronted him, Mr. Mukwena dropped the bag and ran. It contained three rhinoceros horns, two from a cow and one from her calf.

Apprehended, Mr. Mukwena admitted to killing the cow but said an accomplice had killed the calf because it was bothering him.

The Golden State Killer Is Tracked Through a Thicket of DNA, and Experts Shudder

BY GINA KOLATA AND HEATHER MURPHY | APRIL 27, 2018

GENETIC TESTING SERVICES have become enormously popular with people looking for long-lost relatives or clues to hereditary diseases. Most never imagined that one day intimate pieces of their DNA could be mined to assist police detectives in criminal cases.

Even as scientific experts applauded this week's arrest of the Golden State Killer suspect, Joseph James DeAngelo, 72, some expressed unease on Friday at reports that detectives in California had used a public genealogy database to identify him. Privacy and ethical issues glossed over in the public's rush to embrace DNA databases are now glaringly apparent, they said.

"This is really tough," said Malia Fullerton, an ethicist at the University of Washington who studies DNA forensics. "He was a horrible man and it is good that he was identified, but does the end justify the means?"

Coming so quickly on the heels of the Cambridge Analytica scandal, in which Facebook data on more than 70 million users was shared without their permission, it is beginning to dawn on consumers that even their most intimate digital data — their genetic profiles — may be passed around in ways they never intended.

"There is a whole generation that says, 'I don't really care about privacy,' " said Peter Neufeld, a co-founder of The Innocence Project, which uses DNA to exonerate people who were wrongly convicted. "And then they do, once there is a Cambridge Analytica. No one has thought about what are the possible consequences."

The trail of the Golden State Killer had gone cold decades ago. The police had linked him to more than 50 rapes and 12 murders from 1976 to 1986, and he had eluded all attempts to find him.

In the years since, scientists have developed powerful tools to identify people by tiny variations in their DNA, as individual as fingerprints. At the same time, the F.B.I. and state law enforcement agencies have been cultivating growing databases of DNA not just from convicted criminals, but also in some cases from people accused of crimes.

The California police had the Golden State Killer's DNA and recently found an unusually well-preserved sample from one of the crime scenes. The problem was finding a match.

But these days DNA is stored in many places, and a near-match ultimately was found in a genealogy website beloved by hobbyists called GEDmatch, created by two volunteers in 2011.

Anyone can set up a free profile on GEDmatch. Many customers upload to the site DNA profiles they have already generated on larger commercial sites like 23andMe.

The detectives in the Golden State Killer case uploaded the suspect's DNA sample. But they would have had to check a box online certifying that the DNA was their own or belonged to someone for whom they were legal guardians, or that they had "obtained authorization" to upload the sample.

"The purpose was to make these connections and to find these relatives," said Blaine Bettinger, a lawyer affiliated with GEDmatch. "It was not intended to be used by law enforcement to identify suspects of crimes."

But joining for that purpose does not technically violate site policy, he added.

Erin Murphy, a law professor at New York University and expert on DNA searches, said that using a fake identity might raise questions about the legality of the evidence.

The matches found in GEDmatch were to relatives of the suspect, not the suspect himself.

Since the site provides family trees, detectives also were able to look for relatives who might not have uploaded genetic data to the site themselves.

On GEDmatch, "it just happens they got lucky," said Dr. Ashley Hall, a forensics science expert at the University of Illinois in Chicago.

23andMe has more than 5 million customers, and Ancestry.com has 10 million. But the DNA in databases like these are relevant to tens of millions of others — sisters, parents, children. A lot can be learned about a family simply by accessing one member's DNA.

"Suppose you are worried about genetic privacy," Ms. Murphy said. "If your sibling or parent or child engaged in this activity online, they are compromising your family for generations."

DNA profiles can be held indefinitely, and the data can be handed over to police who have warrants or subpoenas. You may never commit a crime. But how should you feel if your DNA was used to locate a distant relative who did?

On a Facebook page dedicated to genealogy, hobbyists debated this new use of DNA data.

"I'll volunteer to give my DNA and out any of my cousins who may be rapist/murderers. So much drama over nothing," wrote Stu Pike, who said he had used GEDmatch to track down relatives.

But others expressed outrage. "My relatives consented for their data to be used for genealogy but not for criminal investigations," wrote Leah LaPerle Larkin, who adjusted her settings to make sure her family's data was private on the GEDmatch site.

"I've had many sleepless nights the last few years, realizing that it's coming," CeCe Moore, a genetic genealogist, said of the possibility that an online site might be used to identify a suspect.

The founder of DNA Detectives, a group that helps adoptees find their biological parents and reunite long-lost relatives, Ms. Moore said that she has been approached numerous times by law enforcement asking her help in solving murder and rape cases.

She declined, she said, "because I was still wrestling with the ethical questions of using genealogy databases for criminals."

It's not clear how often law enforcement turns to burgeoning DNA databases. Andy Kill, a spokesman for 23andMe, said the company has "had a handful of inquiries over the course of 11 years," and that no data were "given out in any circumstance."

It is unlikely that the apparent success of the method in the Golden State Killer case will spur a rush to use genealogy databases to solve crimes.

"Using a database of this kind will generate an extraordinary number of leads, and running them all down using both nongenetic and genetic information requires a lot of police power," Ms. Murphy said. "So I doubt it will be run of the mill any time soon."

But it clearly is time for a wider discussion about law-enforcement access to stored DNA, Mr. Neufeld said. "What really needs to happen is for ethicists, lawyers and minorities likely to be disproportionately affected to think of the unintended consequences of this genetic data."

CHAPTER 4

Ethical Issues in Genetic Testing

Genetics as a discipline has long raised ethical questions. The potential to determine the fate of one's offspring, either positively or negatively, has been considered from the perspective of class and disability rights. The rise of personal genetic testing has intensified older debates about genetics, disability and "designer babies," while raising new controversies. In the current charged climate around race, many have turned to genetics to settle their ancestry or prove their assumptions, while scientists and critics have complicated this view.

Ethics Questions Arise as Genetic Testing of Embryos Increases

BY GINA KOLATA | FEB. 3, 2014

HER FIRST THOUGHT after she heard the news, after she screamed and made her mother and boyfriend leave the room, was that she would never have children. Amanda Baxley's doctor had just told her, over a speakerphone in her psychiatrist's office, that she had the gene for Gerstmann-Straussler-Scheinker disease, or GSS, which would inevitably lead to her slow and terrible death.

This rare neurological disease had stalked her family for generations. Her father, 56, was even then in its final throes.

On the spot, Ms. Baxley, 26, declared she would not let the disease take another life in her family line, even if that meant forgoing childbirth. "I want it stopped," she said. The next day, her boyfriend, Bradley Kalinsky, asked her to marry him.

But the Kalinskys' wedded life has taken a completely unexpected turn, one briefly described on Monday in The Journal of the American Medical Association Neurology. Like a growing number of couples who know a disease runs in the family, they chose in vitro fertilization, and had cells from the embryos, created in a petri dish with her eggs and his sperm, tested first for the disease-causing gene. Only embryos without the gene were implanted. The Kalinskys are now parents of three children who will be free of the fear of GSS.

Genetic testing of embryos has been around for more than a decade, but its use has soared in recent years as methods have improved and more disease-causing genes have been discovered. The in vitro fertilization and testing are expensive — typically about $20,000 — but they make it possible for couples to ensure that their

NATHAN MORGAN FOR THE NEW YORK TIMES

Amanda and Bradley Kalinsky with their children, who were born after embryos for in vitro fertilization were found to be free of the gene for the deadly disease that Ms. Kalinsky carries.

children will not inherit a faulty gene and to avoid the difficult choice of whether to abort a pregnancy if testing of a fetus detects a genetic problem.

But the procedure also raises unsettling ethical questions that trouble advocates for the disabled and have left some doctors struggling with what they should tell their patients. When are prospective parents justified in discarding embryos? Is it acceptable, for example, for diseases like GSS, that develop in adulthood? What if a gene only increases the risk of a disease? And should people be able to use it to pick whether they have a boy or girl? A recent international survey found that 2 percent of more than 27,000 uses of preimplantation diagnosis were made to choose a child's sex.

In the United States, there are no regulations that limit the method's use. The Society for Assisted Reproductive Technology, whose members provide preimplantation diagnosis, says it is "ethically justified" to prevent serious adult diseases for which "no safe, effective interventions are available." The method is "ethically allowed" for conditions "of lesser severity" or for which the gene increases risk but does not guarantee a disease.

There is no question that the method's use is increasing rapidly, though no group collects comprehensive data, said Dr. Joe Leigh Simpson, vice president for research at the March of Dimes and past president of the American Society for Reproductive Medicine.

The center in Chicago that tested the Kalinskys' embryos for the GSS gene, the Reproductive Genetics Institute, has tested embryos from more than 2,500 couples and sought to identify 425 gene mutations. The institute's caseload has risen 40 percent in just the past two years, according to its director, Svetlana Rechitsky, an author of the new paper on the Kalinskys' case.

Ms. Kalinsky's gene causes a particularly dire disease. Her grandfather, great-aunt, uncle, father and cousins died of it. Sometime between her mid-30s and her mid-50s, Ms. Kalinsky, who is now 30, will begin to stumble like a drunk. Dementia will follow, and possibly blindness or deafness. Five years after the onset of symptoms, she will most likely be dead.

The Kalinskys went to a fertility clinic in Chicago, the Institute for Human Reproduction, which created embryos with in vitro fertilization. Then the Reproductive Genetics Institute tested the embryos for the GSS gene.

The procedure cost $20,000 for the first round, and the Kalinskys paid for it out of pocket. Many insurers do not cover the procedure, or pay only for the genetic analysis, not the in vitro fertilization required to obtain the embryos for testing, saying the patients are not infertile.

Preimplantation diagnosis often goes unmentioned by doctors. In a recent national survey, Dr. Robert Klitzman, a professor of clinical psychiatry and bioethicist at Columbia University, found that most internists were unsure about whether they would suggest the method to couples with genes for diseases like cystic fibrosis or breast cancer. Only about 6 percent had ever mentioned it to patients and only 7 percent said they felt qualified to answer patients' questions about it.

"In the medical community, the lack of knowledge about P.G.D. is a serious concern," said Dr. P. Murali Doraiswamy, a dementia researcher at Duke University Medical Center and an author of the new paper, referring to preimplantation genetic diagnosis. In his area — brain disorders — he adds, there are no guidelines about using the method, even though there are hundreds of inherited neurological conditions. Ms. Kalinsky, a nurse, and her husband, a doctor, only learned about the testing from a genetic counselor.

Ethicists are divided about use of the method.

Janet Malek, a bioethicist at the Brody School of Medicine at East Carolina University, said that people who carry a gene like GSS have a moral duty to use preimplantation diagnosis — if they can afford it — to spare the next generation.

"If there is a paradigm example in which a parent can have an obligation to use this technology, this is it," she said.

But David Wasserman, an ethicist at Yeshiva University and consultant to the department of bioethics at the National Institutes of Health, says there is no obligation to use it for diseases that do not start until adulthood. Eliminating embryos with such genes is essentially saying someone like Ms. Kalinsky should never have been born, he said.

And discarding embryos that carry gene mutations that increase the risk for disease — for example, breast cancer — is problematic, he said.

"To someone who says, 'I can't deal with a risk of breast cancer,' I would say: 'Look, there are all kinds of risks. You and your children are going to be hostage to fortune and no amount of testing is going to change that,' " Mr. Wasserman said.

Dr. Klitzman calls diseases like breast cancer the "gray areas." And, he said, "with the exploding use of the technology, we are increasingly confronting gray areas."

Patients can avoid all testing and hope for the best, playing what Dr. Ilan Tur-Kaspa, the founder and director of the Institute for Human Reproduction, calls "reproductive roulette." Or, he said, they can conceive on their own and have the fetus tested. If the gene is present, they face the difficult choice of whether to abort the pregnancy. Preimplantation genetic diagnosis provides another option.

Dr. Tur-Kaspa said that after having done the procedure a thousand times, he cannot think of a gene he would not test for if a patient requested it.

Ms. Kalinsky and her husband ended up with 12 embryos from in vitro fertilization. Six that had the GSS gene were discarded. "That was a really hard thing to do," she said. But getting pregnant and then deciding what to do would have been more difficult. "For me, destroying a fetus that is already growing inside of me was much different than discarding embryos that had not yet implanted," she said.

Dr. Tur-Kaspa said the majority of his patients differ from Ms. Kalinsky in one crucial way: they do not want to know if they have a gene that will cause them eventually to have a disease or a higher risk of it. In such cases, he said, if all the embryos carry the faulty gene, the couple is told that none of their embryos was viable, which can happen with or without a mutated gene.

Ms. Kalinsky never considered not finding out, but the knowledge shadows her. "Every little trip, every little stumble, I think, 'This could be the disease starting,' " she said.

Her husband, Dr. Kalinsky, says he will be there with her. He never considered abandoning her when they learned she had the gene. "That would be the cruelest thing," he said.

He had been planning to ask her to marry him and was saving up for a ring — all he had was a loose diamond. But he decided not to wait after she got the news that she had the gene. He gave her the diamond in a field outside his parents' home.

"There were a lot of emotions," he said, "a lot of sadness." But, he said, "I wanted her to know she had someone with her throughout this journey."

They decided together to have children and fell in love with them — twin 3-year-olds, Ava and Cole, and 9-month-old Tatum — more deeply than they could have imagined.

"I would travel that road a million times over if I had to because in the end I was given the privilege of being their mother," Ms. Kalinsky said.

Until a couple of months ago, she worked part time as a hospice nurse, but has given that up to be with her children full time. She and her husband plan to tell their children about GSS while they are still young in hopes of preparing them for her inevitably slow and painful death.

And the Kalinskys still have two frozen embryos left at the Chicago clinic and plan to try for two more children.

"We have our time here now, and we try to live in the now," Dr. Kalinsky said. "We try to love each other and the kids every single day that we can."

The Fault in Our DNA

BY DAVID DOBBS | JULY 10, 2014

IN HIS 2007 BOOK "A Farewell to Alms," the economic historian Gregory Clark argued that the English came to rule the world largely because their rich outbred their poor, and thus embedded their superior genes and values throughout the nation. In her comprehensive takedown, the historian Deirdre N. McCloskey noted that Clark's idea was a "bold hypothesis, and was bold when first articulated by social Darwinists such as Charles Davenport and Francis Galton in the century before last." Indeed, over the past 150 years, various white Western scientists and writers have repeatedly offered biological explanations for Caucasian superiority. They have repeatedly failed because, as McCloskey noted, none ever mounted a credible quantitative argument.

Now, in "A Troublesome Inheritance," Nicholas Wade, a longtime science writer for The New York Times, says modern genetics shows that "the three major races," Africans, Caucasians and East Asians, are genetically distinct races that diverge much as subspecies do, and that their genetic differences underlie "the rise of the West."

This racial divide started, Wade says, when humans began migrating out of Africa some 50,000 years ago. As groups entered diverse environments, they faced differing pressures that selected for gene variants creating different traits, including dissimilar social behaviors. Genetic selection for distinctive physical traits in different populations, such as lighter skin to maximize sunlight absorption, is well established and widely accepted. Decidedly not well established, however, is Wade's proposal that genetic selection gives different human populations distinct behaviors. Because this is the heart of his argument, and because social behavior is far more complex than, say, skin color, it seems fair to ask that his evidence clear a high bar. Does it?

Wade builds much of his case around historical ideas like Gregory Clark's hypothesis about English breeding; the political scientist

Francis Fukuyama's notion that Western democracies represent a high point in the evolution of social institutions; and the economic historian Niall Ferguson's view that the West "succeeded because it was an open society." These values and institutions, Wade says, were both shaped by and drove the evolution of Caucasian genes.

As a key event he cites Europe's adoption, starting around A.D. 1000, of the principle that law is the ultimate ruler. This, Wade argues, allowed a transition from closed, insular tribal social organizations to more open, interactive nation-states, and Europe then entered a self-reinforcing cycle: Its rules-based, trade-oriented culture selected for gene variants generating trusting and productive social behavior, and these genes in turn made the culture more trusting and rewarding of hard work.

Meanwhile, the other two major races developed their own distinctions: East Asians (and their genes) evolved to embrace a disciplined, state-dominated culture more respectful of rigid authority. Sub-Saharan Africans evolved to better fit and support their culture's greater allegiance to tribal imperatives than to wider forms of social organization.

Wade runs into much trouble making this argument. He indulges in circular logic. He tells just-so stories. While warning us to avoid filtering science through politics, he draws heavily from conservative historians who minimize the roles played by political power, geographic advantage, momentum, disease and dumb luck. Conveniently, this leaves more historical questions for genetics to answer.

And despite his protests to the contrary, Wade often sounds as if he sees the rise of the West as a sort of stable endpoint of human history and evolution — as if, having considered 5,000 years in which history has successively blessed the Middle East, the Far East and the Ottoman Empire, he observes the West's current run of glory and thinks the pendulum has stilled.

If Wade could point to genes that give races distinctive social behaviors, we might overlook such shortcomings. But he cannot.

He tries. He tells, for instance, of specific gene variants that reputedly create less trust and more violence in African-Americans and, he says, explain their resistance to modern economic institutions and practices. Alas, the scientific literature he draws on is so uneven and disputed that many geneticists dismiss it outright. Wade also cites a 2008 paper that analyzed the genomes of almost 1,000 people from 51 populations around the globe. That paper found that people from different regions do indeed tend to have distinctive genomes. But Wade errs in saying the paper supports his idea that genetic selection has created races with particular social inclinations.

To begin with, the 2008 study mentions nothing about race. It merely establishes that many of the slight differences between human genomes cluster by geography at many scales, including continents, and that genomes from any given location will most likely be similar, just as two people from a particular place will most likely speak with similar accents.

Second, and far more serious, the paper's authors specifically state that while selection may sometimes create genetic differences between populations, they saw little evidence that selection shaped the small genetic differences they found. In fact, they say the differences can be largely explained by "random drift" — arbitrary changes in genes having little to no effect on people's biology or behavior. All of this directly contradicts Wade's argument. Yet he baldly claims the study as support.

And he does this sort of thing repeatedly: He constantly gathers up long shots, speculations and spurious claims, then declares they add up to substantiate his case.

The result is a deeply flawed, deceptive and dangerous book. Its most pernicious conceit is that it's finally safe to talk of racial genetics because "opposition to racism is now well entrenched." The daily news — a black teenager's killer walks free in Florida; a former Ku Klux Klansman shoots up a Jewish community center; and tearful survivors observe the 20th anniversary of the Rwanda genocide, in which 100 days of mass murder rose from ethnic distinctions pressed on the populace by European colonists a century before — says otherwise.

One can find more productive ways to think about genes. As a physician who researches and treats rare genetic disorders, Sharon Moalem, the author of "Inheritance," sees firsthand how sharply DNA can constrain our lives. Yet "our genes aren't as fixed and rigid as most of us have been led to believe," he says, for while genetic defects often create havoc, variable gene expression (our genes' capacity to respond to the environment with a flexibility only now being fully recognized) can give our bodies and minds surprising resilience. In his new book, Moalem describes riveting dramas emerging from both defective genes and reparative epigenetics.

Moalem sometimes tries too hard to entertain, and he may overstate the extent to which trauma-related gene expression changes tend to be lasting and heritable. But the man is loaded with weird findings and great stories. For example, researchers have found they can predict which teenagers will shed pounds at a weight-loss camp by examining methylation patterns — "the way their genes were turned off or on" — in about five sites on their genomes.

Most fascinating are the genetic conditions Moalem describes, like fibrodysplasia ossificans progressiva, or F.O.P., in which the bone-repair genetic machinery works overtime, and muscles are turned to bone. There is no effective treatment as yet.

Moalem's earthy, patient-focused account reminds us that whatever its promise, genetics yet stands at a humble place.

A TROUBLESOME INHERITANCE
Genes, Race and Human History
By Nicholas Wade
278 pp. The Penguin Press. $27.95.

INHERITANCE
How Our Genes Change Our Lives — And Our Lives Change Our Genes
By Sharon Moalem with Matthew D. LaPlante
255 pp. Grand Central Publishing. $28.

DAVID DOBBS is writing a book about theories of human sensitivity to experience.

White? Black? A Murky Distinction Grows Still Murkier

BY CARL ZIMMER | DEC. 24, 2014

IN 1924, THE State of Virginia attempted to define what it means to be white.

The state's Racial Integrity Act, which barred marriages between whites and people of other races, defined whites as people "whose blood is entirely white, having no known, demonstrable or ascertainable admixture of the blood of another race."

There was just one problem. As originally written, the law would have classified many of Virginia's most prominent families as not white, because they claimed to be descended from Pocahontas.

So the Virginia legislature revised the act, establishing what came to be known as the "Pocahontas exception." Virginians could be up to one-sixteenth Native American and still be white in the eyes of the law.

People who were one-sixteenth black, on the other hand, were still black.

In the United States, there is a long tradition of trying to draw sharp lines between ethnic groups, but our ancestry is a fluid and complex matter. In recent years geneticists have been uncovering new evidence about our shared heritage, and last week a team of scientists published the biggest genetic profile of the United States to date, based on a study of 160,000 people.

The researchers were able to trace variations in our genetic makeup from state to state, creating for the first time a sort of ancestry map.

"We use these terms — white, black, Indian, Latino — and they don't really mean what we think they mean," said Claudio Saunt, a historian at the University of Georgia who was not involved in the study.

The data for the new study were collected by 23andMe, the consumer DNA-testing company. When customers have their genes analyzed, the company asks them if they'd like to make their results available for study by staff scientists.

Over time the company has built a database that not only includes DNA, but also such details as a participant's birthplace and the ethnic group with which he or she identifies. (23andMe strips the data of any information that might breach the privacy of participants.)

The scientists also have been developing software that learns to recognize the origins of the short segments of DNA that make up our genomes. Recently they used their program to calculate what percentage of each subject's genomes was inherited from European, African or Native American forebears.

"This year we saw that we were in a great position to do the analysis," said Joanna L. Mountain, senior director of research at 23andMe.

On average, the scientists found, people who identified as African-American had genes that were only 73.2 percent African. European genes accounted for 24 percent of their DNA, while .8 percent came from Native Americans.

Latinos, on the other hand, had genes that were on average 65.1 percent European, 18 percent Native American, and 6.2 percent African. The researchers found that European-Americans had genomes that were on average 98.6 percent European, .19 percent African, and .18 Native American.

These broad estimates masked wide variation among individuals. Based on their sample, the resarchers estimated that over six million European-Americans have some African ancestry. As many as five million have genomes that are at least 1 percent Native American in origin. One in five African-Americans, too, has Native American roots.

Dr. Mountain and her colleagues also looked at how ancestry might influence ethnic identification.

Most Americans with less than 28 percent African-American ancestry say they are white, the researchers found. Above that threshold, people tended to describe themselves as African-American.

Katarzyna Bryc, a 23andMe researcher and co-author of the new study, didn't want to speculate about why people's sense of ethnic identity pivots at that point.

"We can only take it so far as geneticists," she said.

The scientists also linked geographical patterns to their subjects' ancestries. Latinos in the Southwest had high levels of Native American DNA, they found, while Latinos in the Southeast had high levels of African DNA.

The genes of African-Americans varied strikingly from state to state. In Oklahoma, the researchers estimated, 14 percent of African-Americans have genomes that are at least 2 percent Native American. This high percentage is probably due to the unique history of the state.

Some Native American tribes in the South, such as the Cherokee and Choctaw, kept African slaves. When they were expelled to Oklahoma in the 1830s, they brought the slaves with them. In some tribes, Native Americans and African slaves intermarried, and their descendants continue to live in Oklahoma today.

Dr. Saunt was fascinated in particular by the genetic findings among people in South Carolina. Dr. Mountain and her colleagues estimated that 13.3 percent of European-Americans in South Carolina have genes that are at least 1 percent African in origin.

But the researchers also found that African-Americans in South Carolina have among the lowest percentages of European DNA of any African-American population in the United States.

At one point, Dr. Saunt noted, the percentage of South Carolina residents who were slaves was greater than in any other state. But there was also a large population of freed slaves in Charleston permitted to interact with whites.

"We know lots of planters had mistresses in Charleston, and they obviously had children together," said Dr. Saunt. "So what happened to those children? Some remained in the African-American community, and some moved into the white community when they were able to."

Jeffrey C. Long, an anthropologist at the University of New Mexico who was not involved in the study, cautioned that the research was not based on a random sample of Americans. Instead, Dr. Mountain and her colleagues studied only people who were curious enough about their DNA to pay for a test.

"Perhaps people who have mixed ancestry are more interested in their ancestry than people who don't think they have mixed ancestry," Dr. Long said.

David Reich, a geneticist at Harvard University and a co-author on the new study, acknowledged this was a reasonable concern. "It's classic survey bias," he said. But Dr. Reich also noted that the new results were consistent with smaller studies done in the past.

As genetic databases grow, Dr. Reich predicted it would be possible to get even more detailed insights into American history. DNA may be able to illuminate the movements of people across the United States, such as the Great Migration that took African-Americans from the South to Chicago.

"We're in striking distance of that now," Dr. Reich said.

Disability and the Right to Choose

OPINION | BY JENNIFER BARTLETT | MAY 10, 2017

AS A YOUNG WOMAN, I had no particular desire to be a mother. I was neither for nor against having and raising a child, and as things were at the time, the opportunity had not presented itself. That changed when I was 29 and met Jim, the man who would become my husband. In 2002, not long after we married, I gave birth to my son.

In my 20s, I was neutral about parenthood partly because, as a woman with cerebral palsy, I was spared the usual intrusive questioning and expectations about having children that most women are subject to. People never pressured me to have children; they just assumed that I could not. In fact, it became clear very fast that women like me are expected not to reproduce. Now, in my 40s, I find these attitudes ignorant and prejudicial, but as a young woman, it seemed like a bit of freedom to be excused from the usual problems women complain about.

My disability is not genetic and it does not hamper pregnancy. Being pregnant was physically, emotionally and spiritually easy for me, but socially, it was complicated. Moving around in New York City as a pregnant woman with a disability opened me up for constant commentary. I am used to having my body be an object of attention. The real difficulty came from elsewhere — it was dealing with the medical establishment during my pregnancy that I was not prepared for.

Navigating the medical system as a pregnant woman is difficult; as a disabled pregnant woman, it is nearly impossible. The first OB/GYN I went to told me condescendingly, "You sure know what's going on for someone in your condition." By "condition" she meant cerebral palsy.

She referred me to her colleague to get a sonogram because the clinic did not have the necessary equipment. This doctor was more respectful, so I wanted to be under his care. He told me that he could not treat me because it would be unethical "to take work" from his colleague.

I found a third doctor. This doctor was very traditional and although she did not infantilize me, there was a conflict because I wanted to have natural childbirth, and this was not in her vocabulary. In fact, she called my birth plan a "wish list." As my pregnancy developed, after taking a Bradley class and hiring a doula, I became more and more adamant about natural childbirth. At one point, I called the now-defunct Elizabeth Seton Natural Birth Center in Manhattan in an attempt to get a midwife. Without even an examination, I was told that the center would not take me as a client because I was "high risk." When I protested, the midwife told me if a woman at the center had trouble during labor, she would have to walk to the nearby hospital. There was no possibility that this was the case, but she managed to get rid of me. I had no choice but to stay with the third doctor.

In my fifth month of pregnancy, my doctor sent me to the hospital to have a transvaginal ultrasound to "check" the fetus. My doctor did not give the reason for the procedure or what it would determine. I later learned that in addition to determining the viability of the pregnancy, this type of ultrasound is used to detect Down syndrome and other birth "defects." I was already beginning to understand the ways in which modern medicine could be used to devalue, or even weed out, people with disabilities.

When I got pregnant, my husband and I discussed what we would do if our child had a disability. I didn't have any anxiety about it. In some ways, I viewed the possibility as an opportunity. If my son ended up with cerebral palsy, he would be like me. If he ended up with a different disability, we would have a chance to see the world in a different light. Either way, there was no question in my mind that I would not have an abortion, no matter what the circumstance. We wanted our son, whether or not he had a disability. As it turned out, he did not.

In 2004, when my son was 3, I read an article in The New York Times that deeply upset me and has stayed with me. In it, Amy Harmon wrote about fetal genetic testing and the hundreds of "defects" that, even then, could be predicted before birth (this technology has since evolved

DADU SHIN

rapidly, as we know). If an abnormality is detected, parents must make the decision whether to continue with the pregnancy or abort. One woman, with a genetic condition that caused her to have an extra finger, which she'd had surgically removed, chose to end two of her pregnancies because tests detected her fetuses' having the same condition. This instance is the extreme, but it is by no means an exception.

I support legal abortion and am not criticizing women who have made the difficult decision to terminate a pregnancy because of a disabled fetus. There are situations in which the life of the child would be so painful and short that abortion would be the most compassionate option.

I do believe, however, that aborting a fetus with a disability should not be a given. In his book "Far From the Tree," Andrew Solomon theorizes that families might abort fetuses if their sexual orientation could be determined. What he is touching upon is that there is sometimes a social and prejudicial component in the decision making. (We already know this danger is real; gender-selective abortions still take place in the hundreds of thousands in India and China each year, and in lesser numbers in dozens of countries across the globe.) Genetic testing should be given for the purpose of preparation and decision-making, not as a tool for predicting the quality of a child's life.

The right to legal and safe abortion is a core element of American feminism and the struggle for women's rights. This puts me in a strange position. When I think about this issue, I feel my very existence questioned. As a disabled woman, I have been told flat out, "I'd rather be dead than be like you." Even the Dalai Lama has said that aborting a fetus with a disability is understandable. How do I begin to hold this contradiction in my mind? That I am a valid, beautiful human being — as are all my friends, some of whom have much severer impairments — and that I also support women's right to choose, a right that logically must extend to a woman who ends a pregnancy because of the prospect of an extra finger? I don't know the answer, but somehow, I believe the treatment I received as a disabled woman who chose to conceive — the disrespect, the testing, the constant questioning of my capacity to give birth and to be a mother — and my response to it fit into this equation.

Some days, I look at my son, who is now 14, and I want to pull my hair out. O.K., most days. Here I am tempted to compile a list of the ways he makes my life difficult and tedious. But that list is unnecessary. That's not because my son is perfect, but because he's perfect to me. Because I love the person he has become, not the person I wish him to be.

JENNIFER BARTLETT is a co-editor of "Beauty Is a Verb: The New Poetry of Disability," and the author of "Autobiography/Anti-Autobiography," a book of poetry.

My ‘Orphan Disease’ Has Given Me a New Family

OPINION | BY ROSEMARIE GARLAND-THOMSON | OCT. 26, 2017

THE MEMBERS OF my family share a number of traits, but not one of them looks quite like me.

Many of us have the same sturdy physique, blue eyes, fine Northern European hair and skin that should never see bright sun. I look pretty much like that except for one very unusual characteristic. I was born with asymmetrical, atypical hands and forearms into a world where symmetry and typicality are the marks of good looks and proper function. In fact, I am so unusual that in the half century of my lifetime, I have encountered only one other person who looks precisely like me. In other words, I'm rare.

I recently learned that I am distinguished in this way because I have a rare genetic condition — complex syndactyly. Before I learned this, no medical doctor had ever presented a diagnosis more helpful than a shrug.

Before being able to identify and give a name to what I have, I was subject to plenty of unsavory terms: “freak of nature,” “funny-looking kid,” “deformed,” “birth anomaly,” “sporadic limb deficiency.” The most disagreeable and persistent was “birth defect,” the unfortunate outcome of whatever sin or defilement could be guessed at or imagined — alcohol consumption, pollution, environmental contamination. With no impressive diagnosis to offer to the perpetual query about “what happened” to me, I usually resorted to, “I was born that way.”

I'm glad to now have a “rare genetic condition” instead of a “birth defect.” Anything “rare” has prestige, suggesting something sought after and prized by important collectors, archaeologists or scientists. Indeed, so exceptional is my way of being that fewer than one in 90,000 people are enough like me to receive the same diagnosis. It's a bit like winning the lottery.

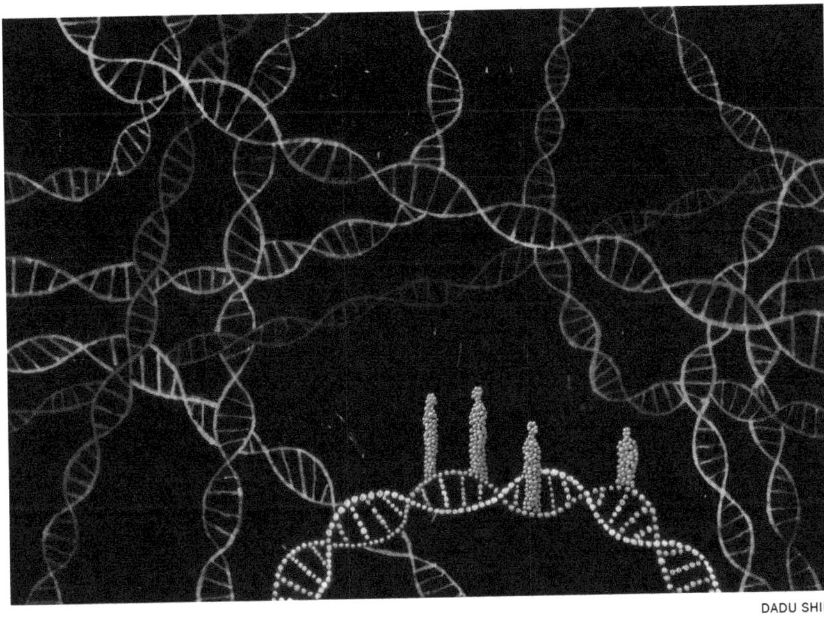

DADU SHIN

Before decades of scientific work gave us the genome map in 2003, our ways to explain unexpected human variation were limited. People like me were inexplicable. As often happens with the inexplicable, supernatural and superstitious reasoning rushed in. Mother-blaming and divine retribution were prominent. Mortal sins, erotic thoughts or any violation of the social code was thought to produce a disabled child.

Modern versions of this superstition haunt the mothers of congenitally disabled children; they experience corrosive guilt about exposure to toxins ranging from face cream and nail polish, alcohol and cigarettes, to thalidomide and the BPA in our plastic bottles. People with disabilities were then and are now taken as cautions or warnings of bad things past or future, canaries in the coal mine of human existence.

But things have changed. "Rare" is now an inflection in my personal dignity tool kit, a status upgrade. Even "syndrome" has an air of sophistication, an augmentation rather than the lessening that "deficit" or "defect" brings. It's something you have instead of something you don't have. More important, my form is not a mistake, some random whack from a menacing outside world. My shape is intentional, manifesting deliberately from some mysterious purpose at the very core of my being. Evolution's purposive caprice, some inexplicable force beyond our puny human imagination, is trying out a new design.

Today, identifying genetic diseases is a growth industry, powered by scientific-research funding and lucrative commercial interests. With testing available everywhere now, from private companies to clinics, people whose genetic diseases have been identified are an increasing population. All of us, it turns out, are carriers for at least eight to 10 common, significant genetic diseases and even more rare, enigmatic conditions.

What this tells us is that we are all related to one another through a system of genetic lineage that almost no one understood until recently. These genetic kinship circles are expanding and connecting us through networks of recessive, dominant and autosomal genes; mitochondrial DNA; and complex interactions with the environment that shape how genes express themselves as we develop. Medical science has discovered more than 7,000 genetic diseases, and new ones emerge every day.

People in my world of disability pride and advocacy sometimes call themselves by tribal names such as "a thalidomide" or "a polio" or even "crips." Our new genetic identities now yield more complex affinities. Rare genetic conditions are also called "orphan diseases." Now that I have an orphan disease instead of a birth defect, I'm no longer an orphan but instead newly a member of several distinctive tribes, a heretofore hidden web of kinship and clan affiliations. Resemblances are crucial to kinship, whether familial, tribal or ethnic. What we look like tells us and other people to whom we belong. Our distinctive traits gather us in kinship networks that often provide us with alternative families of mutual care and support.

In a recent conversation about Crispr, the newest genetic editing tool, the geneticist and Nobel laureate Mario R. Capecchi told me, "The purpose of evolution is to anticipate the unexpected." Random genetic variation is what moves evolution forward, yielding new forms that are fresh solutions to changing environments both natural and human designed.

The short span of human life and imagination limits our capacities to anticipate the unexpected. Ways of being that meet the demands of human life as we live it here and now may not serve our distant descendants so well. Characteristics we think of as intelligence, strength, vision, uprightness, dexterity, body mass or whiteness will outlive their usefulness, morphing from advantages to disadvantages, counterintuitive though that seems today, especially perhaps to those who have those valued traits and benefit from them.

Capecchi's framing of evolution's purpose as anticipating the unexpected can give us progressive perceptions about living with disabilities and stand as a caution against hubris and narcissism in our aspirations to shape our human communities according to the traits valued by the majority.

People with disabilities are the unexpected made flesh. The challenges of living in a world not built for us are occasions for resourcefulness and adaptability, especially for those of us who start out disabled early in life. We are innovators, early adopters, expert users and technology hackers as we respond to the adversity that the built and natural environments present us.

We don't know which human variations will be advantages and which will be disadvantages in the long arc of our struggle to prevail in an ever-changing environment. My blind friend with excellent orientation skills quips that she will be leading all of us out of burning buildings and planes when the lights go out. My deaf friends avoid the stress of noise pollution and the exhaustion of talking over the incessant din in fashionable bars in which social and professional life takes place now. Another friend, who is a small person, remarks that he consumes fewer resources and fits better into airplane spaces than big guys good at fighting and football. Some people with autism have a capacity to focus that boosts creativity. Expertise at composing with my voice instead of clunky keyboards puts me ahead in new communication technology.

The bright line between the healthy and the diseased, those who "have" a disease and those that don't, grows dimmer every day. Each of us carries within us many "orphan diseases" — that faintly Dickensian phrase that typically severs the connection between people like me and the human family of ordinary people. All of us are anything but "orphans." Instead, we are all second or third cousins, inextricably linked through a chain of quickly vanishing ancestors and descendants. We are all patients-in-waiting, bound together on a wait list of inheritance hidden deep in the elegant whirls of that double helix in every one of our cells — silently paused in its inscrutable determination to shape our lives. All those clichés of connectedness are now encoded in our genes. The human community is quite literally the human family.

We disabled are no longer orphans. We are instead a sturdy tribe, blood kin, navigating a changing world, living well, bonding fast and passing it on.

ROSEMARIE GARLAND-THOMSON is a bioethicist and professor of English at Emory University, where she is a founding director of the Disability Studies Initiative.

How Genetics Is Changing Our Understanding of 'Race'

OPINION | BY DAVID REICH | MARCH 23, 2018

IN 1942, THE ANTHROPOLOGIST Ashley Montagu published "Man's Most Dangerous Myth: The Fallacy of Race," an influential book that argued that race is a social concept with no genetic basis. A classic example often cited is the inconsistent definition of "black." In the United States, historically, a person is "black" if he has any sub-Saharan African ancestry; in Brazil, a person is not "black" if he is known to have any European ancestry. If "black" refers to different people in different contexts, how can there be any genetic basis to it?

Beginning in 1972, genetic findings began to be incorporated into this argument. That year, the geneticist Richard Lewontin published an important study of variation in protein types in blood. He grouped the human populations he analyzed into seven "races" — West Eurasians, Africans, East Asians, South Asians, Native Americans, Oceanians and Australians — and found that around 85 percent of variation in the protein types could be accounted for by variation within populations and "races," and only 15 percent by variation across them. To the extent that there was variation among humans, he concluded, most of it was because of "differences between individuals."

In this way, a consensus was established that among human populations there are no differences large enough to support the concept of "biological race." Instead, it was argued, race is a "social construct," a way of categorizing people that changes over time and across countries.

It is true that race is a social construct. It is also true, as Dr. Lewontin wrote, that human populations "are remarkably similar to each other" from a genetic point of view.

But over the years this consensus has morphed, seemingly without questioning, into an orthodoxy. The orthodoxy maintains that the average genetic differences among people grouped according to today's racial terms are so trivial when it comes to any meaningful biological traits that those differences can be ignored.

The orthodoxy goes further, holding that we should be anxious about any research into genetic differences among populations. The concern is that such research, no matter how well-intentioned, is located on a slippery slope that leads to the kinds of pseudoscientific arguments about biological difference that were used in the past to try to justify the slave trade, the eugenics movement and the Nazis' murder of six million Jews.

I have deep sympathy for the concern that genetic discoveries could be misused to justify racism. But as a geneticist I also know that it is simply no longer possible to ignore average genetic differences among "races."

Groundbreaking advances in DNA sequencing technology have been made over the last two decades. These advances enable us to measure with exquisite accuracy what fraction of an individual's genetic ancestry traces back to, say, West Africa 500 years ago — before the

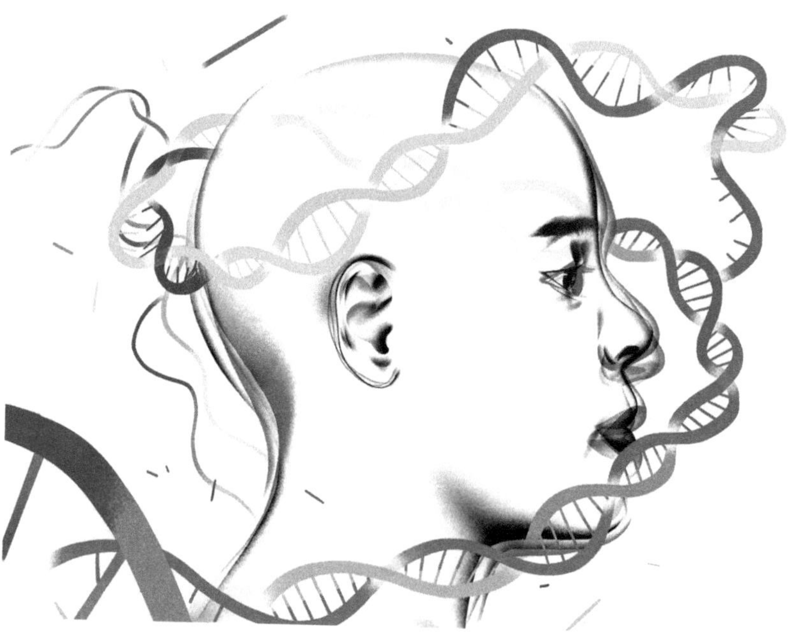

ANGIE WANG

mixing in the Americas of the West African and European gene pools that were almost completely isolated for the last 70,000 years. With the help of these tools, we are learning that while race may be a social construct, differences in genetic ancestry that happen to correlate to many of today's racial constructs are real.

Recent genetic studies have demonstrated differences across populations not just in the genetic determinants of simple traits such as skin color, but also in more complex traits like bodily dimensions and susceptibility to diseases. For example, we now know that genetic factors help explain why northern Europeans are taller on average than southern Europeans, why multiple sclerosis is more common in European-Americans than in African-Americans, and why the reverse is true for end-stage kidney disease.

I am worried that well-meaning people who deny the possibility of substantial biological differences among human populations are digging themselves into an indefensible position, one that will not survive the onslaught of science. I am also worried that whatever discoveries are made — and we truly have no idea yet what they will be — will be cited as "scientific proof" that racist prejudices and agendas have been correct all along, and that those well-meaning people will not understand the science well enough to push back against these claims.

This is why it is important, even urgent, that we develop a candid and scientifically up-to-date way of discussing any such differences, instead of sticking our heads in the sand and being caught unprepared when they are found.

To get a sense of what modern genetic research into average biological differences across populations looks like, consider an example from my own work. Beginning around 2003, I began exploring whether the population mixture that has occurred in the last few hundred years in the Americas could be leveraged to find risk factors for prostate cancer, a disease that occurs 1.7 times more often in self-identified African-Americans than in self-identified European-

Americans. This disparity had not been possible to explain based on dietary and environmental differences, suggesting that genetic factors might play a role.

Self-identified African-Americans turn out to derive, on average, about 80 percent of their genetic ancestry from enslaved Africans brought to America between the 16th and 19th centuries. My colleagues and I searched, in 1,597 African-American men with prostate cancer, for locations in the genome where the fraction of genes contributed by West African ancestors was larger than it was elsewhere in the genome. In 2006, we found exactly what we were looking for: a location in the genome with about 2.8 percent more African ancestry than the average.

When we looked in more detail, we found that this region contained at least seven independent risk factors for prostate cancer, all more common in West Africans. Our findings could fully account for the higher rate of prostate cancer in African-Americans than in European-Americans. We could conclude this because African-Americans who happen to have entirely European ancestry in this small section of their genomes had about the same risk for prostate cancer as random Europeans.

Did this research rely on terms like "African-American" and "European-American" that are socially constructed, and did it label segments of the genome as being probably "West African" or "European" in origin? Yes. Did this research identify real risk factors for disease that differ in frequency across those populations, leading to discoveries with the potential to improve health and save lives? Yes.

While most people will agree that finding a genetic explanation for an elevated rate of disease is important, they often draw the line there. Finding genetic influences on a propensity for disease is one thing, they argue, but looking for such influences on behavior and cognition is another.

But whether we like it or not, that line has already been crossed. A recent study led by the economist Daniel Benjamin compiled information on the number of years of education from more than 400,000 people, almost all of whom were of European ancestry. After controlling for differences in socioeconomic background, he and his colleagues identified 74 genetic variations that are over-represented in genes known to be important in neurological development, each of which is incontrovertibly more common in Europeans with more years of education than in Europeans with fewer years of education.

It is not yet clear how these genetic variations operate. A follow-up study of Icelanders led by the geneticist Augustine Kong showed that these genetic variations also nudge people who carry them to delay having children. So these variations may be explaining longer times at school by affecting a behavior that has nothing to do with intelligence.

This study has been joined by others finding genetic predictors of behavior. One of these, led by the geneticist Danielle Posthuma, studied more than 70,000 people and found genetic variations in more than 20 genes that were predictive of performance on intelligence tests.

Is performance on an intelligence test or the number of years of school a person attends shaped by the way a person is brought up? Of course. But does it measure something having to do with some aspect of behavior or cognition? Almost certainly. And since all traits influenced by genetics are expected to differ across populations (because the frequencies of genetic variations are rarely exactly the same across populations), the genetic influences on behavior and cognition will differ across populations, too.

You will sometimes hear that any biological differences among populations are likely to be small, because humans have diverged too recently from common ancestors for substantial differences to have arisen under the pressure of natural selection. This is not true. The ancestors of East Asians, Europeans, West Africans and Australians were, until recently, almost completely isolated from one another for 40,000 years or longer, which is more than sufficient time for the forces of evolution to work. Indeed, the study led by Dr. Kong showed that in Iceland, there has been measurable genetic selection against the genetic variations that predict more years of education in that population just within the last century.

To understand why it is so dangerous for geneticists and anthropologists to simply repeat the old consensus about human population differences, consider what kinds of voices are filling the void that our silence is creating. Nicholas Wade, a longtime science journalist for The New York Times, rightly notes in his 2014 book, "A Troublesome Inheritance: Genes, Race and Human History," that modern research is challenging our thinking about the nature of human population differences. But he goes on to make the unfounded and irresponsible claim that this research is suggesting that genetic factors explain traditional stereotypes.

One of Mr. Wade's key sources, for example, is the anthropologist Henry Harpending, who has asserted that people of sub-Saharan African ancestry have no propensity to work when they don't have to because, he claims, they did not go through the type of natural selection for hard work in the last thousands of years that some Eurasians did. There is simply no scientific evidence to support this statement. Indeed, as 139 geneticists (including myself) pointed out in a letter to The New York Times about Mr. Wade's book, there is no genetic evidence to back up any of the racist stereotypes he promotes.

Another high-profile example is James Watson, the scientist who in 1953 co-discovered the structure of DNA, and who was forced to retire as head of the Cold Spring Harbor Laboratories in 2007 after he stated in an interview — without any scientific evidence — that research has suggested that genetic factors contribute to lower intelligence in Africans than in Europeans.

At a meeting a few years later, Dr. Watson said to me and my fellow geneticist Beth Shapiro something to the effect of "When are you guys going to figure out why it is that you Jews are so much smarter than everyone else?" He asserted that Jews were high achievers because of genetic advantages conferred by thousands of years of natural selection to be scholars, and that East Asian students tended to be conformist because of selection for conformity in ancient Chinese society. (Contacted recently, Dr. Watson denied having made these statements, maintaining that they do not represent his views; Dr. Shapiro said that her recollection matched mine.)

What makes Dr. Watson's and Mr. Wade's statements so insidious is that they start with the accurate observation that many academics are implausibly denying the possibility of average genetic differences among human populations, and then end with a claim — backed by no evidence — that they know what those differences are and that they correspond to racist stereotypes. They use the reluctance of the academic community to openly discuss these fraught issues to provide rhetorical cover for hateful ideas and old racist canards.

This is why knowledgeable scientists must speak out. If we abstain from laying out a rational framework for discussing differences among populations, we risk losing the trust of the public and we actively contribute to the distrust of expertise that is now so prevalent. We leave a vacuum that gets filled by pseudoscience, an outcome that is far worse than anything we could achieve by talking openly.

If scientists can be confident of anything, it is that whatever we currently believe about the genetic nature of differences among populations is most likely wrong. For example, my laboratory discovered in 2016, based on our sequencing of ancient human genomes, that "whites" are not derived from a population that existed from time immemorial, as some people believe. Instead, "whites" represent a mixture of four ancient populations that lived 10,000 years ago and were each as different from one another as Europeans and East Asians are today.

So how should we prepare for the likelihood that in the coming years, genetic studies will show that many traits are influenced by genetic variations, and that these traits will differ on average across human populations? It will be impossible — indeed, anti-scientific, foolish and absurd — to deny those differences.

For me, a natural response to the challenge is to learn from the example of the biological differences that exist between males and females. The differences between the sexes are far more profound than those that exist among human populations, reflecting more than 100 million years of evolution and adaptation. Males and females differ by huge tracts of genetic material — a Y chromosome that males have and that females don't, and a second X chromosome that females have and males don't.

Most everyone accepts that the biological differences between males and females are profound. In addition to anatomical differences, men and women exhibit average differences in size and physical strength. (There are also average differences in temperament and behavior, though there are important unresolved questions about the extent to which these differences are influenced by social expectations and upbringing.)

How do we accommodate the biological differences between men and women? I think the answer is obvious: We should both recognize that genetic differences between males and females exist and we should accord each sex the same freedoms and opportunities regardless of those differences.

It is clear from the inequities that persist between women and men in our society that fulfilling these aspirations in practice is a challenge. Yet conceptually it is straightforward. And if this is the case with men and women, then it is surely the case with whatever differences we may find among human populations, the great majority of which will be far less profound.

An abiding challenge for our civilization is to treat each human being as an individual and to empower all people, regardless of what hand they are dealt from the deck of life. Compared with the enormous differences that exist among individuals, differences among populations are on average many times smaller, so it should be only a modest challenge to accommodate a reality in which the average genetic contributions to human traits differ.

It is important to face whatever science will reveal without prejudging the outcome and with the confidence that we can be mature enough to handle any findings. Arguing that no substantial differences among human populations are possible will only invite the racist misuse of genetics that we wish to avoid.

DAVID REICH is a professor of genetics at Harvard and the author of the forthcoming book "Who We Are and How We Got Here: Ancient DNA and the New Science of the Human Past," from which this article is adapted.

The Racial Spectacle of DNA Test Result Videos

BY AMANDA HESS | MAY 6, 2018

THE TRY GUYS, a quartet of BuzzFeed personalities who film themselves undergoing often absurd and humiliating experiences on camera (skiing in Speedos, posing for beefcake photos, suffering simulated labor pains), subjected themselves last year to a different kind of bodily experimentation: genetic testing.

In the video, the guys spit into vials and ship them off to 23andMe, a DNA mapping service that extracts genealogical data from saliva. Then they invite a 23andMe representative on camera to dramatically reveal the exciting results.

But when the Try Guy Zach Kornfeld learns about his precise ethnic makeup — 99.6 percent European — he's a little bummed. "Is it weird that I'm, like, disappointed that I don't have more of a mix?" he asks. His colleague Eugene Lee Yang volleys the question to the 23andMe analyst: "Do you always come across white people being disappointed that they're not mixed?" Like, "I wish I was a little more spicy, but I'm just vanilla like I thought."

23andMe is among a crop of new services that have arrived to help us mine our genetic material for answers to questions we didn't even know we had. These services' ancestral algorithms are based on estimates and probabilities, not certainties, but they nevertheless claim to distill the self into a series of appealingly specific data points onto which personal narratives can be written. Helix has created what it calls the first "app store for DNA," offering insights into a host of topics, from how "your ancestors' diets influenced yours" to your genetically ideal wine pairings. AncestryDNA, the testing arm of the online family tree service Ancestry.com, promises that "your DNA is just one part of the story that leads to you." Then there's the

DNA dating app, Pheramor, which matches users based on what it calls "the science of genetics-based human attraction."

All this focus on the self belies the broader consequences of widespread DNA testing. Recently, DNA and genealogical data were used to track down a suspected California serial killer, raising concerns about how else our most intimate information could be wielded by the state. And as DNA test results are shared publicly — spawning their own YouTube genre ("Am I REALLY Hispanic? DNA Test Results!") and Twitter memes — they transform into a tool for talking not just about ourselves, but about race, often in ways that obscure its realities.

It's probably not a coincidence that these mechanisms of biological self-discovery are on the rise now, amid seething tensions over racism, immigration and what constitutes a "real American." White supremacists are drawn to DNA testing to prove their racial purity, excitedly publicizing their exclusively European ancestries (or else dismissing any trace of outside DNA as a Jewish conspiracy.) But progressive white people seem to be using these services in a different way: as methods for performing racial harmony and assuaging white guilt.

These DNA spectacles offer a rare public forum where people of all backgrounds are encouraged to talk about their heritages in very similar ways, with a shared sense of suspense and excitement about "where they come from." Over the past decade, genealogical edutainment shows — including TLC's "Who Do You Think You Are?" and PBS's "Finding Your Roots" — have proliferated. The trend has exploded on YouTube, where you can watch "Asian-Americans Take a DNA Test," "Irish People Take a DNA Test" and "Latinos Get Their DNA Tested." In each, footage of a physical process — spitting into vials or swabbing cheeks — cuts quickly, as if by magic, to computerized results. We see people from the outside, then (surprise!) learn who they "really" are inside.

Ethnic backgrounds are distinct from social constructions of race, which are tied up in perceptions of skin color, shared cultures and historical oppression — and these public airings of DNA results often read as an attempt to transcend race by revealing hidden, scientific-seeming insights that expose our "true" origins. In "Latinos Get Their DNA Tested," Gadiel Del Orbe — a producer for the Latino BuzzFeed channel Pero Like — learns that his DNA is more than 50 percent European, and exclaims, half-jokingly: "Hold on, time out. Am I white?"

Meanwhile, for actual white users, DNA testing services helpfully atomize whiteness into a series of percentage-point allegiances to various European countries. (The Try Guys episode teased out such associations; Mr. Kornfeld's revelation of some Iberian DNA was punctuated with a flourish of Spanish music.) They also allow white people to seize on an even more transformative ethnic narrative. 23andMe, for instance, tracks genealogical lines so deeply that it claims to pinpoint ancestors that migrated to Europe from Siberia or the Middle East as far back as 10,000 years ago. In these genetic tales, modern racial dynamics become flattened into a kind of shared origin story.

In contrast to the white supremacist DNA testing fans, many white users perform delight at any hint of non-European origins in their

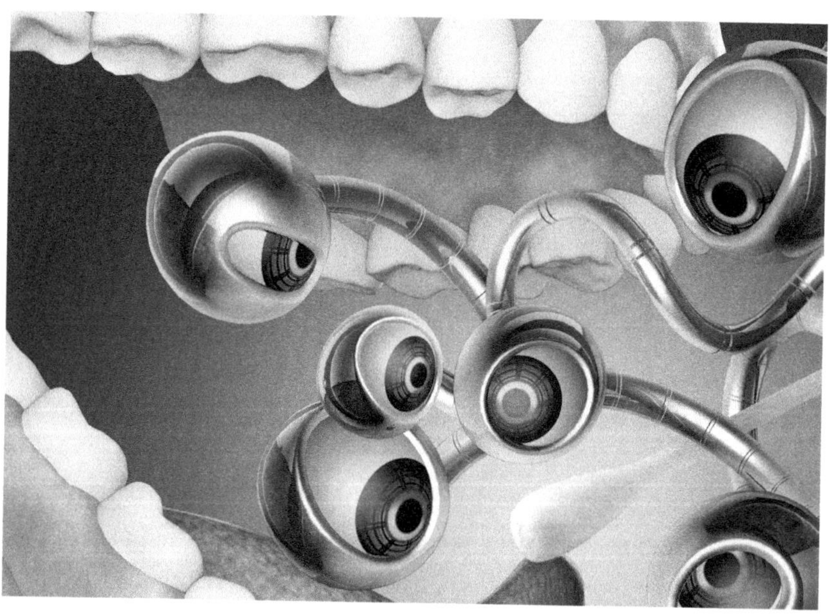

SALLY THURER

results. In "Irish People Take a DNA Test," one woman rejoices when she learns that she is 4.2 percent Jewish. "I knew there was a bit of Jew in me!" she exclaims. "I'm glad that I have other bits in me." She calls it "a really nice surprise."

And in the Try Guys episode, Keith Habersberger introduces himself as "the whitest man," only to learn that 0.2 percent of his DNA could be traced to sub-Saharan Africa. To Mr. Yang, who had pegged him as 100 percent European, Mr. Habersberger gleefully says, "Suck it!" But when the 23andMe representative reveals that the African DNA was introduced in Mr. Habersberger's bloodline between 1720 and 1810, the mood sours. As Mr. Kornfeld puts it: "I thought this was real cool until I remembered what the British were doing in the 1700s, and now I'm thinking it's less cool."

Even in videos that seek to dispel racism through multicultural celebration, historical realities sneak in. And that leads to another form of performance, where white people deny the grotesque aspects of their heritage, or else detach from them with self-deprecating wokeness. When Mr. Kornfeld raises the specter of imperialism in Mr. Habersberger's ancestral past, Mr. Habersberger defensively suggests that "love happens in a lot of places" and that "spit will never tell us that kind of thing."

The exchange recalled Ben Affleck's controversial appearance on "Finding Your Roots," in which (it was later revealed) he successfully lobbied PBS to omit any mention of his slaveholding ancestor. When Anderson Cooper appeared on the show, he modeled a different approach to such revelations. "Your ancestor was beaten to death" by a slave, Henry Louis Gates told him. "Honestly," Mr. Cooper replied, "part of me thinks that's awesome."

If these YouTube videos treat DNA testing with credence and awe, a Twitter meme parodying 23andMe results pokes at these tests' specious scientific certainty and pushes back at the idea that these ethnic ancestral breakdowns say much at all about us and our place in the world.

One version plays off the lyrics to Meredith Brooks's "Bitch," editing a 23andMe results page to reveal a person who is 31 percent bitch, 9.2 percent lover, 17 percent child and 11 percent mother. Another makes fun of Gov. Andrew Cuomo's frequent rhetorical strategy of claiming membership to disadvantage groups, revealing his 23andMe results as 9.2 percent Muslim, 10.1 percent gay and 21.7 percent "woman trying to control her health."

These jokes ridicule the idea that anything truly relevant about our social realities can be measured to a fraction of a percent. As it turns out, DNA tests reveal plenty about us — just not what they claim to.

Scientists Can Design 'Better' Babies. Should They?

BY CLYDE HABERMAN | JUNE 10, 2018

FOR NINE FRUSTRATING YEARS, Lesley and John Brown tried to conceive a child but failed because of her blocked fallopian tubes. Then in late 1977, this English couple put their hopes in the hands of two men of science. Thus began their leap into the unknown, and into history.

On July 25, 1978, the Browns got what they had long wished for with the arrival of a daughter, Louise, a baby like no other the world had seen. She came into being through a process of in vitro fertilization developed by Robert G. Edwards and Patrick Steptoe. Her father's sperm was mixed with her mother's egg in a petri dish, and the resulting embryo was then implanted into the womb for normal development.

Louise was widely, glibly and incorrectly called a "test-tube baby." The label was enough to throw millions of people into a moral panic, for it filled them with visions of Dr. Frankenstein playing God and throwing the natural order of the universe out of kilter. The reality proved far more benign, maybe best captured by Grace MacDonald, a Scottish woman who in January 1979 gave birth to the second in vitro baby, a boy named Alastair. Nothing unethical was at work, she told the BBC in 2003. "It's just nature being given a helping hand."

In this installment of its video documentaries, Retro Report explores how major news stories of the past shape current events by harking back to Louise Brown's birth. If anything, more modern developments in genetics have raised the moral, ethical and political stakes. But the fundamental questions are essentially what they were in the 1970s with the advent of in vitro fertilization:

Are these welcome advances that can only benefit civilization? Or are they incursions into an unholy realm, one of "designer babies," with potentially frightening consequences?

In vitro fertilization, or I.V.F., is by now broadly accepted, though it still has objectors, including the Roman Catholic Church. Worldwide, the procedure has produced an estimated six million babies, and is believed to account for 3 percent of all live births in some developed countries. Designer-baby fears have proved in the main to be "overblown," said Dr. Paula Amato, a professor of obstetrics and gynecology at Oregon Health & Science University in Portland. "We have not seen it with I.V.F. in general," she told Retro Report. "We have not seen it with P.G.D."

P.G.D. is shorthand for pre-implantation genetic diagnosis, developed more than two decades ago and an offshoot of in vitro fertilization. Couples with family histories of serious diseases — cystic fibrosis, Tay-Sachs and Down syndrome are among the more common — can have their lab-created embryos tested for the probability of passing the flaws to their offspring. Technology in effect gives them a measure of control over their genetic fate. An embryo that looks O.K. under a microscope can be implanted in the mother's uterus for normal development. (Typically, the others are discarded, itself a morally fraught practice for some people).

But what if the issue isn't averting a dreadful disease? What if would-be parents, rather than leaving the matter to an old-fashioned roll of the genetic dice, resort to embryonic selection to guarantee the child is of a particular sex? It can be done with pre-implantation genetic diagnosis. Dr. Jeffrey Steinberg, director of The Fertility Institutes in New York, does it as matter of course.

"The technology was out there — it was being applied only to diseases," Dr. Steinberg told Retro Report. He continued: "I've decided to open the door and expand it and say, 'Listen, this is something that people are interested in, causes no harm, makes people happy. Let's expand it.' " Though many doctors are strongly skeptical, he also offers P.G.D. to improve the odds that a baby will have a desired eye color, practically casting himself as the Benjamin Moore of the laboratory with his "choice of 30 shades of blue eyes."

Still other gene-altering techniques are now in play. Mitochondrial transfer, for one, is intended for a woman whose genetic makeup makes it likely she will bear a child with a severe birth defect. DNA is removed from her egg and implanted in an egg from another woman that contains healthy energy-generating components known as mitochondria. This has given rise to the discomfiting term "three-parent baby."

Then there is a gene-editing method called Crispr, the acronym for a mouthful of a procedure: Clustered Regularly Interspaced Short Palindromic Repeats. A team led by Shoukhrat Mitalipov, an American reproductive biologist, announced last year that it had applied the technique to change a human genome. With an enzyme called Cas9 acting as a scalpel, Crispr snipped away a mutated gene that can lead to thickened heart muscles and cause sudden death in young athletes.

In theory, it meant that if this embryo were implanted in a womb — it wasn't in this team's research — the child eventually born would not carry the mutation, and nor would any grandchildren. In short, that family's germ line, the genetic material governing cellular lineage from one generation to the next, would have been permanently altered.

As Louise Brown prepares for her 40th birthday next month, moral debates over the new capabilities echo those that swirled around her parents, both now dead.

Some ethicists see only good in the prospect of eliminating diseases that condemn families to misery. After all, don't childhood vaccinations amount to using technology for that very same purpose? Yet few people regard measles or polio shots as unacceptable fiddling with the natural world.

In a different camp are those who invoke slippery slopes, fearing unpredictable genies that may be unleashed. What, they ask, is to prevent gene editing from being used someday not to combat disease but, rather, to design people who are stronger or smarter than everyone else, able themselves to produce children programmed genetically for SAT scores of 1,600 or LeBron James point totals?

Then again, selecting genes to produce, say, a star basketball player is hardly a snap; height alone is influenced by tens of thousands of genetic variations. On the other hand (there is almost always another hand) the sheer expense of the procedures threatens to widen an already substantial gap between the wealthy and everyone else.

In 2017, an advisory group formed by the National Academy of Sciences and the National Academy of Medicine endorsed gene editing in principle, but with a proviso that it be used only to deal with "serious diseases and disability" and only when no "reasonable alternative" exists.

Some scientists say it is unwise to be paralyzed by fear of the unknown. But Marcy Darnovsky, executive director of the Center for Genetics and Society in Berkeley, Calif., is more skeptical. "We have to ask where is the stopping point," Ms. Darnovsky said, and she suggested that policy discussions include "a much broader range of voices" than just scientists.

Perhaps Shakespeare can enter the conversation. He bequeathed words often invoked to encapsulate both hope for and dread of human capability. They're from "The Tempest": "O brave new world, that has such people in't."

Why Many Native Americans Are Angry With Elizabeth Warren

BY MAGGIE ASTOR | OCT. 17, 2018

IF SENATOR ELIZABETH WARREN thought that releasing her DNA test results showing Native American ancestry would neutralize a Republican line of attack, she was wrong.

The test — part of her strategic preparations for a likely presidential campaign — did not placate President Trump, who has mocked Ms. Warren as "Pocahontas" and once promised $1 million to a charity of her choice if a DNA test substantiated her claims of Cherokee and Delaware heritage. And her announcement of the results angered many Native Americans, including the Cherokee Nation, the largest of the country's three federally recognized Cherokee tribes.

DNA testing cannot show that Ms. Warren is Cherokee or any other tribe, the secretary of state of the Cherokee Nation, Chuck Hoskin Jr., said in a statement. Tribes set their own citizenship requirements, not to mention that DNA tests don't distinguish among the numerous indigenous groups of North and South America. The test Ms. Warren took did not identify Cherokee ancestry specifically; it found that she most likely had at least one Native American ancestor six to 10 generations ago.

Ms. Warren defended herself by saying she was not claiming to be eligible for membership in the Cherokee Nation — and she isn't, given that her ancestors do not appear on the Dawes Rolls, early-20th-century government documents that form the basis of the Cherokee citizenship process. She said she was simply corroborating the family stories of Native American lineage that she has often recounted.

But that distinction actually cuts to the heart of why Native Americans are so upset with her. Fundamentally, their anger is about what it means to be Native American — and who gets to decide.

"The American public doesn't understand the difference" between ancestry and tribal membership, said Kim TallBear, a professor at the

University of Alberta who wrote a book titled "Native American DNA: Tribal Belonging and the False Promise of Genetic Science."

While many people see "Native American" as simply a racial category, she said, "we have additional ideas about how to identify when one is Native American that aren't really consistent with the way most Americans think. Our definitions matter to us."

And so when someone like Ms. Warren emphasizes undocumented lineage over tribal citizenship criteria, said Dr. TallBear, who is a member of the Sisseton-Wahpeton Oyate tribe in South Dakota, "what they're telling us is they are privileging nonindigenous definitions of being indigenous."

Membership in a Native American tribe is "very precious to us," Mr. Hoskin, the Cherokee Nation secretary of state, said in a phone interview. "It's not just a card that we hold. It's something that we consider a dear possession, and so we don't take it lightly."

This perspective is grounded in a long history of persecution, displacement and massacre. Over many decades of United States history, the government took the land of Native American tribes, including the Cherokee, and pushed them steadily west. President Andrew Jackson's policies, continued under Martin Van Buren, forced the Cherokee into their current territory in Oklahoma in the Trail of Tears during 1838 and 1839. Administration after administration signed treaties with tribes and then violated them. It was not until the 1930s that tribes gained the sovereignty they now have on their reservations.

"Those of us who are Cherokee citizens, we know our ancestors in some cases perished along the Trail of Tears," Mr. Hoskin said.

"Most reasonable people can understand," in that context, why claims to Native American heritage based on a DNA test are fraught, he added.

Neither Ms. Warren nor anyone on her staff contacted the Cherokee Nation before publicizing the DNA results, Mr. Hoskin said. A spokeswoman for Ms. Warren's re-election campaign, Kristen Orthman, declined to comment on this point.

Ms. Warren's announcement was clearly intended to put to rest one of Mr. Trump's favorite lines of attack. (Mr. Hoskin criticized Mr. Trump, too, for his repeated use of "Pocahontas" as a slur.) Instead, the DNA test brought a barrage of negative headlines and opinion pieces, in liberal-leaning publications like HuffPost as well as conservative-leaning ones like The New York Post.

Asked about the criticism, the senator's campaign spokeswoman, Ms. Orthman, sent links to a tweet by Ms. Warren and to a statement posted on Facebook by the Eastern Band Cherokee, a separate tribe from the Cherokee Nation.

The Eastern Band Cherokee's statement was supportive of Ms. Warren, saying that she "has not used her family story or evidence of Native ancestry to gain employment or other advantage" and that she "demonstrates respect for tribal sovereignty by acknowledging that tribes determine citizenship and respecting the difference between citizenship and ancestry." It also listed Native-friendly bills she had supported in the Senate.

"Some people who have family stories or evidence of Native ancestry have sought to appropriate Cherokee culture, claim a preference in hiring, claim that their art is 'Indian art,' or advance their careers based on a family story or evidence of Native ancestry," Principal Chief Richard G. Sneed added in the statement, which argued that Ms. Warren had not done any of those things. "We strongly condemn such actions as harmful to our tribal government and Cherokee people."

By Wednesday, the post had been deleted from the Facebook page of the tribe's newspaper, but Ashleigh Stephens, a spokeswoman for Principal Chief Sneed, said he stood by it.

CHAPTER 5

Scientific Frontiers Opened by Genetic Testing

As genetic testing advances, people are making discoveries beyond the fields of health and criminology. These discoveries are adding nuance to older assumptions about genes. Research on epigenetics has demonstrated the effects of lived experience on future generations, while genes commonly associated with disease are proving to have additional value. DNA evidence found in fossils is rewriting human evolutionary history, while the new gene editing technology, Crispr, is allowing "biohackers" to rewrite their own DNA.

DNA Double Take

BY CARL ZIMMER | SEPT. 16, 2013

FROM BIOLOGY CLASS to "C.S.I.," we are told again and again that our genome is at the heart of our identity. Read the sequences in the chromosomes of a single cell, and learn everything about a person's genetic information — or, as 23andme, a prominent genetic testing company, says on its Web site, "The more you know about your DNA, the more you know about yourself."

But scientists are discovering that — to a surprising degree — we contain genetic multitudes. Not long ago, researchers had thought it was rare for the cells in a single healthy person to differ genetically in a significant way. But scientists are finding that it's quite common for an individual to have multiple genomes. Some people, for example, have groups of cells with mutations that are not found in the rest of the body. Some have genomes that came from other people.

"There have been whispers in the matrix about this for years, even decades, but only in a very hypothetical sense," said Alexander Urban, a geneticist at Stanford University. Even three years ago, suggesting that there was widespread genetic variation in a single body would have been met with skepticism, he said. "You would have just run against the wall."

But a series of recent papers by Dr. Urban and others has demonstrated that those whispers were not just hypothetical. The variation in the genomes found in a single person is too large to be ignored. "We now know it's there," Dr. Urban said. "Now we're mapping this new continent."

Dr. James R. Lupski, a leading expert on the human genome at Baylor College of Medicine, wrote in a recent review in the journal Science that the existence of multiple genomes in an individual could have a tremendous impact on the practice of medicine. "It's changed the way I think," he said in an interview.

Scientists are finding links from multiple genomes to certain rare diseases, and now they're beginning to investigate genetic variations to shed light on more common disorders.

Science's changing view is also raising questions about how forensic scientists should use DNA evidence to identify people. It's also posing challenges for genetic counselors, who can't assume that the genetic information from one cell can tell them about the DNA throughout a person's body.

HUMAN BLUEPRINT

When an egg and sperm combine their DNA, the genome they produce contains all the necessary information for building a new human. As the egg divides to form an embryo, it produces new copies of that original genome.

JOHN HERSEY

For decades, geneticists have explored how an embryo can use the instructions in a single genome to develop muscles, nerves and the many other parts of the human body. They also use sequencing to understand genetic variations that can raise the risk of certain diseases. Genetic counselors can look at the results of genetic screenings to help patients and their families cope with these diseases — altering their diet, for example, if they lack a gene for a crucial enzyme.

The cost of sequencing an entire genome has fallen so drastically in the past 20 years — now a few thousand dollars, down from an estimated $3 billion for the public-private partnership that sequenced the first human genome — that doctors are beginning to sequence the entire genomes of some patients. (Sequencing can be done in as little as 50 hours.) And they're identifying links between mutations and diseases that have never been seen before.

Yet all these powerful tests are based on the assumption that, inside our body, a genome is a genome is a genome. Scientists believed that they could look at the genome from cells taken in a cheek swab and be able to learn about the genomes of cells in the brain or the liver or anywhere else in the body.

In the mid-1900s, scientists began to get clues that this was not always true. In 1953, for example, a British woman donated a pint of blood. It turned out that some of her blood was Type O and some was Type A. The scientists who studied her concluded that she had acquired some of her blood from her twin brother in the womb, including his genomes in his blood cells.

Chimerism, as such conditions came to be known, seemed for many years to be a rarity. But "it can be commoner than we realized," said Dr. Linda Randolph, a pediatrician at Children's Hospital in Los Angeles who is an author of a review of chimerism published in The American Journal of Medical Genetics in July.

Twins can end up with a mixed supply of blood when they get nutrients in the womb through the same set of blood vessels. In other cases, two fertilized eggs may fuse together. These so-called embryonic chimeras may go through life blissfully unaware of their origins.

One woman discovered she was a chimera as late as age 52. In need of a kidney transplant, she was tested so that she might find a match. The results indicated that she was not the mother of two of her three biological children. It turned out that she had originated from two genomes. One genome gave rise to her blood and some of her eggs; other eggs carried a separate genome.

Women can also gain genomes from their children. After a baby is born, it may leave some fetal cells behind in its mother's body, where they can travel to different organs and be absorbed into those tissues. "It's pretty likely that any woman who has been pregnant is a chimera," Dr. Randolph said.

EVERYWHERE YOU LOOK

As scientists begin to search for chimeras systematically — rather than waiting for them to turn up in puzzling medical tests — they're finding them in a remarkably high fraction of people. In 2012, Canadian scientists performed autopsies on the brains of 59 women. They found neurons with Y chromosomes in 63 percent of them. The neurons likely developed from cells originating in their sons.

In The International Journal of Cancer in August, Eugen Dhimolea of the Dana-Farber Cancer Institute in Boston and colleagues reported that male cells can also infiltrate breast tissue. When they looked for Y chromosomes in samples of breast tissue, they found it in 56 percent of the women they investigated.

A century ago, geneticists discovered one way in which people might acquire new genomes. They were studying "mosaic animals," rare creatures with oddly-colored patches of fur. The animals didn't inherit the genes for these patches from their parents. Instead, while embryos, they acquired a mutation in a skin cell that divided to produce a colored patch.

Mosaicism, as this condition came to be known, was difficult to study in humans before the age of DNA sequencing. Scientists could only discover instances in which the mutations and the effects were big.

In 1960, researchers found that a form of leukemia is a result of mosaicism. A blood cell spontaneously mutates as it divides, moving a big chunk of one chromosome to another.

Later studies added support to the idea that cancer is a result of mutations in specific cells. But scientists had little idea of how common cases of mosaicism were beyond cancer.

"We didn't have the technology to systematically think about them," said Dr. Christopher Walsh, a geneticist at Children's Hospital in Boston who recently published a review on mosaicism and disease in Science. "Now we're in the midst of a revolution."

BENIGN DIFFERENCES

The latest findings make it clear that mosaicism is quite common — even in healthy cells.

Dr. Urban and his colleagues, for example, investigated mutations in cells called fibroblasts, which are found in connective tissue. They

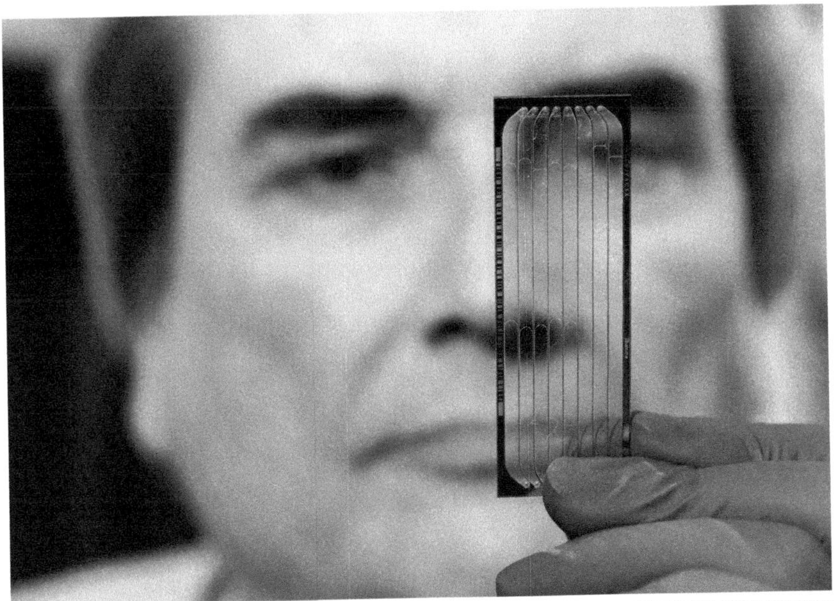
KATHY KMONICEK FOR THE NEW YORK TIMES

A DNA sample. Sequencing has become faster and relatively cheaper in the last 20 years.

searched in particular for cases in which a segment of DNA was accidentally duplicated or deleted. As they reported last year, 30 percent of the fibroblasts carried at least one such mutation.

Michael Snyder of Stanford University and his colleagues searched for mosaicism by performing autopsies on six people who had died of causes other than cancer. In five of the six people they autopsied, the scientists reported last October, they found cells in different organs with stretches of DNA that had accidentally been duplicated or deleted.

Now that scientists are beginning to appreciate how common chimerism and mosaicism are, they're investigating the effects of these conditions on our health. "That's still open really, because these are still early days," Dr. Urban said.

Nevertheless, said Dr. Walsh, "it's safe to say that a large proportion of those mutations will be benign." Recent studies on chimeras suggest that these extra genomes can even be beneficial. Chimeric cells from fetuses appear to seek out damaged tissue and help heal it, for example.

But scientists are also starting to find cases in which mutations in specific cells help give rise to diseases other than cancer. Dr. Walsh, for example, studies a childhood disorder of the brain called hemimegalencephaly, in which one side of the brain grows larger than the other, leading to devastating seizures.

"The kids have no chance for a normal life without desperate surgery to take out half of their brain," he said.

Dr. Walsh has studied the genomes of neurons removed during those surgeries. He and his colleagues discovered that some neurons in the overgrown hemisphere have mutations to one gene. Two other teams of scientists have identified mutations on other genes, all of which help to control the growth of neurons. "We can get our hands on the mechanism of the disease," said Dr. Walsh.

Other researchers are now investigating whether mosaicism is a factor in more common diseases, like schizophrenia. "This will play itself out over the next 5 or 10 years," said Dr. Urban, who with his colleagues is studying it.

MOVING CAUTIOUSLY

Medical researchers aren't the only scientists interested in our multitudes of personal genomes. So are forensic scientists. When they attempt to identify criminals or murder victims by matching DNA, they want to avoid being misled by the variety of genomes inside a single person.

Last year, for example, forensic scientists at the Washington State Patrol Crime Laboratory Division described how a saliva sample and a sperm sample from the same suspect in a sexual assault case didn't match.

Bone marrow transplants can also confound forensic scientists. Researchers at Innsbruck Medical University in Austria took cheek swabs from 77 people who had received transplants up to nine years earlier. In 74 percent of the samples, they found a mix of genomes — both their own and those from the marrow donors, the scientists reported this year. The transplanted stem cells hadn't just replaced blood cells, but had also become cells lining the cheek.

While the risk of confusion is real, it is manageable, experts said. "This should not be much of a concern for forensics," said Manfred Kayser, a professor of Forensic Molecular Biology at Erasmus University in Rotterdam. In the cases where mosaicism or chimerism causes confusion, forensic scientists can clear it up by other means. In the Austrian study, for example, the scientists found no marrow donor genomes in the hair of the recipients.

For genetic counselors helping clients make sense of DNA tests, our many genomes pose more serious challenges. A DNA test that uses blood cells may miss disease-causing mutations in the cells of other organs. "We can't tell you what else is going on," said Nancy B. Spinner, a geneticist at the University of Pennsylvania, who published a review about the implications of mosaicism for genetic counseling in the May issue of Nature Reviews Genetics.

That may change as scientists develop more powerful ways to investigate our different genomes and learn more about their links to diseases. "It's not tomorrow that you're going to walk into your doctor's office and they're going to think this way," said Dr. Lupski. "It's going to take time."

The Upside of Bad Genes

OPINION | BY MOISES VELASQUEZ-MANOFF | JUNE 17, 2017

THERE'S A WELL-TO-DO COUPLE thinking about having children. They order a battery of genetic tests to ensure that there's nothing untoward lurking in their genomes. And they discover that they each carry one copy of the sickle cell gene.

If their children inherit two copies of the gene, they could develop anemia, which can cause joint pain, weakness and even death. So what should the couple do?

For the last two decades, they've had the option of artificially fertilizing embryos and selecting only those that lack the sickle cell trait. Now a new possibility is on the horizon: They may soon be able to edit the offending gene right out of their own sperm, eggs or embryos, erasing it from their bloodline forever.

The technology that will allow this is called Crispr-Cas9. It's relatively cheap and it permits scientists to change DNA with an ease and precision that until now has been impossible. The promise is that it will transform medicine by vanquishing previously incurable diseases. The method is probably at least a few years away from being applied in clinical settings. Still, some are already worried that, when it comes to improving our own genome, we don't yet know enough about how genes work to wield this power without unintended consequences.

In 2015, the journal Science declared Crispr the "breakthrough of the year," and researchers in China edited human embryos for the first time. Scientists also convened a meeting in Napa, Calif., to talk through the ethical implications of this new technology, and to draft guidelines. A fundamental issue that came up, says Jennifer Doudna, a biochemist at the University of California, Berkeley, and a pioneer in Crispr research, was that scientists really don't understand enough about the upside of genes we consider "bad" to begin editing them willy-nilly.

Sickle cell was a case in point. The gene is usually found in people who live in, or whose ancestors came from, sub-Saharan Africa, the Arab world and India; in those places, having one copy of the gene can prevent the worst symptoms of malaria. Of every four children our imaginary couple might have, one will probably be afflicted with sickle cell disease, but two would most likely be protected from malarial disease.

Ditto with the gene variants that cause the lung disease cystic fibrosis. In parts of northwest Europe, about 1 in 25 people carries a single copy of the gene. And while two copies cause disease, it has long been hypothesized that having just one protects against tuberculosis — the White Plague that ravaged Europe for a few hundred years.

Both these genes probably helped us survive in the past, so is it wise to remove them now?

Earlier this year, the National Academy of Sciences and the National Academy of Medicine issued recommendations on editing embryos and other germ line cells, calling for a high degree of caution but not prohibition. An obvious counterargument to the precautionary approach is that the world has changed. We in the developed world don't inhabit an environment rife with malaria and TB anymore. We have drugs to protect us when infection strikes. So doomsday preppers notwithstanding, removing injurious and outdated genes is a logical step in our (now self-directed) evolution.

The problem, Dr. Doudna points out, is that new pathogens for which we don't have cures continue to emerge — like H.I.V. and SARS and drug-resistant variants of TB. In fact, as the world has become more crowded and interconnected, the emergence of new pathogens has accelerated. Those "bad" gene variants might still come in handy, she says.

More broadly, genetically diverse populations tend to be more resilient, precisely because they have more genetic resources to draw on when unforeseen challenges arise.

To further complicate matters, some of the gene variants now linked with disease probably don't cause as many problems in other environments. Consider the border between Finland and Russia, where there's a sharp gradient in the prevalence of autoimmune disorders like celiac disease and Type 1 diabetes. As I've pointed out before, these conditions have become worrisomely common in Finland in recent decades, but are between one-fifth and one-sixth as common on the Russian side, despite the fact that the Russians are just as genetically predisposed to developing them.

What protects the Russians from their own genetic inheritance? Or better phrased, what makes the Finns vulnerable?

Finnish scientists think that exposure to a particular community of microbes — one that more resembles the microbiota of our less hygienic past — prevents the diseases from emerging in Russia. That's important because at least some of the gene variants associated with autoimmune disease are probably useful; they most likely helped us battle infections in the past.

So instead of rewriting our genetic code, a better approach might be to change the interplay between our genes and environment — in this case by altering the microbes we encounter.

This dynamic may also apply to a gene linked with dementia. Carriers of the ApoE4 variant have an up-to-fourfold increased risk of Alzheimer's disease. In 2010, scientists at Northwestern University found that the gene was more prevalent in tropical and polar populations than in those from mid-latitudes, presumably because it served some function in those regions. Then, strangely, the gene was linked to enhanced cognitive performance in children living in Brazilian slums. And last year, Ben Trumble, an anthropologist at Arizona State University, and colleagues published an intriguing study suggesting that the gene might improve brain function in elderly people living in the Bolivian Amazon.

The tribe he studied, called the Tsimane, subsist mostly on what they grow and hunt in the jungle, and about two-thirds have intestinal parasites. Dr. Trumble discovered that if elderly ApoE4 carriers harbored parasites, their cognitive abilities improved relative to noncarriers with parasites. Only carriers without parasites suffered cognitively.

How this might work is unclear. The gene seems to increase the absorption of cholesterol, which is necessary for brain health. Parasites, of course, steal cholesterol and other fats, either by extracting them from your food or by drinking your blood. Maybe people who have the gene are better at countering this thievery. Or perhaps their superior fat absorption affords them more energy to fight parasites, too many of which can also erode brain function. And maybe because the Tsimane exercise plenty and eat low-fat fare, the gene never becomes problematic for them as it does in the developed world — unless they lack parasites.

Whatever the mechanism, here's the point: A gene that we now think increases the risk of cognitive decline may actually protect against it in other environments.

Most biomedical research is done on modernized populations in industrialized cities. But if we edit out genes based on how they work in those populations exclusively, "we might disrupt processes that we didn't realize were important," Dr. Trumble says.

Finally, there's diet. Back in the late 1980s, the anthropologist Fatimah Jackson discovered that the prevalence of the sickle cell trait varied considerably across Liberia, a small country. It was more common in the northwest than the southeast, even though the infection that makes the trait advantageous — malaria — was everywhere.

Scientists at Albert Einstein College of Medicine in New York City had recently discovered that ingesting cyanate salts could prevent the "sickling" of red blood cells that leads to the anemia and pain of sickle cell disease. Dr. Jackson knew that a related compound, cyanide, was common in foods across Africa, particularly in the staple crop cassava (which you may know as tapioca). She was also aware that, at the right dose, cyanide could directly protect against the malaria parasite. She realized that regular consumption of cassava — more common in the Southeast than the Northwest — could, by working as an antimalarial drug, affect the prevalence of the sickle cell trait, by making it less advantageous.

Something different was happening in the Northwest, though. Dr. Jackson, who is now at Howard University, thinks that while cassava consumption in the region was insufficient to protect against malaria directly, people who had two copies of the sickle cell gene still ate enough to partly avoid sickling. In that population, diet may have prevented a genetic disease from fully manifesting.

Certainly, some genes will turn out to be only detrimental, and provide no advantage. But there are bound to be other cases like these, in which genes deemed harmful can aid survival or at least cause less damage in other surroundings. As the epidemiologist David Barker said, "genes are not Stalinist dictators." They respond to what's going on around them — to environment.

We evolved in environments that are radically different from today's, and some of our genes may work better in those environments. This complicates the idea of trying to perfect the human genome with technology. Given how much the world has changed in just the past 150 years, and how much it's likely to change again in the next 150, the question is, "What environment will we optimize our genes for?"

MOISES VELASQUEZ-MANOFF, the author of "An Epidemic of Absence: A New Way of Understanding Allergies and Autoimmune Disease," is a contributing opinion writer.

The Famine Ended 70 Years Ago, but Dutch Genes Still Bear Scars

BY CARL ZIMMER | JAN. 31, 2018

IN SEPTEMBER 1944, trains in the Netherlands ground to a halt. Dutch railway workers were hoping that a strike could stop the transport of Nazi troops, helping the advancing Allied forces.

But the Allied campaign failed, and the Nazis punished the Netherlands by blocking food supplies, plunging much of the country into famine. By the time the Netherlands was liberated in May 1945, more than 20,000 people had died of starvation.

The Dutch Hunger Winter has proved unique in unexpected ways. Because it started and ended so abruptly, it has served as an unplanned experiment in human health. Pregnant women, it turns out, were uniquely vulnerable, and the children they gave birth to have been influenced by famine throughout their lives.

When they became adults, they ended up a few pounds heavier than average. In middle age, they had higher levels of triglycerides and LDL cholesterol. They also experienced higher rates of such conditions as obesity, diabetes and schizophrenia.

By the time they reached old age, those risks had taken a measurable toll, according to the research of L.H. Lumey, an epidemiologist at Columbia University. In 2013, he and his colleagues reviewed death records of hundreds of thousands of Dutch people born in the mid-1940s.

They found that the people who had been in utero during the famine — known as the Dutch Hunger Winter cohort — died at a higher rate than people born before or afterward. "We found a 10 percent increase in mortality after 68 years," said Dr. Lumey.

The patterns that Dr. Lumey and his colleagues documented are not disputed, but scientists still are struggling to understand how they come about.

"How on earth can your body remember the environment it was exposed to in the womb — and remember that decades later?" wondered Bas Heijmans, a geneticist at Leiden University Medical Center in the Netherlands.

Dr. Heijmans, Dr. Lumey and their colleagues published a possible answer, or part of one, on Wednesday in the journal Science Advances. Their study suggests that the Dutch Hunger Winter silenced certain genes in unborn children — and that they've stayed quiet ever since.

While all cells in a person's body share the same genes, different ones are active or silent in different cells. That program largely is locked in place before birth.

But scientists have learned that later experiences — say, exposure to a virus — can cause cells to quiet a gene or boost its activity, sometimes permanently.

The study of this long-term gene control is called epigenetics. Researchers have identified molecules that cells use to program DNA, but how those tools work isn't entirely clear. One of the best studied is a molecular cap called a methyl group.

At millions of spots across our DNA, genes may carry a methyl group. They seem to silence genes — at least, researchers have found that silenced genes often have a collection of methyl groups lurking nearby.

Many researchers have speculated that prenatal conditions can influence people's health across their lifetime, and some have speculated that methyl groups or other forms of epigenetics put this so-called fetal programming into action.

But it's hard to put that idea to a firm test. The Dutch Hunger Winter might offer an opportunity, Dr. Heijmans and Dr. Lumey realized.

When Dr. Lumey first started studying the Dutch Hunger Winter cohort in the 1990s, he took blood samples from thousands of middle-aged subjects. He also took samples from their siblings, born before or after the famine.

Over a decade later, he and his colleagues were able to take advantage of powerful new technology for detecting methyl groups in blood cells. They retrieved DNA from the samples and placed it in a device able to find methyl groups at nearly 350,000 spots on the genome.

Next, the researchers looked for odd patterns. They searched for methyl groups that were common in the Dutch Hunger Winter cohort, for example, but missing from their siblings.

Then they turned their attention to the health of their subjects. They sorted people according to their body mass index, for example, and looked for methyl groups that were unusually common in overweight people.

Finally, the researchers merged the results — and found a few methyl groups that were linked both to the famine and to health conditions later in life. "We were able to connect the three dots," said Dr. Lumey.

Dr. Lumey and his colleagues propose that these methyl groups disrupt how cells normally use genes. One methyl group that is linked to a higher body mass index may be able to quiet a gene called PIM3, which is involved in burning the body's fuel.

So here's the theory: Perhaps the Dutch Hunger Winter added a methyl group to fetuses born to starving mothers, which made the PIM3 gene less active — and continued to do so for life.

The result? "Maybe your metabolism is in a lower gear," Dr. Heijmans said.

Dalton Conley, a biosociologist at Princeton University who was not involved in the new study, said that there might be other explanations for the results. Perhaps putting on extra weight as you age triggers an epigenetic change to PIM3, rather than the other way around.

And the Dutch famine probably led to many miscarriages and early deaths. It's possible that the survivors had some genetic variant that made them resilient and gave them a distinctive epigenetic profile not captured in this study.

John M. Greally, the director of the Center for Epigenomics at Albert Einstein College of Medicine, noted that blood is made up of many different types of cells, each with its own epigenetic profile.

Maybe the Dutch famine made some types of cells more common, he said, rather than altering the epigenetics.

But Dr. Heijmans and his colleagues studied the same methyl groups in muscle cells, fat cells and other tissues they got from cadavers. In any given person, the pattern was roughly the same.

Still, Dr. Heijmans said that the new study would need to be followed up — for example, with carefully controlled experiments on animals that can shed more light on how a pregnant mother's food supply affects the epigenetics of her offspring.

If scientists can solve the Dutch Hunger Winter's lingering mysteries, they might also get some clues to how other kinds of stress can reprogram children's health even before they're born.

Dr. Lumey speculated that epigenetic profiles might someday allow doctors to detect changes that would lead to problems much later in life. "You don't have to wait for sixty years," he said.

David Reich Unearths Human History Etched in Bone

BY CARL ZIMMER | MARCH 20, 2018

The geneticist at Harvard Medical School has retrieved DNA from more than 900 ancient people. His findings trace the prehistoric migrations of our species.

BOSTON — David Reich wore a hooded, white suit, cream-colored clogs, and a blue surgical mask. Only his eyes were visible as he inspected the bone fragments on the counter.

Dr. Reich, a geneticist at Harvard Medical School, pointed out a strawberry-sized chunk: "This is from a 4,000-year-old site in Central Asia — from Uzbekistan, I think."

He moved down the row. "This is a 2,500-year-old sample from a site in Britain. This is Bronze Age Russian, and these are Arabian samples. These people would have never met each other in time or space."

Dr. Reich hopes that his team of scientists and technicians can find DNA in these bones. Odds are good that they will.

In less than three years, Dr. Reich's laboratory has published DNA from the genomes of 938 ancient humans — more than all other research teams working in this field combined. The work in his lab has reshaped our understanding of human prehistory.

"They often answer age-old questions and sometimes provide astonishing unanticipated insights," said Svante Paabo, the director of the Max Planck Institute of Paleoanthropology in Leipzig, Germany.

Dr. Reich, Dr. Paabo and other experts in ancient DNA are putting together a new history of humanity, one that runs in parallel with the narratives gleaned from fossils and written records. In Dr. Reich's research, he and his colleagues have shed light on the peopling of the planet and the spread of agriculture, among other momentous events.

In a book to be published next week, "Who We Are and How We Got Here," Dr. Reich, 43, explains how advances in DNA sequencing and analysis have helped this new field take off.

KAYANA SZYMCZAK FOR THE NEW YORK TIMES

David Reich in his office at Harvard. He and his colleagues have sequenced the genomes of more than 900 ancient individuals, shedding light on how humans spread across the globe.

"It's really like the invention of a new scientific instrument, like a microscope or a telescope," he said. "When an instrument that powerful is invented, it opens up all these horizons, and everything is new and surprising."

Dr. Reich oversees a team with many different skills, from genetics to mathematics. But the "clean lab" is where the raw material for all their work — ancient DNA — is recovered. The head-to-toe suits that the researchers don in an airlock each morning ensure that no stray flake of skin or bead of sweat contaminates the bones with modern DNA. Each night the entire lab is bathed in gene-destroying ultraviolet light.

The clean lab feels like it belongs in a computer chip factory. But Dr. Reich has not forgotten that these are human remains, not widgets on a conveyor belt.

"This is a bone from a person's body who lived four thousand years ago, and we're destroying it," he said, gazing down at the

Uzbek remains. "I think we need to do well by the individuals we're studying."

Doing well means understanding who these people were, and how they were linked to one another — and to us.

Standing next to Dr. Reich was a suited technician, Ann Marie Lawson. She picked up the Uzbek bone and lowered it into a box, which she covered with a clear plastic lid. She pushed her gloved hands through two rubber-lined holes on its sides.

She picked up the bone in her left hand; with her right hand, she switched on a sandblasting hose and pointed it at the bone. An outer layer of dirt flew upward, quickly sucked away by a fan in the box.

Ms. Lawson then inspected the freshly white bone. It came from the base of a skull, and deep inside was the inner ear. The bone that surrounds the inner ear turns out to be the best place in the body to search for ancient DNA.

Ms. Lawson began sandblasting again, chiseling away chunks of

KAYANA SZYMCZAK FOR THE NEW YORK TIMES

Mr. Oppenheimer at work in Dr. Reich's lab. DNA recovered from a small piece of bone can tell scientists about human migrations over thousands of years.

bone. Eventually, she was left holding a remnant only as big as a grain of rice.

"That's the motherlode," said Dr. Reich.

AN EXTRAORDINARY INVITATION

Dr. Reich grew up in Washington, the son of the novelist Tova Reich and Walter Reich, the first director of the Holocaust Memorial Museum and now a professor at George Washington University.

Dr. Reich began studying sociology as a Harvard undergraduate, but later he turned to physics and then to medicine. After graduating, he went to Oxford to prepare for medical school.

There he met Dr. David B. Goldstein, who at the time was comparing the DNA of living people for clues to what their distant ancestors were like.

"When I first met him, he was obviously smart, but he gave an impression of being a little bit shy and not having a very forceful personality," said Dr. Goldstein.

"It turned out that's the most misleading impression he could possibly give. He knows exactly what he wants to do."

It was obvious that his student was captivated by the research. But Dr. Goldstein had come to view it as a scientific dead end.

"I said, 'My God, don't spend your career on human evolutionary genetics," recalled Dr. Goldstein, who now studies disease genetics at Columbia University.

"He just listened very politely and wasn't persuaded an iota," he added with a laugh. "He wasn't just proven right. He was proved dramatically right."

Abandoning medical school, Dr. Reich continued with genetics research and was hired by Harvard Medical School in 2003. By then, he had developed a close partnership with a mathematician named Nick Patterson, who had come late in life to genetics after twenty years working as a cryptographer in British intelligence and then joining a hedge fund.

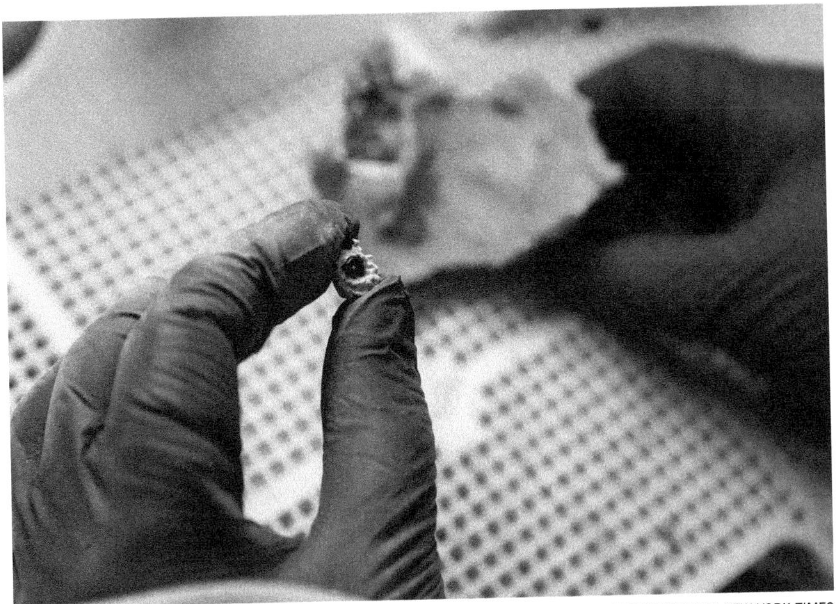

KAYANA SZYMCZAK FOR THE NEW YORK TIMES

The cochlea, or inner ear, extracted by Mr. Oppenheimer. It may contain DNA that is tens of thousands of years old.

Dr. Reich appointed Dr. Patterson deputy head of the newly formed genetics lab, and together they began developing new statistical techniques to plumb genetic data for hidden patterns.

The two researchers devised a way to determine whether a single population descended from two or more distinct groups. Collaborating with researchers at the Center for Cellular and Molecular Biology in Hyderabad, India, they put their method to its first big test.

Analyzing DNA from hundreds of villages, they discovered that just about every living Indian descends from two distinct groups. One, which the researchers called Ancestral North Indians, is related to Central Asians, Near Easterners and Europeans.

The second group, Ancestral South Indians, is a mysterious population that is not closely related to any living people outside of India. The two populations mixed together, Dr. Reich estimated, 2,000 to 4,000 years ago.

As Dr. Reich and his colleagues gained attention for their new methods, they got an extraordinary invitation: to study the DNA of Neanderthals.

A MYSTERIOUS LINEAGE

The invitation came from Dr. Paabo. In the 1990s, he had pioneered methods to extract ancient DNA from fossils dating back tens of thousands of years. While he studied many extinct species — such as cave bears, mastodons and ground sloths — Neanderthals were his deepest passion.

Fossils of these heavy-browed individuals date back over 200,000 years in Europe and the Near East. They made tools, weapons and even cave art. But they vanished about 40,000 years ago.

Dr. Paabo gradually filled in gaps to reconstruct the entire Neanderthal genome. In 2006, he invited Dr. Reich's team to help figure out how modern humans and Neanderthals were related.

Dr. Reich threw himself into the project, and over the next few years, the scientists made a series of landmark discoveries.

The DNA of Neanderthals indicates that their ancestors split from our own about 600,000 years ago. But Dr. Reich's tests revealed that living humans outside of Africa still carry traces of Neanderthal DNA.

How is that possible? Before Neanderthals became extinct in Europe, they encountered and interbred with the ancestors of modern humans as they departed Africa.

As the scientists searched in more fossils for Neanderthal DNA, they got another surprise. In 2010, a nondescript pinkie bone recovered in a Siberian cave called Denisova yielded the entire genome of a previously unknown, and extinct, lineage of humans.

The Denisovans, as they came to be known, split off from Neanderthals about 400,000 years ago, genetic analysis revealed.

Denisovan DNA has turned up only in a few additional teeth discovered in that Siberian cave. The oldest such fossils date to over 100,000 years old; the pinkie bone belonged to a Denisovan who lived sometime between 48,000 and 60,000 years ago.

Dr. Reich and his colleagues discovered that Denisovans, like Neanderthals, left a genetic legacy in living people, mostly in Australia, New Guinea and Asia.

Their research also suggested that Denisovans divided early in their history into two lineages. "They were isolated from each other for many hundreds of thousands of years," said Dr. Reich.

A study published on Thursday by Princeton geneticist Joshua Akey and his colleagues confirmed this finding and brought Denisovans into sharper focus.

Each branch, the new study suggests, interbred with the ancestors of living humans. One Denisovan group left behind DNA in modern-day Asians and Oceanians. The other branch left genetic traces only in living people in China and Japan.

Ancient DNA has summoned the genetic shadows of a long-vanished people, one that fossils alone could not reveal. Many scientists now suspect that ancient DNA will reveal other extinct kinds of humans in the future.

"The discovery of Denisovan DNA was a landmark in my thinking about ancient DNA," said Dr. Reich. "It can reveal things about the past that are completely unexpected, that are not dreamed of in our philosophy."

SETTING THE 'TRAPS'

Dr. Reich's voyage through prehistory left him wondering about what DNA could reveal about more recent events. Museums around the world were loaded with bones of people who lived within the last 20,000 years, after all.

Since those remains were younger, they'd be more likely to still have some DNA in them. To begin retrieving it, Dr. Reich retooled his laboratory, copying Dr. Paabo's facility in Germany to the last detail.

"We even cloned the linoleum from Leipzig," he said.

But in important ways, Dr. Reich broke from the standard scientific strategy for searching for ancient DNA.

Dr. Paabo and other experts typically examine many fossils to find a rare one packed with DNA. They then try to reconstruct the entire genome.

Dr. Reich's lab instead designed DNA "traps" that snag hundreds of thousands of genetic fragments from the human genome. The result is far from a complete genome sequence, but enough to divine ancestries and even get some clues about the traits of ancient people.

In 2015, the first results emerged from Dr. Reich's new research pipeline. He and his colleagues published DNA from 69 ancient Europeans who lived 3,000 to 8,000 years ago.

According to their results, farmers with Near East ancestry displaced hunter-gatherers already living in Europe. Then, about 4,500 years ago, another wave of people arrived, descended from the horse-riding nomads of what are now the Russian steppes.

Less than three years since that study, Dr. Reich's team has published a torrent of similar findings. They have traced the spread of the first farmers in the Near East, for example, and have tracked the rise and fall of various populations in ancient Africa.

While some of these results describe migrations across continents, Dr. Reich's team also focuses on smaller regions to reconstruct the genetic makeup of people over thousands of years.

Recently, for example, Dr. Reich and his colleagues published the DNA of people who lived on what are now the British Isles 3,500 to 10,000 years ago. It, too, tells a story.

When the Ice Age glaciers retreated from the islands, hunter-gatherers moved in from what is now Europe. About 6,000 years ago, farmers with Near Eastern ancestry reached Britain, and mostly replaced the hunter-gatherers.

About 4,500 years ago, archaeologists have found, there was a sudden shift in Britain to new styles of pottery and metalworking, known collectively as the Beaker culture. Many experts have argued that farmers borrowed the techniques from the European continent.

But the DNA says otherwise, Dr. Reich and his colleagues found.

While the Beaker culture spread from society to society on the mainland, it was brought to Britain by immigrants descended from the nomads of what are now the Russian steppes.

These people almost entirely replaced the earlier farmers. Today, British people trace 90 percent of their ancestry to this immigrant wave.

Were it not for the genetic findings, "nobody would have believed the scale of the turnover," said Ian Armit, an archaeologist at the University of Bradford who collaborated with Dr. Reich on the research.

"Archaeologists will need to get to grips with this 90 percent replacement, and what this might really mean in human terms," he added.

A DRAMATIC VOYAGE

The Beaker people needed only to cross the English Channel to get to the British Isles. A far more spectacular voyage took place about 3,300 years ago, when humans first sailed to remote islands in the Pacific.

Dr. Reich and his colleagues have shed light on that migration by analyzing ancient DNA from the skeletons of early Pacific voyagers.

"It's changed the game," said Matthew Spriggs, an archaeologist at Australian National University, who has collaborated with Dr. Reich.

Until recently, many archaeologists argued that the ancestors of Pacific Islanders were related to the indigenous people of Taiwan. They had sailed south to the islands around New Guinea, the idea went, later mixing with the population, known as Papuans. Only later did their descendants sail east to Pacific islands.

This theory helped account for the kinds of languages spoken in the Pacific, the agriculture, and styles of pottery, as well as the mix of East Asian and New Guinea DNA found in the islanders.

Dr. Spriggs and other archaeologists provided Dr. Reich with bones from Vanuatu and Tonga, and his team succeeded in recovering DNA where others had failed. And what did it say about the prevailing theory?

"We found genetically that wasn't right at all," Dr. Reich said. He and his colleagues published their results last month in the journal Current Biology.

Instead, the people who first arrived on Vanuatu and other Pacific islands came directly from Asia — perhaps Taiwan or the Philippines — without ever stopping in New Guinea. Only later did a wave of Papuans arrive.

"We know now when that wave hits — it hits before 2,400 years ago," said Dr. Reich. "And it's a total replacement."

And that second wave actually was made up of at least two migrations. The Papuans who came to what is now Vanuatu probably sailed from the Bismarck Islands. But the Papuans who arrived further east, in Polynesia, came from other islands, possibly New Britain.

As of last month, Dr. Reich's team has published about three-quarters of all the genome-wide data from ancient human remains in the scientific literature. But the scientists are only getting started.

They also have retrieved DNA from about 3,000 more samples. And the lab refrigerators are filled with bones from 2,000 more denizens of prehistory.

Dr. Reich's plan is to find ancient DNA from every culture known to archaeology everywhere in the world. Ultimately, he hopes to build a genetic atlas of humanity over the past 50,000 years.

"I try not to think about it all at once, because it's so overwhelming," he said.

As D.I.Y. Gene Editing Gains Popularity, ‘Someone Is Going to Get Hurt’

BY EMILY BAUMGAERTNER | MAY 14, 2018

After a virus was created from mail-order DNA, scientists are sounding the alarm about the genetic tinkering carried out in garages and living rooms.

WASHINGTON — As a teenager, Keoni Gandall already was operating a cutting-edge research laboratory in his bedroom in Huntington Beach, Calif. While his friends were buying video games, he acquired more than a dozen pieces of equipment — a transilluminator, a centrifuge, two thermocyclers — in pursuit of a hobby that once was the province of white-coated Ph.D.’s in institutional labs.

“I just wanted to clone DNA using my automated lab robot and feasibly make full genomes at home,” he said.

Mr. Gandall was far from alone. In the past few years, so-called biohackers across the country have taken gene editing into their own hands. As the equipment becomes cheaper and the expertise in gene-editing techniques, mostly Crispr-Cas9, more widely shared, citizen-scientists are attempting to re-engineer DNA in surprising ways.

Until now, the work has amounted to little more than D.I.Y. misfires. A year ago, a biohacker famously injected himself at a conference with modified DNA that he hoped would make him more muscular. (It did not.)

Earlier this year, at Body Hacking Con in Austin, Tex., a biotech executive injected himself with what he hoped would be a herpes treatment. (Verdict: No.) His company already had live-streamed a man injecting himself with a home-brewed treatment for H.I.V. (His viral load increased.)

In a recent interview, Mr. Gandall, now 18 and a research fellow at Stanford, said he only wants to ensure open access to gene-editing technology, believing future biotech discoveries may come from the least expected minds.

But he is quick to acknowledge that the do-it-yourself genetics revolution one day may go catastrophically wrong.

"Even I would tell you, the level of DNA synthesis regulation, it simply isn't good enough," Mr. Gandall said. "These regulations aren't going to work when everything is decentralized — when everybody has a DNA synthesizer on their smartphone."

The most pressing worry is that someone somewhere will use the spreading technology to create a bioweapon.

Already a research team at the University of Alberta has recreated from scratch an extinct relative of smallpox, horsepox, by stitching together fragments of mail-order DNA in just six months for about $100,000 — without a glance from law enforcement officials.

ERIN BRETHAUER FOR THE NEW YORK TIMES

Keoni Gandall, in his laboratory at home in Palo Alto, Calif. He barely earned a high school diploma, he said, and was kicked out of a local science fair for reckless genetic engineering.

The team purchased overlapping DNA fragments from a commercial company. Once the researchers glued the full genome together and introduced it into cells infected by another type of poxvirus, the cells began to produce infectious particles.

To some experts, the experiment nullified a decades-long debate over whether to destroy the world's two remaining smallpox remnants — at the Centers for Disease Control and Prevention in Atlanta and at a research center in Russia — since it proved that scientists who want to experiment with the virus can now create it themselves.

The study's publication in the journal PLOS One included an in-depth description of the methods used and — most alarming to Gregory D. Koblentz, the director of the biodefense graduate program at George Mason University — a series of new tips and tricks for bypassing roadblocks.

"Sure, we've known this could be possible," Dr. Koblentz said. "We also knew North Korea could someday build a thermonuclear weapon, but we're still horrified when they actually do it."

Experts urged the journal to cancel publication of the article, one calling it "unwise, unjustified, and dangerous." Even before publication, a report from a World Health Organization meeting noted that the endeavor "did not require exceptional biochemical knowledge or skills, significant funds or significant time."

But the study's lead researcher, David Evans, a virologist at the University of Alberta, said he had alerted several Canadian government authorities to his poxvirus venture, and none had raised an objection.

Many experts agree that it would be very difficult for amateur biologists of any stripe to design a killer virus on their own. But as more hackers trade computer code for the genetic kind, and as their skills become increasingly sophisticated, health security experts fear that the potential for abuse may be growing.

"To unleash something deadly, that could really happen any day now — today," said Dr. George Church, a researcher at Harvard and a leading synthetic biologist. "The pragmatic people would just engineer drug-resistant anthrax or highly transmissible influenza. Some recipes are online."

"If they're willing to inject themselves with hormones to make their muscles bigger, you can imagine they'd be willing to test more powerful things," he added. "Anyone who does synthetic biology should be under surveillance, and anyone who does it without a license should be suspect."

Authorities in the United States have been hesitant to undertake actions that could squelch innovation or impinge on intellectual property. The laws that cover biotechnology have not been significantly updated in decades, forcing regulators to rely on outdated frameworks to govern new technologies.

The cobbled-together regulatory system, with multiple agencies overseeing various types of research, has left gaps that will only widen as the technologies advance.

Academic researchers undergo strict scrutiny when they seek federal funding for "dual-use research of concern": experiments that, in theory, could be used for good or ill. But more than half of the nation's scientific research and development is funded by nongovernmental sources.

In 2013, a quest to create a glowing plant via genetic engineering drew almost half a million dollars through Kickstarter, the crowdfunding website.

"There really isn't a national governance per se for those who are not federally or government funded," said Dr. William So, a biological countermeasures specialist at the Federal Bureau of Investigation.

Instead, he said, the agency relies on biohackers themselves to sound the alarm regarding suspicious behavior.

"I do believe the F.B.I. is doing their best with what they have," said Dr. Thomas V. Inglesby, director of the Johns Hopkins Center for Health Security in Baltimore.

"But if you really want to do this, there isn't a whole lot stopping you."

UNDERGROUND EXPERIMENTERS

The F.B.I. has befriended many white-hat biohacking labs, among them Genspace in Sunset Park, Brooklyn. Behind an inconspicuous steel door on a gritty, graffiti-lined street, biohackers-in-training — musicians, engineers, retirees — routinely gather for crash courses in genetic engineering.

Participants in "Biohacker Boot Camp" learn basic technical skills to use in homegrown genetics projects, like concocting algae that glows.

"The double helix is the most iconic image of the 20th century, perhaps rivaled only by the mushroom cloud," the bootcamp's leader, Michael Flanagan, said to a recent class.

Genspace's entryway resembles a college dorm room, complete with sagging couch, microwave, mini-fridge. But the lab itself is palatial: two stories of white brick walls, industrial kitchen counters marked with dry-erase notes, shelves towering with glassware and reagents.

ERIN BRETHAUER FOR THE NEW YORK TIMES

Josiah Zayner, a former NASA scientist turned biohacker, in Oakland, Calif.

It's a significant upgrade for Genspace. Daniel Grushkin, the co-founder, used to host bacterial experiments in his living room over pizza and beer.

The group later moved into a rental for creatives — roboticists, organic fashion designers, miniature-cupcake makers — and constructed a makeshift lab using old patio screen doors. It was Mr. Grushkin who reached out to the F.B.I.

"People might be calling you because we are nonscientists doing science in a busted-up old building," he recalled telling bureau agents. "But we aren't a meth lab, and we aren't bioterrorists."

Mr. Grushkin has become a trailblazer in biohacking risk management, in part because he recognizes that letting neophytes manipulate live organisms is "less like a 'hackerspace,' more like a pet store."

He has posted community guidelines, forbidden infectious agents in the lab, and accepted a grant of almost $500,000 to design security practices for some four dozen similar labs across the country.

Most of them report not having heard so much as a greeting from the F.B.I. At many, the consequence for breaking safety guidelines is simply the loss of membership — leaving the perpetrator to experiment in isolation, but still among thousands of enthusiasts huddled online in Facebook groups, email listservs and Reddit pages.

Many find their inspiration in Josiah Zayner, a NASA scientist turned celebrity biohacker who straps a GoPro camera to his forehead and streams experiments on himself from his garage. He's the man who tried to make his muscles bigger.

"This is just normal Scotch packing tape," Mr. Zayner, chief executive of a biohacking start-up called The Odin, told his YouTube audience one summer night, muttering expletives as he stripped the top layer of skin from his forearm. "This is Day 1 of my experiment to genetically engineer myself."

In an interview, Mr. Zayner conceded that among his biohacking followers, an accident — not a premeditated offense — was conceivable.

"I guess I can see why they don't let the entire public have access to Ebola," he said. "The risk is, if they're working with Ebola and their house burns down, the Ebola could somehow get out."

Even Mr. Zayner is apprehensive of the movement he helped begin; he plans to include live frogs in The Odin's D.I.Y.-Crispr kits to encourage his followers to experiment on animals instead of themselves — or others.

"I have no doubt that someone is going to get hurt," he said. "People are trying to one-up each other, and it's moving faster than any one of us could have ever imagined — it's almost uncontrollable. It's scary."

A BIOLOGICAL ARMS RACE

If nefarious biohackers were to create a biological weapon from scratch — a killer that would bounce from host to host to host, capable of reaching millions of people, unrestrained by time or distance — they would probably begin with some online shopping.

A site called Science Exchange, for example, serves as a Craigslist for DNA, a commercial ecosystem connecting almost anyone with online access and a valid credit card to companies that sell cloned DNA fragments.

Mr. Gandall, the Stanford fellow, often buys such fragments — benign ones. But the workarounds for someone with ill intent, he said, might not be hard to figure out.

Biohackers will soon be able to forgo these companies altogether with an all-in-one desktop genome printer: a device much like an inkjet printer that employs the letters AGTC — genetic base pairs — instead of the color model CMYK.

A similar device already exists for institutional labs, called BioXp 3200, which sells for about $65,000. But at-home biohackers can start with DNA Playground from Amino Labs, an Easy Bake genetic oven that costs less than an iPad, or The Odin's Crispr gene-editing kit for $159.

Tools like these may be threatening in the wrong hands, but they also helped Mr. Gandall start a promising career.

At age 11, he picked up a virology textbook at a church book fair. Before he was old enough for a driver's permit, he was urging his mother to shuttle him to a research job at the University of California, Irvine.

He began dressing exclusively in red polo shirts to avoid the distraction of choosing outfits. He doodled through high school — correcting biology teachers — and was kicked out of a local science fair for what was deemed reckless home-brew genetic engineering.

Mr. Gandall barely earned a high-school diploma, he said, and was rebuffed by almost every college he applied to — but later gained a bioengineering position at Stanford University.

"Pretty ironic, after they rejected me as a student," he said.

He moved to East Palo Alto — with 14 red polo shirts — into a house with three nonbiologists, who don't much notice that DNA is cloned in the corner of his bedroom.

His mission at Stanford is to build a body of genetic material for public use. To his fellow biohackers, it's a noble endeavor.

To biosecurity experts, it's tossing ammunition into trigger-happy hands.

"There are really only two things that could wipe 30 million people off of the planet: a nuclear weapon, or a biological one," said Lawrence O. Gostin, an adviser on pandemic influenza preparedness to the World Health Organization.

"Somehow, the U.S. government fears and prepares for the former, but not remotely for the latter. It baffles me."

Glossary

algorithm A precise sequence of steps, often used by a computer program, to make decisions based on a large amount of data.

artificial selection The use of breeding to influence genetic traits in organisms.

benign Not dangerous, the opposite of malignant.

biohacker An individual experimenting in editing their own genes.

chromosome The larger chemical structure that carries DNA, contained in the nucleus of the cell.

codon A short DNA sequence that forms a unit of genetic code.

Crispr A gene editing process developed in 2015 that promises many novel applications in genetic engineering.

designer babies Term for the proposed practice of genetically engineering children to have desired traits.

direct-to-consumer genetic testing Genetic testing sold by companies, independent from medical or scientific organizations.

DNA Deoxyribonucleic acid, the chemical carrier of genetic information. The genetic information is represented in a sequence of bases, held in place by a double helix structure.

DNA sequencing The process of determining the precise order of genetic information in DNA.

embryo A fertilized egg in the early stage of development.

epigenetics The modification of gene expression in the life of an organism, caused by external factors.

essentialism The belief that certain human traits have an underlying internal cause or essence, rather than being caused by their environment.

fabricate To invent or falsify.

forensics The science of criminal investigations.

genealogy The study of family lineages and ancestry over time.

genetic counseling The practice of giving medical advice to parents about risks of genetic disorders in their children.

genome The complete genetic sequence of a living organism. The first complete human genome was mapped in 2003.

genomics The science of mapping and studying genomes.

genotype The genetic makeup of an individual organism.

in vitro fertilization A reproductive technology that fertilizes an egg using a sperm sample, then implants the egg in the womb.

mutation A change in the structure of a gene, occasionally causing the appearance of new traits.

phenotype The observable characteristics of an individual organism, often studied in relation to the genotype.

pseudoscience False or unverifiable claims that appear scientific but have no scientific evidence.

prenatal genetic testing Genetic testing that occurs before a child is born, screening for possible disease risks.

sickle cell anemia A genetic disorder causing red blood cells to be misshapen.

Tay-Sachs disease A severe genetic disorder affecting the brain and spinal cord, primarily affecting Ashkenazi Jews.

Trisomy 21 An accidental replication of the 21st chromosome, causing Down syndrome.

Media Literacy Terms

"Media literacy" refers to the ability to access, understand, critically assess and create media. The following terms are important components of media literacy, and they will help you critically engage with the articles in this title.

angle The aspect of a news story that a journalist focuses on and develops.

attribution The method by which a source is identified or by which facts and information are assigned to the person who provided them.

balance Principle of journalism that both perspectives of an argument should be presented in a fair way.

bias A disposition of prejudice in favor of a certain idea, person or perspective.

byline Name of the writer, usually placed between the headline and the story.

chronological order Method of writing a story presenting the details of the story in the order in which they occurred.

credibility The quality of being trustworthy and believable, said of a journalistic source.

editorial Article of opinion or interpretation.

feature story Article designed to entertain as well as to inform.

headline Type, usually 18 point or larger, used to introduce a story.

human interest story Type of story that focuses on individuals and how events or issues affect their life, generally offering a sense of relatability to the reader.

impartiality Principle of journalism that a story should not reflect a journalist's bias and should contain balance.

intention The motive or reason behind something, such as the publication of a news story.

interview story Type of story in which the facts are gathered primarily by interviewing another person or persons.

inverted pyramid Method of writing a story using facts in order of importance, beginning with a lead and then gradually adding paragraphs in order of relevance from most interesting to least interesting.

motive The reason behind something, such as the publication of a news story or a source's perspective on an issue.

news story An article or style of expository writing that reports news, generally in a straightforward fashion and without editorial comment.

op-ed An opinion piece that reflects a prominent individual's opinion on a topic of interest.

paraphrase The summary of an individual's words, with attribution, rather than a direct quotation of their exact words.

quotation The use of an individual's exact words indicated by the use of quotation marks and proper attribution.

reliability The quality of being dependable and accurate, said of a journalistic source.

rhetorical device Technique in writing intending to persuade the reader or communicate a message from a certain perspective.

tone A manner of expression in writing or speech.

Media Literacy Questions

1. Steven Pinker's article, "My Genome, My Self" (page 10), is an op-ed. This op-ed combines personal experience with his scientific research. What perspective does this offer to the discussion on personal genetic testing?

2. Gina Kolata's article, "With a Simple DNA Test, Family Histories Are Rewritten" (page 36), is a human interest story. What types of personal issues does it depict in its subject?

3. J. David Goodman's article, "New York's Chief Medical Examiner Seeks to Lead in DNA Research" (page 62), has a specific angle. What is that angle, and how does that angle reflect more broadly on the discipline of genetics research?

4. Robert Pear's article, "U.S. Introduces New DNA Standard for Ensuring Accuracy of Genetic Tests" (page 70), is written in the inverted pyramid format. What decisions did the author and editor make when choosing which material was most important?

5. Reed Abelson and Julie Creswell's article, "Pursuit of Cash Taints Promise of Gene Tests" (page 73), is written in chronological order. Why did the authors choose to tell the story in this way?

6. Claudia Dreifus's article, "Biologist Teaches the Nation's Judges About Genetics" (page 92), is an interview story. What unique perspective does interviewee James P. Evans offer, and what questions does Dreifus ask?

7. Patricia Cohen's article, "Genetic Basis for Crime: A New Look" (page 104), addresses a heavily debated topic. How does Cohen achieve the journalistic principle of balance in her article?

8. Gina Kolata and Heather Murphy's article, "The Golden State Killer Is Tracked Through a Thicket of DNA, and Experts Shudder" (page 128), includes extensive quotations. What backgrounds do these quotations represent, and how do they shed light on the criminal investigation the article describes?

9. Carl Zimmer's article, "White? Black? A Murky Distinction Grows Still Murkier" (page 142), attributes much of its information to scientists. How does the article set up their background to show how the attribution is relevant to the article?

10. Rosemarie Garland-Thomson's article, "My 'Orphan Disease' Has Given Me a New Family" (page 150), is an op-ed. Garland-Thomson is a professor of disability studies. How does her expertise inform the argument of her article?

11. What is the motive of Moises Velasquez-Manoff's article, "The Upside of Bad Genes" (page 184)? What particular assumptions is Velasquez-Manoff responding to?

12. Why does Emily Baumgaertner's headline, "As D.I.Y. Gene Editing Gains Popularity, 'Someone Is Going to Get Hurt' " (page 203), contain a quote? What does the quote convey, and who says it in the article?

Citations

All citations in this list are formatted according to the Modern Language Association's (MLA) style guide.

BOOK CITATION

THE NEW YORK TIMES EDITORIAL STAFF. *DNA Testing: Genealogy and Forensics*. New York: New York Times Educational Publishing, 2019.

ONLINE ARTICLE CITATIONS

ABELSON, REED, AND JULIE CRESWELL. "Pursuit of Cash Taints Promise of Gene Tests." *The New York Times*, 24 June 2015, https://www.nytimes.com/2015/06/25/technology/genetic-testing-case-highlights-the-fields-hope-and-hype.html.

ASTOR, MAGGIE. "Why Many Native Americans Are Angry With Elizabeth Warren." *The New York Times*, 17 Oct. 2018, https://www.nytimes.com/2018/10/17/us/politics/elizabeth-warren-dna-test.html.

BARTLETT, JENNIFER. "Disability and the Right to Choose." *The New York Times*, 10 May 2017, https://www.nytimes.com/2017/05/10/opinion/disability-and-the-right-to-choose.html.

BAUMGAERTNER, EMILY. "As D.I.Y. Gene Editing Gains Popularity, 'Someone Is Going to Get Hurt.' " *The New York Times*, 14 May 2018, https://www.nytimes.com/2018/05/14/science/biohackers-gene-editing-virus.html.

COHEN, PATRICIA. "Genetic Basis for Crime: A New Look." *The New York Times*, 19 June 2011, https://www.nytimes.com/2011/06/20/arts/genetics-and-crime-at-institute-of-justice-conference.html.

DOBBS, DAVID. "The Fault in Our DNA." *The New York Times*, 10 July 2014, https://www.nytimes.com/2014/07/13/books/review/a-troublesome-inheritance-and-inheritance.html.

DREIFUS, CLAUDIA. "Biologist Teaches the Nation's Judges About Genetics."

The New York Times, 1 July 2008, https://www.nytimes.com/2008/07/01/science/01conv.html.

EISENBERG, ANNE. "The Path to Reading a Newborn's DNA Map." *The New York Times*, 8 Feb. 2014, https://www.nytimes.com/2014/02/09/business/the-path-to-reading-a-newborns-dna-map.html.

FACKLER, MARTIN. "Falsely Convicted, Freed and No Longer Quiet." *The New York Times*, 13 Aug. 2010, https://www.nytimes.com/2010/08/14/world/asia/14japan.html.

GARLAND-THOMSON, ROSEMARIE. "My 'Orphan Disease' Has Given Me New Family." *The New York Times*, 26 Oct. 2017, https://www.nytimes.com/2017/10/26/opinion/my-orphan-disease-has-given-me-a-new-family.html.

GOODMAN, J. DAVID. "New York's Chief Medical Examiner Seeks to Lead in DNA Research." *The New York Times*, 9 Feb. 2015, https://www.nytimes.com/2015/02/10/nyregion/new-yorks-chief-medical-examiner-seeks-to-lead-in-dna-research.html.

HABERMAN, CLYDE. "Scientists Can Design 'Better' Babies. Should They?" *The New York Times*, 10 June 2018, https://www.nytimes.com/2018/06/10/us/11retro-baby-genetics.html.

HESS, AMANDA. "Ethics Questions Arise as Genetic Testing of Embryos Increases." *The New York Times*, 3 Feb. 2014, https://www.nytimes.com/2014/02/04/health/ethics-questions-arise-as-genetic-testing-of-embryos-increases.html.

HESS, AMANDA. "The Racial Spectacle of DNA Test Result Videos." *The New York Times*, 6 May 2018, https://www.nytimes.com/2018/05/06/arts/dna-testing-race.html.

KOLATA, GINA. "In Africa, Geneticists Are Hunting Poachers." *The New York Times*, 8 Jan. 2018, https://www.nytimes.com/2018/01/08/science/dna-rhinos-ivory-poachers.html.

KOLATA, GINA. "New Gene Tests Pose a Threat to Insurers." *The New York Times*, 12 May 2017, https://www.nytimes.com/2017/05/12/health/new-gene-tests-pose-a-threat-to-insurers.html.

KOLATA, GINA. "The Online Gene Test Finds a Dangerous Mutation. It May Well Be Wrong." *The New York Times*, 2 July 2018, https://www.nytimes.com/2018/07/02/health/gene-testing-disease-nyt.html.

KOLATA, GINA. "Seeking Answers in Genome of Gunman." *The New York Times*, 24 Dec. 2012, https://www.nytimes.com/2012/12/25/science

/scientists-to-seek-clues-to-violence-in-genome-of-gunman-in-newtown-conn.html.

KOLATA, GINA. "The Struggle to Build a Massive 'Biobank' of Patient Data." *The New York Times*, 19 Mar. 2018, https://www.nytimes.com/2018/03/19/health/nih-biobank-genes.html.

KOLATA, GINA. "With a Simple DNA Test, Family Histories Are Rewritten." *The New York Times*, 28 Aug. 2017, https://www.nytimes.com/2017/08/28/science/dna-tests-ancestry.html.

KOLATA, GINA, AND HEATHER MURPHY. "The Golden State Killer Is Tracked Through a Thicket of DNA, and Experts Shudder." *The New York Times*, 27 Apr. 2018, https://www.nytimes.com/2012/12/25/science/scientists-to-seek-clues-to-violence-in-genome-of-gunman-in-newtown-conn.html.

KRUEGER, ALYSON. "Are Genetic Testing Sites the New Social Networks?" *The New York Times*, 16 June 2018, https://www.nytimes.com/2018/06/16/style/23-and-me-ancestry-dna.html.

PEAR, ROBERT. "U.S. Introduces New DNA Standard for Ensuring Accuracy of Genetic Tests." *The New York Times*, 14 May 2015, https://www.nytimes.com/2015/05/15/health/new-way-to-ensure-accuracy-of-dna-tests-us-announces.html.

PINKER, STEVEN. "My Genome, My Self." *The New York Times*, 7 Jan. 2009, https://www.nytimes.com/2009/01/11/magazine/11Genome-t.html.

POLLACK, ANDREW. "DNA Blueprint for Fetus Built Using Tests of Parents." *The New York Times*, 6 June 2012, https://www.nytimes.com/2012/06/07/health/tests-of-parents-are-used-to-map-genes-of-a-fetus.html.

POLLACK, ANDREW. "DNA Evidence Can Be Fabricated, Scientists Show." *The New York Times*, 17 Aug. 2009, https://www.nytimes.com/2009/08/18/science/18dna.html.

POLLACK, ANDREW. "23andMe Will Resume Giving Users Health Data." *The New York Times*, 21 Oct. 2015, https://www.nytimes.com/2015/10/21/business/23andme-will-resume-giving-users-health-data.html.

REICH, DAVID. "How Genetics Is Changing Our Understanding of 'Race.' " *The New York Times*, 23 Mar. 2018, https://www.nytimes.com/2018/03/23/opinion/sunday/genetics-race.html.

ROBBINS, LIZ. "Helping Decide Guilt or Innocence." *The New York Times*, 15 Dec. 2012, https://www.nytimes.com/2012/12/16/nyregion/a-forensic-tool-helps-decide-guilt-or-innocence.html.

SOUTHALL, ASHLEY. "Using DNA to Sketch What Victims Look Like; Some Call

It Science Fiction." *The New York Times*, 19 Oct. 2017, https://www.nytimes.com/2017/10/19/nyregion/dna-phenotyping-new-york-police.html.

VELASQUEZ-MANOFF, MOISES. "The Upside of Bad Genes." *The New York Times*, 17 June 2017, https://www.nytimes.com/2017/06/17/opinion/sunday/crispr-upside-of-bad-genes.html.

ZIMMER, CARL. "David Reich Unearths Human History Etched in Bone." *The New York Times*, 20 Mar. 2018, https://www.nytimes.com/2018/03/20/science/david-reich-human-migrations.html.

ZIMMER, CARL. "DNA Double Take." *The New York Times*, 16 Sept. 2013, https://www.nytimes.com/2013/09/17/science/dna-double-take.html.

ZIMMER, CARL. "The Famine Ended 70 Years Ago, but Dutch Genes Still Bear Scars." *The New York Times*, 31 Jan. 2018, https://www.nytimes.com/2018/01/31/science/dutch-famine-genes.html.

ZIMMER, CARL. "In Iceland's DNA, New Clues to Disease-Causing Genes." *The New York Times*, 25 Mar. 2015, https://www.nytimes.com/2015/03/26/science/in-icelands-dna-clues-to-what-genes-may-cause-disease.html.

ZIMMER, CARL. "White? Black? A Murky Distinction Grows Still Murkier." *The New York Times*, 24 Dec. 2014, https://www.nytimes.com/2014/12/25/science/23andme-genetic-ethnicity-study.html.

Index

A

ABCA7 gene, 67
ABDB4 gene, 67
Abelson, Reed, 73–80
abortion, 53, 56, 148, 149
ACTN3 gene, 30, 31
adoption, 15, 16, 17, 20, 41, 43, 44, 45, 107, 130
Advanced Science and Technology Adjudication Resource Center, 92
All of Us, 86–91
alpha thalassemia, 20
Alzheimer's disease, 8, 19, 66, 67, 70, 81, 83, 95, 186
Ambry Genetics, 50, 51
Amgen, 66, 69
AncestryDNA, 44, 45, 47, 164
apolipoprotein E gene (APOE), 19, 81, 84, 186
Ashkenazi Jews, 20, 40, 51
Astor, Maggie, 173–175
atrial fibrillation, 67

B

balancing selection, 25–26, 27
Bartlett, Jennifer, 146–149
Baumgaertner, Emily, 203–210
Beaker culture, 200–201
behavioral genetics, 14, 15–18, 23, 25, 94
Benjamin, Daniel, 158
biobank, creation of, 86–91
"Biohacker Boot Camp", 207
biohackers, 9, 176, 203–210
biological determinism, 14–15
Bloom syndrome, 72
BRCA2, 68, 95
Burken, Mitchell, 77, 78, 79
Bush, George W., 12

C

cancer, 8, 21, 22, 48, 50, 51, 68, 70, 74, 93, 95, 135, 136, 158, 180, 181, 182
Capecchi, Mario, 152, 153
Caragine, Theresa A., 108, 109, 110, 111, 112, 113
cardiac channelopathies, 64
Cas9 enzyme, 171
cassava, 187
celiac disease, 81, 186
Centers for Medicare and Medicaid Services, 72
cerebral palsy, 146–149
chimerism, 179, 181, 183
Church, George, 11
Clayton, Joshua, 48, 50, 52
Cohen, Patricia, 104–107
complex syndactyly, 150–154
Counsyl, 20
Creswell, Julie, 73–80
"crime gene," 9, 104–107, 114–117
crime victims, using DNA testing to determine appearance of, 118–122
Crick, Francis, 7, 19
Crispr, 9, 53, 152, 171, 176, 184–188, 203, 209
cystic fibrosis, 20, 34, 55, 66, 70, 135, 170, 185

D

DeAngelo, James (Golden State Killer), 128–131, 165
Decode, 66, 67, 68, 69, 88
Denisovans, 198, 199
Denissen, Jaap, 26, 27
"designer babies," 9, 132, 169–172
diabetes, 21, 22, 88, 186, 189
DNA blueprint, of unborn children, 53, 57
DNA detectives, 130
DNA evidence, fabrication of, 97–98
DNA Playground, 209
DNA testing standards, 70–72
Dobbs, David, 138–141
dopamine, 28
Down syndrome, 7, 147, 170
Dreifus, Claudia, 92–96
Dutch Hunger Winter, 189–192

E

Eisenberg, Anne, 58–61
epigenetics, 9, 176, 189–192

eugenics, 14, 15
Evans, James, 92–96

F

Fackler, Martin, 99–103
false convictions, 99–103
"Falsely Convicted," 99
familial dysautonomia, 20
fibroblasts, 180–181
fibrodysplasia ossificans progressiva, 141
"Finding Your Roots," 165, 167
Fisher, Ronald, 27
Forensic Statistical Tool, 108–113
Frye hearing, 109

G

gallstones, 66, 67
Garland-Thomson, Rosemarie, 150–154
Garner, Eric, 62, 64
GEDmatch, 129, 130
Geisinger, 86, 87, 88, 89, 90
gene editing, 9, 53, 152, 171, 172, 176, 184–188, 203–210
Genelex, 80
Genentech, 35
Genetic Information Nondiscrimination Act, 12, 82–83
genetic testing
 ethical concerns, 132–175
 popularity of personal testing, 8, 10–52
 scientific discoveries based in, 176–210
 use in law enforcement, 7, 9, 63–64, 92–131, 182
 use in medicine, 7, 9, 33–35, 48–52, 53–91
Geno's Paradox, 23
Genspace, 207
Gerstmann-Straussler-Scheinker disease (GSS), 132, 133, 134, 135, 136, 137
Goodman, J. David, 62–65
Griffith, Barry, 76, 77

H

Haberman, Clyde, 169–172
Harpending, Henry, 160
Harris, Judith Rich, 18
Health Diagnostic Laboratory, 75, 80
health insurance, 11, 12, 52, 71, 81–85
heart disease, 66, 69
Heijmans, Bas, 190,192
hemimegalencephaly, 182
heritable diseases, genetic screening to determine risk of, 8, 19–21, 33–35, 48–52, 54–56, 58–61, 66–69, 70–72, 73, 81–85, 128, 132–137, 152, 184–188
Hess, Amanda, 164–168
Hirsch, Charles, 63, 65
Human Genome Project, 7
Huntington's disease, 14–15, 19, 95

I

Iceland, 66–69, 88, 160
Ilumina, 60
imputation, 68
Innocence Project, 128

J

Jackson, Fatimah, 187, 188
Jolly, Tarun, 76, 77, 78, 80

K

Kasirajan, Karthikeshwar, 76, 77, 78, 79, 80
kidney disease, 157
Knome, 11
Kolata, Gina, 36–42, 48–52, 81–85, 86–91, 114–117, 123–127, 128–131, 132–137
Kong, Augustine, 159
Krueger, Alyson, 43–47

L

Lanza, Adam, 114
leukemia, 180
Lewontin, Richard, 155
Li-Fraumeni syndrome, 50
Lumey, L.H., 189, 190
Lynch syndrome, 48, 51, 52

M

malaria, 185, 187
"Man's Most Dangerous Myth: The Fallacy of Race,"155
Marfan syndrome, 55
Mendel, Gregor, 7, 12
Mendelian disorders, 55
methyl groups, 190–191
Miller, Geoffrey, 26, 27
Million Veteran Program, 89
Mitchell, Adele A., 108, 110, 111
mitochondrial transfer, 171
monoamine oxidase A enzyme, 105, 115
Montagu, Ashley, 155
mosaicism, 180, 181, 182, 183
multiple sclerosis, 157
Murphy, Heather, 128–131
MYL4 gene, 67

N

Native Americans, 8, 40, 47, 142, 143, 144, 173–175
Natural Molecular Testing Corporation, 76, 77

neonatal genetic testing, 7, 58–61
Netherlands, 189–192
New York Commission on Forensic Science, 121
New York Office of the Chief Medical Examiner, 62–65, 108
Nucleix, 97, 98
Nussbaum, Robert, 52, 59

O

Obama, Barack, 74
"orphan diseases," 152, 154

P

Pacific Biosciences, 60
Parabon NanoLabs, 118, 120
Parkinson's disease, 81
Pear, Robert, 70–72
Penke, Lars, 26, 27
Personal Genome Project (P.G.P.), 11, 18, 19, 22, 29
phenotyping, 118–122
Pheramor, 165
PIM3 gene, 191
Pinker, Steven, 10–32, 105–106
poachers, 123–127
"Pocahontas exception," 142
Pollack, Andrew, 33–35, 53–57, 97–98
Powell, Cynthia, 58
prenatal genetic testing, 7, 53–60, 132–137, 147–149, 170–172
Promethease, 48, 50, 51, 52
propylthiouracil, 30

R

racial/ethnic ancestry, 8, 10, 36–42, 43–46, 142–145, 155–163, 164–168, 173–175
Racial Integrity Act, 142
Regeneron, 87, 88, 89
Reich, David, 66, 145, 155–163, 193–202
Renaissance RX, 73–80
Reproductive Genetics Institute, 135
rhinoceroses DNA, using to catch poachers, 123–127
Rhodis, 123, 126
Ridgeway, Patrick, 76, 77
Robbins, Liz, 108–113

S

Sampson, Barbara, 62–65
Scheller, Richard, 35
schizophrenia, 182, 189
Science Exchange, 209
serotonin, 28, 105
Shapiro, Beth, 160, 161
sickle cell anemia, 7, 34, 58, 185, 187–188
Single Nucleotide Polymorphisms (SNPs), 24, 29
Society for Assisted Reproductive Technology, 134
Southall, Ashley, 118–122
Sugaya, Toshikazu, 99–103

T

Tay-Sachs disease, 7, 20, 34, 55, 170
"A Troublesome Inheritance," 138–141, 160
Tsimane, 186, 187
tuberculosis, 185
Turkheimer, Eric, 16
21st Century Cures Act, 86
23andMe, 8, 10, 11, 20, 21, 22, 30, 33–35, 36, 38, 43, 44, 45, 46, 47, 48, 51, 52, 72, 81, 82, 83, 84, 129, 131, 142, 143, 164, 166, 167, 168

U

U.K. Biobank, 89, 90

V

Velasquez-Manoff, Moises, 184–188

W

Wade, Nicholas, 138–141, 160
Warren, Elizabeth, 173–175
Wasser, Sam, 124, 125, 126
Watson, James, 7, 19, 160
"Who Do You Think You Are?," 165
"Who We Are and How We Got Here," 193
Wojcicki, Anne, 33

Z

Zimmer, Carl, 66–69, 142–145, 176–183, 189–192, 193–202

This book is current up until the time of printing. For the most up-to-date reporting, visit www.nytimes.com.